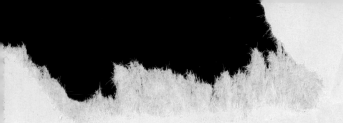

Lt. Col. JP Cross is a retired British officer who served with Gurkha units for nearly forty years. He has been an Indian frontier soldier, jungle fighter, policeman, military attaché, Gurkha recruitment officer and a linguist researcher, and he is the author of nineteen books. He has fought in Burma, Indo-China, Malaya and Borneo and served in India, Pakistan, Hong Kong, Laos and Nepal where he now lives. Well into his nineties, he still walks four hours daily.

Operation Janus is the first in a trilogy of books involving Gurkha military units that may be read in any order and is followed by *Operation Blind Spot* and *Operation Four Rings*. In *Operation Janus*, the author draws on real events he witnessed during his time fighting in the Malayan Emergency and on true characters, including a British officer from his own battalion who attempted to join the Communist terrorists.

'Nobody in the world is better qualified to tell this story of the Gurkhas' deadly jungle battles against Communist insurgency in Malaya in the 1950s. Cross spins his tale with the eye of incomparable experience.'

John le Carré

OPERATION JANUS

JP Cross

monsoon

monsoonbooks

Published in 2017
by Monsoon Books Ltd
www.monsoonbooks.co.uk

No.1 Duke of Windsor Suite, Burrough Court,
Burrough on the Hill, Leicestershire LE14 2QS, UK

ISBN (paperback): 9781912049141
ISBN (ebook): 9781912049158

Cover design by Cover Kitchen.

A Cataloguing-in-Publication data record is available from the British
Library.

MIX
Paper from
responsible sources
FSC® C018072

Printed in Great Britain by Clays Ltd, St Ives plc
20 19 18 17   1 2 3 4 5

List of Characters

PEOPLE ACQUAINTED WITH THE AUTHOR

Mubarak, Ismail, Head of Special Branch, Seremban, known as 'Moby', an 'Ace' operator

Rana, Ksatra Bikram, Lieutenant Colonel, Commanding Officer, The Mahindra Dal Nath, the only Nepalese Contingent unit the Maharaja allowed to operate outside India in WWII

Templer, Sir Gerald, General, High Commissioner and Director of Operations, Malaya

Theopulos, John, Manager, Bhutan Estate, near Seremban

OTHER REAL PEOPLE

Chin Peng, Chairman, Malayan Communist Party

Mao Tse-tung, Chinese Communist leader

Marx, Karl, German founder of modern Communism

Stalin, J, Soviet leader

Stilwell, General Joseph W, United States Army, Northern Burma Combat Command, 1943-44

Too Chee Chew, a.k.a. Mr C C Too, brilliant propagandist, Special Branch, Malayan Police

Zhdanov, Andrei A, Soviet theoretician

FICTITIOUS CHARACTERS

Ah Fat, non-voting member of politburo and police agent

*Chakrabahadur Rai, Rifleman, 1/12 Gurkha Rifles

Clark, Ian, OCPD, Seremban

*Ganeshbahadur Rai, Rifleman, 1/12 Gurkha Rifles

Goh Ah Hok, fresh ration contractor for 1/12 Gurkha Rifles

Hinlea, Alan, Captain, 1/12 Gurkha Rifles

Honker, M CA, Brigadier, Commander 63 Gurkha Infantry
    Brigade

Hung Lo, 'Bear', nickname of Wang Ming, q.v.

Kenny, Richard, Lieutenant Colonel, General Staff Officer (GSO)
    1, HQ Malaya Command

*Kulbahadur Limbu, Rifleman, 1/12 Gurkha Rifles, expert
    tracker

Kwek Leng Joo, barman at Yam Yam and senior Min Yuen
    (Masses Movement)

Lalman Limbu, Rifleman, 1/12 Gurkha Rifles

Lau Beng, Political Commissar, Negri Sembilan Regional
    Committee

Lee Kheng, 'sleeper' in Special Branch, Seremban

*Minbahadur Gurung, wireless operator, Rifleman, 1/12 Gurkha
    Rifles

*Padambahadur Rai, communist in Darjeeling

P'ing Yee, 'Flat Ears', nickname of Ah Fat, q.v.

Rance, Jason Percival Vere, Captain, 1/12 Gurkha Rifles

Shandung P'aau, 'Shandung Cannon', nickname of Captain
    Rance, q.v.

Sik Long, 'Lustful Wolf', nickname of Captain Hinlea, q.v.

Siu Tse, 'Little Miss', cabaret taxi girl in the Yam Yam

Vikas Bugga, secret Bengali communist

Wang Ming, Military Commander, Negri Sembilan Regional Committee

Wang Tao (f); OCPD's table servant

Williams, Robert, Lieutenant Colonel, Commanding Officer, 1/12 Gurkha Rifles

Yap Cheng Wu, manager of Yam Yam nightclub

Yong Kwoh, second in seniority in Malayan Communist Party

* Names ending in 'bahadur' often use the 'é' ending instead, especially when talking.

Abbreviations

2 IC	Second in Command
AVM	Air Vice Marshal
CO	Commanding Officer
DSO	Distinguished Service Order
DWEC	District War Executive Committee
GHQ	General Headquarters
GOC	General Officer Commanding
GR	Gurkha Rifles
GSO 1	General Staff Officer, Grade 1
HQ	headquarters
ID	identity
Int	Intelligence
IO	Intelligence Officer
KGB	Russian initials for the Soviet secret police
LMG	Light Machine Gun, (Bren Gun)
MC	Military Cross
MCP	Malayan Communist Party
MRLA	Malayan Races Liberation Army
MTO	Motor Transport Officer
NCO	non-commissioned officer
NRIC	National registration identity card, also known as ID card
OCPD	Officer Commanding Police District
OSPC	Officer Supervising Police Circle
'O' Group	Orders Group, the staff officers and sub-unit commanders needed to put tactical orders into action

QM	Quartermaster
RV	rendezvous, term used for designated positions to 'close on'
sitrep	situation report
SWEC	State War Executive Committee
Tac Adjutant	Tactical Adjutant, the CO's operational staff officer

WIRELESS JARGON

Acorn	Intelligence Officer
Seagull	Adjutant
Sunray	Commander
Sunray Minor	Second in command
Roger	'message received'
Wilco	'will comply with message'

Glossary

CHINESE

cheongsam	long, tight-fitting dress with slit sides
feng shui	'wind and water': a system of good and bad influences in the environment and correct alignment with nature
foh t'ung	bonfire tree. Family: Sterculiaceae (Cacao family) Species: Sterculia (syn. Firmiana) colorata
Goo K'a	Gurkha
gwai lo	foreigner, 'devil person'
ham sap kwai	salty-wet devil, randy
Min Yuen	Masses Movement: pro-Communist civilians who provided food, shelter, information etc to the Communist Terrorists
seong wai	captain
sinsaang	'elder born', sir
wai	hello

HINDI

bidi	crude cigarette rolled in a leaf
ji	polite suffix

MALAY (1950S SPELLING, PRE-STANDARDISATION)

bukit	hill
gunong	mountain

inche	mister, a polite salutation
jalan	road
siapa chekup?	who's speaking
tuan	sir

NEPALI

Cheena	Chinese
daku	guerilla, (from 'dacoit)
gora	'fair-skinned': when used in a military sense, the meaning was 'British Other Rank'. If used referring to an officer, it implied that the Gurkhas felt that that the officer did not merit officer status
jasus	spy
ningalo	a small type of bamboo, Arundinaria intermedia
ustad	non-commissioned officer, instructor

OTHERS

basha	temporary night shelter
Force 136	secret force, part of which went to Malaya during WWII
gloire	glory (French)
maskirovka	trick, cover plan (Russian)
vlasti	elite (Russian)
wala	person

Author Note

The historical genesis of this story is that of a British officer of a Gurkha battalion who tried to defect to the Communist guerillas during the early days of the Malayan Emergency, 1948-1959. The Malayan Communist Party, with its military wing, the Malayan People's Liberation Army, tried, for eleven years, to take the country over and make it into a communist state. At first it fought against the colonial power, the British and, after Malaya (not yet Malaysia) gained its independence as a democracy, against the Malayan Government. It failed. It was the only time the Communists failed to take over territory of its own choosing.

This story, based on what actually did happen on jungle operations, is fiction. Your author witnessed only the end of the tragic events he writes about.

The battalion concerned has been given a fictitious name for obvious reasons: those who know won't mind and those who mind won't know.

Also it has to be said that this story does not apply to the one case in a British regiment that is still on the Order of Battle when this book was written: it not only still considers itself impeccable but also has covered itself in glory in the past and undoubtedly will again in the future. No one serving in it now, 2017, knows anything about the incident: the thickest and darkest of curtains was drawn so tightly over the unhappy – and, I am glad to say, unsuccessful, albeit only just – incident, that it never passed into regimental legend. It is neither the author's job nor his wish to draw back that curtain.

The four people in the story acquainted with the author were of unusually high calibre and it gives him pleasure to be able to keep their names alive. The other characters are fictitious and any likeness to real characters will be in the reader's imagination.

Author Preface

It is unusual in a novel to acknowledge help but the author feels it incumbent to thank Mr A J V (Gus) Fletcher, OBE, GM and Mr Bernard C C Chan, MBE, AMN for their help with various pieces of Chinese exotica as his own knowledge of Chinese is nowhere near theirs. Mr Fletcher won his George Medal by going into the jungle, several times, with a 2/2 Gurkha Rifles escort and, at night, with face covered and standing at the edge of occupied guerilla camps, persuading, in his impeccable Chinese, even Regional Committee members to surrender. Never were they more surprised to find that a Briton spoke their language probably better than a native Chinese. The author also thanks Lt Col P Shield, MBE, his pilot when serving in the British embassy in Laos, for his input in aviation matters and Major James Devall for his help with maps and the text, read with the eyes of a post-Emergency reader..

During your author's rising forty years military service, he spent approximately ten years of it 'under the canopy' in the jungle. Jungle tactics described in the narrative were either executed by the author with his Gurkhas or someone the author knew, except for ventriloquism. However, even that is not quite as absurd as it may seem as, when on Home Leave in 1951, he took lessons from a professional ventriloquist, thinking that it might well come in useful in jungle operations. His initial aim was to check his sentries from a short distance off. He was taught only on condition that he did not use his skill professionally. Alas, he never progressed far enough to use his new knowledge properly.

Bird calls, calling deer, half rations, not wearing jungle boots but canvas shoes, being scared by kraits, real ones, having a python swallow an arm up to the shoulder, elephants stepping over a soldier in ambush, folded leaves, cigarette smell remaining on leaves and near water, falling trees with frightened monkeys chattering, breathing when hiding under water, putting 'gizmos' in wireless sets, guerillas moving only early and late, out-numbered troops shouting orders to imaginary platoons to confuse the enemy, firing first at a leg then at an arm to prevent running away and firing back, and relieving nature 'within reach' all actually happened: one example of the last mentioned that sticks in the author's memory was when he and a platoon were ambushing the corner of a rubber estate where the 'cover crop' only just hid his camouflaged men. A Chinese female rubber tapper approached the soldier nearest to her, some ten yards from the tree she was tapping, and, turning around, stepped back three paces, lowered her knickers and urinated directly on top of him. He moved his face away just in time to avoid being wetted. He later said he had never seen 'it' from that particular perspective. The author only once came across tiger's pug marks walking backwards. When one of the author's ace sergeants found out valuable intelligence by aping guerilla uniform, he was roundly condemned by the local

Brigadier for adopting 'a ruse de guerre unbecoming to civilised warfare,' -- yes, really. And voice aircraft tapes were used over the wrong areas! Aircraft measured cloud cover in 10/10ths not 8/8ths.

Warfare such as Communist Revolutionary Warfare changed from Passive, Active and Counter-Offensive phases to 'low intensity', 'high intensity' and 'asymmetrical' as the years passed. Some surrendered enemy personnel were used in 'poachers-turned-game-keepers' units and sent back into the jungle on operations.

One of a group of Indonesian infiltrators in Brunei turned away a patrol of Royal Brunei Malay Regiment (the unit's name has since changed) soldiers by calling out to them to turn round and go back, saying it was a ghost. This they did. Your author was initially blamed!

In the narrative the author has used the language of the early Fifties: often 'English' not 'British'; 'Soviet', not 'Russian'; 'wireless' not 'radio'; 'map reference' not 'grid reference'; 'unserviceable' was 'u.s.' until the Americans complained when it became 'unsvc'; 'Gurkhali' not 'Nepali'; designations, such as General Staff Officer Grade 1, which are no longer extant; the LMG (Light Machine Gun), long disappeared and replaced by the General Purpose Machine Gun (GPMG); having studded boots and not the rubberised softer-soled type; Land Rovers reached battalions in 1952 instead of Jeeps; a different phonetic alphabet (which one company's signaller wrongly called 'fanatic' alphabet); surnames used instead of Christian names; some Malay spelling different in place names, e.g. then 'Negri' now 'Negeri', then 'Johore' now 'Johor'; others then 'Ceylon' now 'Sri Lanka'. On operations each man was given a 50-stick tin of cigarettes weekly. Ho, ho! The soldiers always grinned at the fiftieth cigarette: even Authority could not make the ration of seven cigarettes for seven days total of forty-nine without opening each tin and extracting the magic fiftieth!

The author still vividly remembers the English judge, wig and black hat, giving out his death sentence and the look of relief, followed swiftly by one of horror, on the condemned man's face when the verdict was given, finishing with 'And may the Lord have mercy on your soul.' History has yet to tell whether He did or not. Afterwards, wig and black hat lying beside him on the table as he enjoyed a cup of tea, he said that he had a low opinion of army officers as they were not clever enough to be judges.

When the author was in Kathmandu in 1947 (he and his friend probably the 126th and 127th 'swanners' in the past 153 years) he was told about the Maharaja's WWII fears about Japanese retribution if the Allies were to lose the war – which seemed most likely at one time.

Also, in the 1950s there were no 'human rights' to plague us, only 'inhuman lefts', nor did 'political correctness' rear its ugly head: 'gay', meant 'blithe' or 'bonny', while 'queer' meant 'strange' or 'unusual'. Servicemen were still proud to wear uniform in public and 'empire' was not a dirty word. Pounds, shillings and pence, miles, yards and inches were all current measures. One did not have to lock one's front door at night.

And a final historical note: just before this story starts a bomb exploded in the Yam Yam where the real Siu Tse was performing but she was not injured although several taxi-girls were.

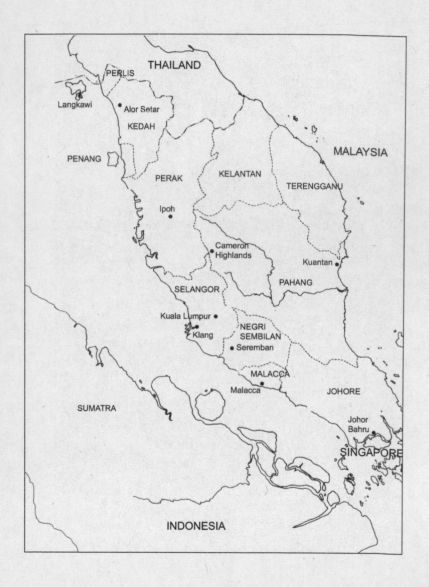

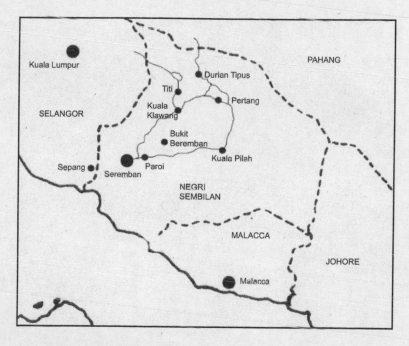

Opposite Peninsular Malaysia
Above Detail of Negri Sembilan

PART ONE

1

Saturday, 17 May 1952

In the nightclub known as the Yam Yam, one that had started life during the Japanese occupation of Malaya and had refused to go away with the returning British liberators, the lights were dim, the room crowded and the noise loud. There was no cooling system and the atmosphere was malodorous with sweaty bodies, cheap powder and alcohol. A small band played and a man, bawling into a microphone, sang the local hits, 'Rose, Rose I love you', 'A slow boat to China' and 'Terang Bulan' over and over again until the slowest numbskull must have learnt every word off pat. Small, skinny Chinese girls, attractively dressed in their long, tight-fitting, slit-sided cheongsams, were taxi-girls trying to earn a pittance of a living. For a fee they would dance with sweaty, red-faced Europeans who, once back at their tables, were inveigled to buy drinks at inflated prices while the girl they had danced with sipped lemonade. Unaccompanied girls either sat silently in small groups waiting to be picked up or else danced with one another. Not official whores – never would the British colonial administration have allowed such! – but girls from poor families, squatters living in the wasteland between the rubber estates and the jungle, or from the poorer end of the town, Seremban, in the state of Negri Sembilan, forty-two miles south of the capital of Malaya, Kuala Lumpur.

The First Battalion of the Twelfth Gurkha Rifles, 1/12 GR, was stationed on the eastern edge of the town at Sikamat Camp, as was 1911 Flight, Air Observation Post, Army Air Corps, with Auster aircraft, but along another road, at Paroi Camp.

Most of the Yam Yam clients were British junior officers and 'other ranks', such as workshop fitters, medical staff and Flight ground crews. Senior rubber planters were never seen there but some younger assistants visited the place on a Saturday night. Gurkhas of 1/12 GR were only allowed to leave the camp at weekends when they had to wear regimental mufti – long, knee-length stockings of black with a green band at the turn-over, black shorts and white shirt with a round black Kilmarnock hat, so even had they been allowed and wanted to go there, they just would not have fitted in. In any case, their miserable pay scales only allowed them to relax in their own canteen.

The Yam Yam's manager, Yap Cheng Wu, was a dedicated senior Communist. He had an upstairs office, not much more than a small cubicle with a telephone, three chairs, a small desk and a cupboard. He had two sets of books, one doctored to show any visiting government auditors, 'snoopers', how little he earned so how little tax he need pay, and the other, the true version, which always showed a far larger profit than did the other. Money: after a certain total had been reached numbers were useful only in keeping the score, not in judging the satisfaction of having it.

The senior Chinese barman, a dedicated ex-guerilla named

Kwek Leng Joo, hid his communistic feelings and good knowledge of English with a bland smile, speaking it only well enough to sustain a conversation with Europeans, without giving away how much he actually did know. He could well understand what the bar-propping *gwai lo* – foreign devils – had to say. With a drink or three inside them they often spoke about matters, even operationally sensitive ones, which he duly reported and were of varying interest to his masters.

When Captain Alan Hinlea first started going to the Yam Yam he didn't seem to mind who his taxi-girl partner was, with lithe body movements and a pulsating lower region, he pleased them all. He was always thirsty after dancing so he'd go and prop up the bar where, with careful prompting, he'd give vent to his feelings about the British in general and his brother officers in particular. 'All the officers are plummy-voiced, public-school snobs who speak with a potato in their mouth and don't like me because of my working-class background. As for their la-di-dah in the Mess with each new officer having to present a silver goblet, cigars and snuff on Mess nights with pipers marching round the table and toasts, first to the King and now to the Queen. Should have made the place a republic when the king died last February – why, it makes me want to puke.' Much of such a tirade was lost on Kwek Leng Joo but he did prick up his ears when Hinlea said, 'If only I had a way in, I'd join the Communists in the jungle and, with the knowledge I have – I'm an officer, aren't I? – lead the comrades in their fight against those cold-blooded shits. That's why I'm trying to learn Chinese.' When worked up, his north-country accent became more pronounced and the barman had difficulty in fully understanding him. Hinlea was ever sure no other British person overheard him.

Over the weeks one particular taxi-girl began to excite his lusts more than did the others. She was the prettiest there: known as Siu Tse, Little Miss, her real name was never mentioned. She refused to show her identity papers to anyone other than a party member or, if she had to, the police. The senior barman noticed Hinlea's attachment to her and, having appraised the manager about it, they decided to put it to good use. Her task was to seduce him. Lead him on, had been her orders, and when you think he's ready for offering to the senior comrades, let the staff know.

'He smells badly from those dreadful cigarettes he smokes,' she had complained. 'I don't like his breath too near me.'

'In that case tell him if he really wants you not to smoke them.'

To steer Hinlea on his way, that evening the senior barman said, 'You are such a good patron, from now on, whenever you want to dance with Siu Tse, who has told me that she has a very soft spot for you, you can have her for free. Pay for the drinks and pay for any other taxi-girl, but regard Siu Tse as yours.' He did not add that Hinlea's prowess with the taxi-girls had earned him the nickname of Lustful Wolf, Sik Long.

As a sweetener, he arranged that, after the place closed for the night, and indeed often before, Hinlea could take his girl to a special room. 'Oh, that's wonderful,' he had said ecstatically. 'I'll look after her properly.'

The senior barman called Siu Tse over and she agreed, as though it was new to her. A little later she said, 'Alan, now we are to be together, please stop smoking those vile-smelling Kling cigarettes. I really hate the smell of them.'

'What cigarettes do you mean? Kling did you say?'

'Yes, Kling. You know, the type of cigarette the Tamils smoke.'

Hinlea knew that many rubber estates had south Indian labourers, Tamils. 'Why call them Klings?'

'Because when they first came to Malaya to work on the estates they were prisoners from India. They had leg chains and, when they walked, the noise the chains made was "cling, cling," so that is what their name became – and still is,' she added with a giggle.

'That sort of thing makes me angry with the British,' he expostulated. *Damn colonials, makes me hate them even more.* But after that he stopped smoking in the Yam Yam.

Saturday, 24 May 1952

This particular Saturday night Hinlea was later at the Yam Yam than usual and Siu Tse had found herself fretting for his arrival. 'Oh, darling, I'm so glad you've come, I was afraid you wouldn't,' she said, rather too breathlessly to be natural when they clasped each other. She was not a natural actor.

'Those damned superiors of mine were fart-arsing about,' he complained. She didn't understand but she was delighted to see that his mood was black enough for her suggestion to be put forward and probably be accepted. 'I know they look down on me. I can hardly wait to do something to show how supremely absurd they are and how right I am.' Accumulated bile had soured his soul and left him prickly, looking for snubs that, in most cases, were unintended with the speaker having no idea how he construed each and every remark they made.

Her English couldn't cope but his tone of voice was enough for her. She took him on to the dance floor when they rubbed groins in the gloom. She let him work some of the rage out of his system and by then it was time to take him away for a talk. After a sit at their table and a drink, 'Darling,' she said, 'I have something important I want to talk to you about. Can we go to a quiet place for a chat?'

Sniffing that there was more to this than just more horizontal refreshment, he quickly agreed. She took him upstairs and knocked on the door of the manager's office. They were invited in and told to sit down. Coffee was waiting on the table and the manager looked serious.

'Comrade Hinlea,' Yap Cheng Wu began after normal courtesies had been exchanged, 'I understand that you're not happy with your life with the army and the arrogant English.'

Alan Hinlea caught his breath in surprise. He pinched the bridge of his nose, narrowing his eyes, taken off guard and wondering how to reply. *How far can I go?* He made his mind up. 'Comrade. Yap, *sinsaang*. Too true. All the way.'

'Listen carefully. I'll tell you a secret. I am a contact for our brothers in the Red Struggle. I'd like to tell them about how much you would like to help them.' Hinlea still looked surprised. 'Oh yes, you told the barman didn't you, last week?'

Hinlea nodded. Mr Yap continued: 'If you're really willing to join them, I feel sure they'd be happy to keep you as an honoured member, protect you, use your knowledge and experience to win final victory – and ensure all so-called colonial upper classes are sent back to their own flea-pits.'

'Wonderful, I would willingly agree,' he said, looking entranced and letting out a long breath of satisfaction. 'Of course it'll have to be properly planned in a way that'll make the break final, once and for all. It can't be done overnight and it won't be all that easy. If it goes off at half-cock I'm finished.'

The manager, not fully understanding that last bit and confused by his emerging north-country twang, merely nodded before smoothly replying, 'Comrade, what you say is so true and of course it must be properly planned. If you will allow me to pass your willingness to work with us back to my comrades, I am sure you can be of real use in our struggle. I know you are the Intelligence Officer in your battalion so have good reasons for making yourself useful to the police. I should think you could find out what sort of sensitive records the Police have. I'm only guessing but I expect that the best way to help would be to collect such data before joining us, bringing it with you. That way, not only will you have scored a great victory but you will make future operational planning more effective.' He let that sink in.

'T'd give me great pleasure to find out all I possibly can,' said Hinlea, liking the idea.

'Now you've given me the assurance that you're willing to try and find out such details, I'll let our brethren know. If they agree, in due course your "escape" details will be worked out in such a way that you will be free.'

Hinlea's upbringing and mindset had him in iron pincers;

there was no escape, even if he had been shown one, even if he had wanted one – which he didn't. 'Done!'

'Good. But for the love of Lenin keep it to yourself and breathe not a word to others.'

Anus twitching at the thought of getting his own back, with dreams and realities playing hide and seek in his mind, he said he would tell nobody at all.

As they left, Siu Tse turned to Mr Yap and gave him a small smile of satisfaction before carnally celebrating her success with 'him'.

Monday, 26 May 1952

Captain Alan Hinlea sat by himself in his office thinking out what had so miraculously happened since he had given vent to his feelings in the Yam Yam. His head was still in a whirl and his stomach was churning at the thought of really doing something for the Party, even more than his father, a party member from an early age, had ever managed to. 'You're dedicated all right, lad,' his father had told him, 'but you'll fail unless you can convince those plutocratic swine that you're with them until you get the chance properly to do them down. When I was in Moscow the KGB taught me about *maskirovka*, a trick to manipulate "them" into looking the other way and not for a moment guessing your real aim. I once learnt that the word January comes from Janus, meaning "looking both forward and back", almost "two-faced". Imagine that you're on a permanent military operation, let's say you give it the code-name "Operation Janus", so that you are always making "them" look at your good record in the past and never guess your real purpose in life for the future.'

Those words had stayed engraved in his mind. He had come from a dirt-poor background in a coal-mining village in Nottinghamshire and had never lost the edge of his working-class accent. His family of six lived in a small, square room that served as kitchen, living room, eating place and, once a week, bathroom, the water used by two or three people before being changed, with a privy in the backyard and candlelight in the shared bedroom. He was culturally unsuited to any other type of society. He became a body-builder and gang leader as he was a big, strong lad. He stood at five feet ten and his otherwise open features were spoilt by an unwavering scowl, a permanent sneer and muddy brown eyes, always a-flicker. He tried hard at the local school and, as would be expected in such a pre-war area, developed a hatred for his despised social superiors. His ideology had turned to Marxism and his hatred of 'the system' made him a ready supporter of anything anti-upper-class. It was a travesty that he was ever considered good enough to be commissioned. His social superiors were apt to look on him as an over-educated nonentity.

During his formative years he had developed a capacity for total resentment which had never left him. As no 'reserved occupation' had stopped him from being conscripted during the war, he had been enlisted in the gunners when called up and, after passing various tests for potential officers, went to India for commissioning because by then there were enough reinforcements for the war in Europe but not enough for the war in Burma against the Japanese, although he was only commissioned after the war had ended. He had started the habit of smoking the offensively smelly *bidis* – primitive Indian cigarette rolled in a leaf. During his time in India he had travelled and been utterly appalled by the outrageous poverty he had seen in the slums of Delhi and other cities. He had witnessed the terrible strife in Calcutta between Hindus and Moslems on 16 August 1946 when many tens of thousands Muslims were massacred and wounded by Hindus – and had been violently sickened by it. *How is it,* he kept on asking himself, *how is it that after so many years the British in India have still done almost nothing to alleviate such dreadful conditions?* comparing European colonial civilian conquerors' nourished contours and elderly double-chins with the deprived faces and skeletal bodies of the under-nourished natives. It had never occurred to him that even before the British had ever set foot in India the native rulers had not done as much as the British had to relieve poverty themselves. He never understood that British officers in the Indian Army generally loved their men and spoke good Urdu, the compulsory *lingua franca*, and maybe another language also, nor were they haughty or superior. When he himself tried to speak to civilian Indians they were too surprised to answer properly but, gradually, he became aware of the overriding yearning for independence. He was deliciously happy when that happened on 15 August 1947, nearly five years earlier, with a smaller India remaining after Pakistan had become separated from it. *So now, no more Sahib-only type clubs!*

He had asked to be excused from the ceremonial parade that had been planned to mark independence –*crass, out-of-date bullshit*, he had illogically summed it up –and to go on leave instead. His Indian CO was secretly happy to have him out of the way – *not a good type* – and he had decided to go to Darjeeling. Wearing plain clothes, he had gone to the Planters' Club to see if, as an army officer, he could become a temporary member and spend a couple of nights there. A smiling Gurkha, wearing a round, black hat with black decorative embellishments, a long, dark-green jacket buttoned to the neck and white trousers – *bloody fancy dress* – asked him in Gurkhali what he wanted. Hinlea answered, in Urdu, that he didn't understand. So the query was rephrased in Urdu for him.

''Follow me, Sahib.'

The Gurkha took him to the office where the club secretary was sitting at his desk and, in Gurkhali, said that this sahib wanted to spend a few nights in the club. The secretary nodded the Gurkha's dismissal and said, 'Who are you and what do you want?' From the look on his face, he quite clearly didn't like what he saw.

Hinlea told him.

'Show me your identification card, please, as you are not in uniform.'

Hinlea produced his wallet. He opened it and put it on the table. He felt a sneeze coming so he took a handkerchief out of his trouser pocket to contain it. The secretary lifted the wallet up and, to his horror, saw a Communist membership card in the name of Alan Hinlea. He put the wallet back on the table. Hinlea finished wiping his nose. 'Sorry about that. A twitch in my snitch. Change in climate.'

Wretched man doesn't even speak like a sahib. 'What is your name?'

'Lieutenant Alan Hinlea.'

'And a Communist I see from your wallet.'

Hinlea was caught off balance. 'I can't and won't deny it.'

The secretary rose and in an icy tone of voice said, 'Get out of my sight, gutter scum. Leave the club immediately. You and your ilk are contagious. It's gutter scum like you that have been the cause of so much trouble in our tea gardens. Leave here immediately.'

Furious to the core and in a particularly foul and uncompromising mood, Hinlea picked up his wallet and left, openly mouthing obscenities of disgust at his treatment. He found a cheap local hotel. That night he rehearsed the three main contagions to guard against: capitalism, colonialism and religion, with a fourth close behind, individuality in a strict party member.

The next day, 15 August, Independence Day, he had wandered around the town, looking at the British tea-planting community traipsing out of St Andrew's church and making their way down to their Club, watching an inter-school football match and just mooching around. He saw a procession of senior schoolboys chanting slogans, being led round the town by a strong, stocky youth in his early twenties. They stopped opposite where he was standing and the leader made a surprisingly ardent speech, the burden of which was 'are we to allow Gurkhas to serve in the British Army, still as slaves of the imperialists?' and 'what must our Branch here in Darjeeling do to stop it? The Communists have the answer.' It was good rabble-rousing stuff. The Artillery officer was surprised that the harangue was delivered in good

English and was transfixed by what he heard.

The monsoon rain held off until people started to go home, then the heavens opened. Hinlea sheltered at the back of the doorway of Pliva's Tea Room next to a Bengali, dressed in a shantung suit and wearing a 'Bombay bowler' pith helmet. The speech maker, tired, sweat-stained, happy and hoarse from haranguing the crowd, now on his way home, was accosted by the Bengali.

'Issst. Not so fast, Padambahadur. I have some soul-shockingly important news for you,' said just loud enough for the youth and Hinlea to hear over the downpour.

Padambahadur stopped in his tracks, utterly taken aback. He obviously recognised the speaker for he said, 'Oh Mr Bugga. You startled me. I was somehow not expecting you. "Soul-shockingly important news" did I hear you say?' he asked huskily.

'Yes. Come in and we will talk. It's raining hard. You've had a tiring day. A cup of tea is what you need, what we both need.' They went inside.

Hinlea, amused, wanted to continue eavesdropping and, so engrossed were the other two, neither took any notice of him as he followed and went to sit at a table where he hoped to continue listening in. They found a quiet corner and ordered a large pot of tea. They drank their first cup talking pleasantries, 'just in case some unexpected suspicions are aroused' said the Bengali. 'Now listen with all your might and main. You have been chosen by the Party for an extraordinarily important mission, utterly secret. It has two parts,' he added tantalisingly, looking out of the window at the rain teeming down.

Vikas Bugga was known by his superior officers as a manipulator but, so clever was he at dissembling, none knew his true Communist role. 'In here is safer than in the Gorkha League office. Normally "hurry spoils curry" but this time "early sow, early mow".'

Gorkha League? Safer here?

'Oh Mr Bugga, I have to ask you, as a joke of course, how is Mrs Bugga and all the little Buggas?' countered Padambahadur with equal levity.

Vikas grinned. 'As a tennis player might say, "that makes the score deuce." But back to the secret.'

At the word 'secret' Padambahadur leant towards the speaker with vibrant interest on his handsome face, with its high forehead and arched eyebrows. 'Vikas-ji. I am ready for whatever you have for me. Have you come all this way from Calcutta just to speak to me alone?'

Party? Party? Still smarting from his brusque dismissal from the club the day before, Hinlea patted his trouser pocket where he kept his party card in his wallet.

Vikas Bugga nodded, 'Yes, and I return tomorrow, hence the hurry. After that I'm wanted back in Delhi.' And then, in mock surprise, 'Nothing to chew on? Go and order some honey sandwiches. I love honey. "Honey is not for donkey's mouth".'

Hinlea could restrain himself no longer. He went over to the Bengali and, politely, said, 'Excuse me. I couldn't help overhearing the magic word "party". I hope it's the same party as this,' and, taking his wallet out of his pocket, he showed him his party card in its protective plastic covering.

The Bengali's eyes ogled in unfeigned delight. 'So, you Britisher, are one of us?'

'Yes,' and he put forward his hand to shake the other's.

Padambahadur came back with a plate of honey sandwiches and Vikas introduced Hinlea as 'one of us, so come and sit with us for a while and share our sandwiches.' He ordered another tea cup.

The matter under discussion thrilled both Padambahadur and Hinlea: Mr Bugga had had a secret message from his controller in Delhi to say that he had recently been contacted by the General Secretary of the Australian Communist Party. 'It is to the effect that the chief Soviet theorist, Comrade Andrei A Zdhanov, has formulated an anti-imperialist policy that has yet to get the approval of Comrade Stalin and the Politburo but will assuredly do so. The Australian is bringing it to Calcutta to discuss it with selected comrades from all colonial countries, not only British but French and Dutch also. This will be big time bobbery and chufferings, I am telling you.'

Both listeners lapped up his every word, Hinlea's fingers steepled on the table as he leant forward, breathing hard.

'Lest we alert our new independent government about anything awkward, we are planning to gather as a Southeast Asia Youth Conference, with the declared accent on regional sport and education. It will take place only a short while before our second Indian Communist Party Plenum. We don't expect to be fully ready for six months. That puts the Conference in February, 1948 – and you will be there with your father.'

He paused, drained his cup and refilled it, along with Hinlea's.

'We have a big opportunity here, you two. "What's God's will, no frost can kill",' and he went into various details. 'Any questions so far?'

'Not about the conference or the Plenum as I'll be with my father. But I can hardly stand to wait for your second point,' he added, so excited he forgot his normally punctilious English grammar.

'Yes, I was keeping that till now. "Haste makes waste." I see you are indeed ready for Stage 2. The second task is – wait for it – you will be needed in Malaya with the British Gurkhas to teach them Communism. There are bound to be many vacancies for clerks and education instructors.'

The two men now wanted to know how Hinlea could help the Cause. Hinlea had his answer ready. 'I am led to believe that one of the Gurkha regiments going to Malaya will be made into a Gunner regiment. I am a Gunner. Do you think that I could help the anti-colonial battle by joining that regiment, finding my way around the Malayan communists who, I hear, are lying low at the moment, and then trying to join them? It will be a great blow against the continued British imperialism. I want to get my own back on them for their snobbish, corrupt and oppressive manners and attitude. They've no sympathy for the underdog. Padambahadur and I could surely secretly work together?'

Both the others were thrilled with the idea, never having heard an Englishman speak in that manner before. With a Communist Party card, there was no thought of his being a double agent. 'But how will I know where to start?' Hinlea pressed.

Mr Bugga said, 'You will know how to talk and who to talk

with. It will happen. You will not have heard that our movement is like a giant spider's web all over the subcontinent and Southeast Asia. Once you're there we'll learn if you have made the right moves or not. If you are still struggling with or without Padambahadur, we can make contact, even from here,' he added , with a wink, 'but we'll give you the address of the Darjeeling Branch of the All-India Gorkha League, to give it its full title, so you can write to them here if you want to.'

As they shook hands on parting, Vikas Bugga said, 'I'll contact you in good time.' Outside, in a heavy downpour, he put up his umbrella and splashed his way back to his hotel, as did Hinlea.

Back in England his demob number came up: leave the army or stay? With the conversation in Darjeeling firmly in his mind he had put his name down to serve on and had been given a short-service peacetime commission that would be reviewed after three years. 12 GR had been made into a Gunner regiment and were short of officers: *my chance to do what had been planned*. He had arrived in the regiment just before it had changed back into its infantry role. To his dismay he discovered that although Padambahadur had become a soldier in the regiment, he had prematurely shown his hand so sent on 'administrative discharge'.

The gap in pay and conditions of service between the British officers and Gurkhas sickened him. He quickly learned some Gurkhali and tried to question the soldiers about their views on the difference but they were never forthcoming. He had no time for his brother officers and did not like any, except a Captain Jason Rance. *There's something about him that's different from the others. If ever I were to be successful and win out as a*

Communist I'll kill all the rest but not him, he concluded, thinking over how he'd deal with his impending challenge. There was now no need to contact the Darjeeling Branch of the Gorkha League as matters had turned out well in his favour. *Whatever else, I'll try not to show anyone in any way anything that I'm planning. My* maskirovka *is still intact. Even the smell of its smell would be disastrous.*

Unthinkingly he folded a piece of paper across the middle and dropped it on the office floor.

2

Sunday, 1 June 1952

The guerilla camp, base of the Negri Sembilan Regional
Committee, the political wing of the Malayan Communist Party
(MCP), was situated in a flat space surrounded by thick jungle
not far from the summit of Bukit Beremban, 3293 feet high, itself
overshadowed by the even higher feature, Gunong Telapak, at
3914 feet, both easily seen from Seremban. It was guarded by
elements of the Malayan Races Liberation Army (MRLA). 1/12
GR's camp could be seen from there.

The camp was always cool by day and chilly at nights,
especially after it had been raining. At that height the noise from
the cicadas in the surrounding jungle was, at times, so loud it
was difficult to hear what a person said in a normal voice. It was
a murderously hard place to attack. Out of sight from below,
the only entrance was up an almost sheer slope, with two lots
of steps, one for 'up' and the other for 'down', cleverly cut and
cunningly camouflaged, invisible to those who did not know they
were there. Tell-tale signs of movement were always carefully
erased. Ropes of plaited vines reached every sentry who only had
to tug their rope to give the alarm: one pull, known visitor; two

pulls, high alert; three, stand-to. At the top was a strong defence post where the one Bren light machine gun was permanently sited, neatly hidden, with rifle positions around the perimeter. Camp sentries alerted their seniors by low whistles.

Water was never a difficulty as there was a spring at the back of the camp and a stream flowed along one edge of it. Rations, though, were a constant problem. Fresh meat was sometimes available – routine patrols were not allowed to shoot for food but traps were set for deer, porcupine and jungle pig. When possible, rice was smuggled in from Seremban, otherwise guerillas 'borrowed' it from villagers on the jungle edge, farther to the east. Cooking, always strictly controlled because of smoke problems, was done in a confined area near the spring, any excess smoke drifting away with the stream. On one side was a cave for stores, rice, flour, a few clothes and sleeping material for any important visitor, as well as a small workshop where arms could be mended. There was enough space for a rudimentary game of volleyball to be played of an evening. Limbs grew stiff sitting around camp all day. Outside patrols were kept to a minimum to avoid leaving tell-tale signs. An evacuation plan was practiced once a month. It had yet to be used.

The guerillas' huts, made of waterproof palm thatch, were almost invisible from the air: orders had been strictly given, and as strictly carried out, for fresh leaves to be put on the roofs as soon as the old ones became the slightest difference in colour. Always tidy and clean, they were built on low bamboo-slatted platforms six inches above the ground as protection both against insects and any possible flash flooding. The two senior men, the

Political Commissar and the Military Commander, both in their late thirties, slept in hammocks. Strung on poles, they too had leafy camouflage on top. It rained heavily almost every afternoon, so near twenty past four that a watch could be set by it, that is, if you had a watch to set. Fronds were laid to sleep on. Men had light-weight blankets. There were no mosquitoes or midges. In front of each guerilla's sleeping place was his pack, always ready with what was needed if an immediate evacuation were ever ordered. Personal weapons were carried at all times: at night they were closer to the owner's body than would a wife have been. Guerillas wore khaki shirt and trousers, puttees and canvas shoes – so easy for leeches to cluster round each ankle – and a round, small-peaked khaki hat with a red star, cloth or enamel, in front.

Some distance off, on the flatter ground, were several guerilla outposts responsible for the safety of the Regional Committee camp by patrolling and ambushing any Security Forces, in order to draw any attacker away from the main camp rather than to engage them decisively. They and the camp's rank-and-file 'defence' guerillas were part of 2 Regiment, MRLA, the regiment assigned for the struggle in Negri Sembilan, attached for the Regional Committee's defence.

Although tactically the camp was easy to defend and in a delightful spot, it did not have good *feng shui*, 'wind and water'. Correct alignment with nature had been disrupted as the stream had been diverted from its natural alignment and the latrines had not been built in the most propitious place. Both were bones of contention between the two senior men in the camp, the political man who overrode the military commander even in military situations, despite when the latter's tactical knowledge was obviously the better but not 'politically sound'. The Regional Commissar, named Lau Beng, was a one-time schoolmaster from Seremban, a veteran activist from pre-war days. Sullen and uncommunicative, with a deeply pockmarked face set above a neck that looked as if it had been screwed on, he had jet-black eyes that sparkled like malevolent jewels and were as venomous as a Black Widow spider's, with lips thin and cruel as a well-healed knife wound. His mouthful of a nickname was Sai Daam Lo Ch'e Dai P'aau, 'Small gall bladder bloke carrying a big cannon', though normally only the first three words were used. Chinese 'guts' lie in the gall bladder and 'big cannon' in this context signifies a 'loud-mouth'. Everybody knew that but woe betide anyone being overheard using it: its owner was ultra sensitive about it. Being of a vicious, irrational, cruel and stupid nature, he punished offenders soundly. He was, in fact, shallow, cowardly and a bully, not as tough physically or mentally as he liked to make out. He did not believe in *feng shui*.

On the other hand, Wang Ming – the military man – trustworthy, stolid and slow-thinking, with limited imagination and who had no hope of promotion, was a proponent of it. He was a short, almost square man, and powerfully built – he looked like a bear and his nickname was Hung Lo, Bear – at low level he was tactically astute. He was liked by the rank-and-file guerillas because he looked after them to the best of his ability. He was patient when training them and would go out on operations with them. A veteran from the Second World War, he had met up with those few British officers and men who had moved into the jungle after the Japanese had conquered both Malaya and Singapore, helping them to fight the invaders. From 1944 onwards, Liberator aircraft, able to fly from Ceylon and back, started parachuting men and stores to augment those sent ashore from submarines, for what was by then known as Force 136. He had helped prepare dropping zones. If the drops were at night it meant preparing fires to be lit when the throb of the aeroplane's engines was heard. On one occasion he was detailed as escort to a British officer who had arranged a meeting with Chin Peng, a senior Politburo member then and now Chairman of the MCP.

Apart from the Political Commissar and his military counterpart neither liking nor trusting one another, normal among any Communist fraternity where didactic diatribes mattered more than the 'cut and thrust' of normal conversation, the mental disparity of belief in *feng shui* acted as an unspoken but rasping grudge between the two men. By now there was an unspoken truce not to mention it.

The camp boasted a wireless set, an old one that needed repair. It picked up the Chinese service of Radio Malaya but only the two senior men were allowed to listen to it. When members of the Min Yuen, officials of the Masses Movement who were the 'eyes and ears' of the guerillas, reported to the camp, current rumour was passed on. The only reading material allowed were copies of *The Beacon*, produced in Johore, and *Battle News* from Pahang, which couriers left in known 'letter box' drops, such as boles in dead trees and clefts in rocks, and which guerillas fetched at odd intervals.

The thirty guerillas in the main camp were divided into a

defence section and a political group. Days were filled by lessons in Marxism and meetings of self-criticism: at the last session one man was told he was 'not hygienic enough', another was praised for 'having the friendly group spirit' and a third was castigated for being 'a little lazy, slipshod in his studies', 'not too agreeable' and, worst of all, 'fearful of the situation' so 'regarded by his comrades as rather immature'. There was no suggestion of friendliness about the Chinese word for 'comrade', 't'ung chi'. It merely meant 'of like purpose', with even less friendly feeling towards each other than was found in any barrack room full of soldiers anywhere: obligatory, all the same. Nobody ever dared let on that these meetings were so mind-numbingly boring it was hard to keep awake. In fact, boredom was their biggest bane.

However, all remembered one discussion on a subject that the Central Committee considered obligatory for dissemination. There had been some trouble with women guerillas and, as the circular had put it: 'We do not prohibit anybody making love. But such love must be proper. Once love is established, one should report it and its exact circumstances to the organisation. The matter will have to undergo investigation, then both parties will be informed in accordance with the resolution.' Even though the camp had no women members, several questions had to be answered:

1. Why is the love of Communists a serious threat?
2. What is the proper view of love?
3. Are the present few kinds of improper love still appearing in our area?

4. Under what circumstances are they appearing?

5. What is the cause?

6. What is our attitude towards love?

7. How are we to overcome improper love and how to deal with it?

It caused a certain amount of ribaldry at 'soldier' level but anything 'touchy-feely' was even more circumspect than before.

This particular day the camp was on high alert, with sentries placed around the bottom of the camp entrance. A high-powered conference was taking place: four men, sitting on spliced bamboo benches around a table made of thin wood, were discussing the latest directive, brought in from the Central Committee of the MCP only the day before by the Deputy Chairman, a bright–looking man named Yong Kwoh. With him had come another Politburo member named Ah Fat. Originally a Kuala Lumpur man, he had made a reputation for himself in the war: by pretending to be a guerilla deserter; he had infiltrated a Japanese camp, promising to lead them to attack some Chinese guerillas who were harassing them, only to lead them into a guerilla ambush. The Japanese had all been killed but frightful revenge had been taken against the residents of the nearest village to where the ambush had taken place. Later Ah Fat had worked with elements of Force 136. Neither the Political Commissar nor the Military Commander had previously met him when he was introduced to them as the Military Consultant to the Central Committee, a non-voting member, but both of them had heard about his exploits.

Ah Fat was well built and solid but his movements were fluid.

His eyes were always alert, never missing a trick, even though his peripheral gaze was not easy to follow. He looked a tad glum, was round of face, with high cheek bones and flat ears. He stood about five and a half feet high. He had a habit of rubbing the palms of his hands together when thinking. His ears, close to his head, had, in some circles, given him the nickname of P'ing Yee, Flat Ears. Normally taciturn, he could turn on the charm when needed. He was well educated and spoke excellent English. However, for safety's sake, he kept that skill a closely guarded secret lest his 'other' role be jeopardised. Whenever he did speak English in front of other Chinese, it was only of middle-school standard.

This was the second occasion in the past six months that such senior men had been in that camp. The earlier visitors had come to explain the new policy that had been issued the previous October. A high-ranking Chinese Army officer had been infiltrated through Thailand and 'suggested' to the Politburo that the original campaign of unrelieved terrorism, from 1948 to the middle of 1949, had misfired. After the Japanese occupation people were tired of living in constant fear so the new policy was to exclude all unnecessary 'inconvenience' and that the Min Yuen, 'Masses Movement', would now control the masses 'legally'.

The Political Commissar had been saddened by the change in strategy. He had been one of the two representatives of the MCP to go to Calcutta for the South Asian Youth Conference that took place in early February, 1948. It was a cover for the dissemination of the Zhdanov Doctrine that, in brief, was designed to wrest all colonial subjects in Asia from British, French and Dutch control to their own, Communist – of course – sovereignty.

Comrade Lau Beng found it difficult to understand some of the lectures and was disappointed in how little it could apply to Malaya: *Surprise is the greatest factor in war. There are two kinds, tactical and strategic. Tactical surprise is an operational art. A skilled unit commander can generally achieve it. Strategic surprise is attained at the political level.* Why quote Soviet doctrine when it was way above the heads of most delegates?

It was the other Malayan delegate who had asked about Mao Tse-tung and his guerilla war. Luckily copies of some of his writings were available for discussion. But they were dated. One was titled *A Single Spark Can Start A Prairie Fire*, published on 3 January 1930. There were some extensive notes on guerilla warfare, written in May 1938, but they were directed against Japan, not western imperialists. But did that matter? It was the Chinese doctrines that delegates could relate to and they certainly brought forth more discussion than had the heavy-handed Soviet stuff. It meant more to simple people. Such points as, for instance, *Six Specific Problems in Guerilla War, Guerilla Zones and Base Areas* and *The Basic Principle of War is to Preserve Oneself and Destroy the Enemy* brought a spark of interest where little or none had previously been observed. But, as ever, there was a negative side to it as much was made of democracy, ideology and education, heady stuff if one was a zealot but pretty meaningless when most of the delegation had no political vocabulary – democracy? fascist? feudal? what are they? – and 'education' merely meant a village school and boring homework. As for 'ideology' ... Lau Beng's education was not good enough to cover such points without more help because, although he had heard the words, he never properly understood what they meant.

The main point raised by a Padamsing Rai, representative from the Darjeeling Branch of the All-India Gorkha League, was about the retention of Gurkha soldiers serving under the British Crown in Malaya and Hong Kong even after the British had left India and his ideas for thwarting them. The conference chairman invited him to initiate them on his plans. Copying other delegates, he started off by thanking the chairman for allowing him the privilege of addressing fellow comrades. Then, 'what I wholly and totally dislike and disagree with is the way the British have continued to make Gurkhas their mercenary slaves by taking them to guard their colonial interests in Malaya and Hong Kong. How can India allow transit facilities for such a colonial-inspired horror? Somehow this conference must bring moral pressure for this immoral project to be stopped.'

Much applause greeted this surprising remark but it was only after Comrade Lau Beng returned to Malaya did it make sense.

When it was the turn of the Australian Communist Party leader to speak, he had backed up Padamsing's project about 'mercenary Gurkha slaves' and said that the Indian government was at fault for letting Gurkhas continue to serve the imperialist British by allowing them transit facilities. He ranted against British Army officers showing the worst side of the Anglo-Saxon character: greed, selfishness, arrogance, intolerance, conceit and chauvinism, 'so *teddibly* Bwitish,' he mincingly mimicked as though he had a potato in this mouth, working himself into such a frenzy that spit-bubbles hung at the corners of his lips and his cheeks, running to fat, wobbled in his intensity. He calmed down enough to insist that the MCP started an armed struggle against the British and finished off by wishing the Indian delegates a glorious red future.

That conference was followed by the Indian Communist Party Plenum, also in Calcutta, and one of the points discussed was the Zhdanov Doctrine. The Indian delegates were smug because India had got rid of the British without means described by the Doctrine.

On his return Lau Beng had briefed Chin Peng, now the Secretary General, about as much as he had been able to absorb on his return at the MCP's 4th Plenary Session. It was then that active, rather than passive measures for a communist take-over, were discussed and, for these, final orders were given at the 5th Plenary Session, at which he was present, on 10th May 1948, at Saling Rubber Estate, 17½ Milestone, Johore Bahru-Kulai Road. *Fancy still remembering those details ...* wrenching himself back to the present. *I must have missed some of what the Politburo representative has been saying because I can't quite place ...* '... military operations, however, have not turned out as well as had been anticipated', he woke up to.

'Comrades, the Central Committee is worried that there is a stool pigeon amongst our comrades who is secretly working for the long-nosed, red-haired, running dogs and their lackeys, the police,' Yong Kwoh was saying. 'We have been taking too many casualties recently, almost as though one of our number was giving the Security Forces details of our movements. The Politburo decided that I and Comrade Ah Fat make personal contact with all southern Regional Committees and you are our last place to visit. It now looks as if the leaks are coming from Negri Sembilan rather Selangor, which one might have expected because Kuala Lumpur has so many more government officials than anywhere else. Seremban is the place to concentrate on. Only the police will know who the spy is. We need two lists, one of any "sleepers" they may have and the other what the police have about us – their Wanted List, not the bland notices put up on police station notice boards for the general public to read, or not to read,' this latter said with a derisory giggle, 'but the confidential lists kept inside. The Central Committee wants to know how many of our higher ranks are still not known about and, if they are known about, a change of name and even a posting may be needed.'

The others nodded wisely. Lau Beng cleared his throat and asked rhetorically how such traitorous behaviour could be tolerated and that its counter needed the most careful planning. 'The defences in Seremban are far too strong for any overt military attack so it'll have to be by stealth, from the inside. Apart from a long-term sleeper, Lee Kheng, in Special Branch and his wife, Wang Tao, who works in the house of the English police officer in charge, is there anyone else trustworthy who can augment Lee Kheng's efforts if the need arose?'

A low whistle from the sentry stopped their conversation. A runner was sent to find out the reason. Was a stand-to necessary? 'No, Comrades,' he said on his return, 'Comrade Kwek Leng Joo has come with a group of Min Yuen with a piece of seriously important information and wishes to tell you about it personally.'

'Bring him in, immediately,' said Yong Kwoh, with a frisson of excitement, eager to find out matters at a lower level than usual.

'Comrade, what important news do you bring us?' he asked after fraternal compliments had been exchanged.

'Comrade, as barman in the Yam Yam, a nightclub in Seremban that employs taxi-girls, I pick up news from talkative foreigners. Recently, I struck gold. My most important girl is the sister of one Comrade Goh Ah Hok, the contractor who supplies fresh rations to the *Goo K'a*', as most Chinese pronounced Gurkha, 'battalion in Seremban and to rifle companies in other areas on detachment. She has skilfully managed to attract a sympathetic English officer to whom, in order to further our cause, she is giving herself on what might be called "an unrestricted basis".'

He paused and looked at his audience: undivided attention. 'His name is Captain Alan Hinlea and he is the Intelligence Officer of the *Goo K'a* battalion,' he continued, 'and liaises with the police whenever he wants to. He has told her that he is a card-carrying Communist but is under the strictest orders not talk about it openly. He hates and despises his brother officers, thinking them clannish, arrogant and utterly worthless. He himself comes from humble parents, his father was also a dedicated member of the Party and, during the war, was locked up by the English police for his activities. Both this woman and her comrade manager, Comrade Yap Cheng Wu, believe in his sincerity in actively wanting to work for us. He has told me that he proposed that, if this officer really wants to help us, the best he can do is to obtain police records about us. The Comrade Manager wants your permission for this officer to be recruited onto our side. I, too, have often spoken to him and he certainly appears genuine, not only in his dislike for the *gwai lo* political system but also he is most favourable for ours. However, he is a promiscuous man,' he added primly, 'and the other workers in the Yam Yam have nicknamed him the Lustful Wolf, Sik Long.' Here he looked away delicately. 'I recommend that if and when we speak of him, we never use his real name and merely refer to him by his nickname or another if that one offends you.'

Four heads nodded and pin-drop silence reigned as they contemplated this timely, unreservedly unanticipated and fortuitous coincidence.

Yong Kwoh nodded thoughtfully. 'Comrade Kwek Leng Joo, thank you for that. You are still serving us well. Wait with us a while.'

On hearing that an English officer wanted to defect from his own people, something at the back of Lau Beng's mind stirred. *What is it?* He stared into the distance, mind delving back. *Where was it?* And then it came to him: *Calcutta! At that meeting ...* And his mind drifted off to the talk at the meeting then on to the sights and sounds of that city that so offended his senses after the clean green Malaya he knew ...

'Comrade Lau Beng. You're not really with us today. I've twice asked you your opinion but you were miles away,' laughed Yong Kwoh. 'Where were you?"

'Forgive me Comrade. I was back in Calcutta, four years ago and I was recalling talk I heard there. An English officer was mentioned as wanting to join us. It was the Darjeeling delegate that brought the matter up: a dedicated English officer, a card-carrying member of the party who wanted to join the *Goo K'a* soldiers and try and prevent their continued imperial exploitation.

If this man is the same man, and it is unlikely there'll be two of them, then his past can vouch for him. Accepting that this Lustful Wolf is fully serious about what we're going to ask him for, do you think it possible that he be introduced to our "sleeper"?'

During that discourse Ah Fat rubbed his hands together as he thought out the implications of this, to him, devastating news. *So unlike anything the English would ever do. How can I prevent such a danger from happening? If only my English childhood friend whom I knew as Shandung P'aau could somehow help out. But where, oh where, is he?*

Comrade Yong Kwoh listened with intense interest. 'If that is really so, then we're more than halfway there. Our Chairman will be delighted with the news.'

Silence reigned once more as this unorthodox and attractive idea was allowed to germinate. Yong Kwoh smiled then said, 'What a stroke of luck! An original and novel idea, indeed! If the Englishman, as battalion Intelligence Officer, can get those police files copied and then get them to us personally, we will have scored a big victory over the *gwai lo*. 'If,' a pause while his brow puckered in concentration, 'if this Lustful Wolf finds he can't come over himself, then to give her the paperwork and she can give it to Yap or to Kwek.' He turned to Kwek who was still standing to one side of the table. 'Anything to say on that?'

'In principle no reason at all, Comrade, but then the ultimate decision's not mine. However, I must say that Comrade Goh Ah Hok is in a difficult position. We want him to continue his work as we can use him even after any documents are handed over – he speaks Gurkhali so can listen into the out-companies' evening situation reports on his wireless as he has found out the frequencies the military set use in the jungle and keeps us informed and he dare not not feed us with information otherwise he'll be dead. If he is blown we'll be without a valuable source.'

Unusually, Hung Lo, the Bear, spoke up. 'Initially I am reminded of our proverb "Hang out a sheep's head but sell dog's meat", and by that I mean, is it a deep-laid, imperialist trick? However, it could be the other side of the coin, "Feigning to be pig he vanquishes tigers". Depending on which way we look we either fall into a deep trap or find ourselves with a unique chance. We have recently had a directive about relations with women: now we have a *ham sap kwai*, a salty-wet devil, wanting to join us. Even though his credentials seem to be of the highest order, do we really know if his basic moral fibre is sufficiently strong to overcome his bourgeois tastes and allow him to become one of us? Apparently our comrades in the Yam Yam think so and have only been indulging him to ensnare him for us. Something as unusual and important as this can only be decided by the Central Committee. Let us vote on which one we think it is, trap or genuine.'

The Political Commissar was furious that he had not thought of making such points himself. He just managed a solemn affirmation in a neutral tone of voice: 'I have taught you better than I had realised, Comrade.' His lack of enthusiasm was noticed by the others.

Yong Kwoh looked serious. 'This might just come off but it is most risky,' he said thoughtfully. 'It most certainly will need Central Committee authority as, were it to happen, it will stir up such a hornets' nest that life for us, never mind him, will become more than merely uncomfortable. You may have to abandon this camp.'

'That would be a great pity,' said Lau Beng pensively, 'but ... we'll make our decision if and when this Sik Long joins us here.'

'How do you see his onward movement if he actually does join us?'

'As you will have seen from the map, we are in a large square of jungle-covered hilly country, enclosed by four main roads. We, on the northern fringe, are protected by a range of high hills running northeast to the top right square not far from which is a group of three small villages, Kuala Kluang, Jelebu and Titi. Your best bet is to plan to move towards the next Regional Committee at Titi, crossing the road somewhere between Jelebu and Kuala Klawang. If you cannot contact anyone at Titi, then make for the Committee at Durian Tipus, farther up to the northeast. That is the way you came.'

'Yes, of course it is. Thank you, Comrade. It will need the most careful planning, a fool-proof cover plan and the closest monitoring,' said Yong Kwoh after a long, long silence. 'Comrade Ah Fat and I will go back and brief the Central Committee and its response will be brought back here by Comrade Ah Fat personally. The need-to-know principle is paramount.'

'Before we set off, you, Comrade Political Commissar, will write two letters, one to the Chairman of the Yam Yam to keep a watching brief of our new recruit and a second to Comrade Goh Ah Hok to tell his sister to continue work on him.'

'Yes, I will certainly do that but I must make the point that you try and get a decision from Central Committee with all possible speed. The Lustful Wolf's impetuosity, his boldness even, should not be allowed to cool off. If there were any suspicion of what he is intending to achieve he will most surely be sent out of the country, so he'll have to behave as the other officers do until the last moment. In my letter I'll stress that the taxi-girl keeps him sweet and that all concerned keep their mouths shut as tight as never before. Speed is essential.'

'Good thinking. Yes, we'll have to work fast. I'll try to get you an answer in a month's time. Let us plan on Comrade Ah Fat being back here by 1 July to be ready for the planning you will have to do if there is an affirmative answer.'

'Do you think it wise to tell the *gwai lo* that the Central Committee is being approached about his working for us?'

The verdict was 'yes it is'. It would keep up his interest and excitement as well as allowing him to try and work out a plan on how to manage what may be expected of him.

'But for the love of Lenin, tell him to keep his mouth most strongly guarded.' Then, to the Min Yuen, 'Comrade Kwek, please take some refreshment before returning to your place of work. We will get any further information to you in due course.'

After a brew of tea, the Min Yuen left them, happy that it was his good luck that two such senior party members happened to be in the camp on his reporting in.

The group from the Central Committee left early the next morning, the letters for delivery in Seremban awaiting the next visit of a Min Yuen representative. Comrade Lau Beng had asked Comrade Yong Kwoh to pass on to the Chairman his personal fraternal greetings. *Never miss a chance!* A personal bodyguard of two guerillas from the defence element of the camp was detailed to go with Ah Fat to guard him at all times and to help him find his way back once they had re-entered 'home territory'. *At least I'll be nearer the problem back here* if *the remotest possibility of defusing it arises ...* Unconsciously he shook his head.

Saturday, 14 June 1952

The returning guerillas were glad to reach the Central Committee camp in the Cameron Highlands after an arduous and dangerous journey. Conditions there were much less austere than in other camps. The core Communist system was based on the *vlasti*, the elite. These were the cats that were fatter than any other – in a mocking distortion of Marx's dreamed-of 'classless society'. In truth, Communist society had become so densely layered and class-ridden, as only a bureaucratic hierarchy can be, that it always showed Ah Fat how fragile the whole Communist system would be without rigid discipline, enforced by overriding fear.

Chin Peng welcomed Yong Kwoh and Ah Fat back after their long and tiring journey. 'Comrades, I really am glad to see you back. It cannot have been an easy journey either way. I hope you managed to do what you went for.' The Secretary General had a large mouth, perfect even teeth and, when animated, his eyes grew round and his eyebrows rose about an inch and a half.

'Comrade Secretary General, indeed we did.' Chin Peng noticed the excitement in Yong Kwoh's eyes. 'We also have a unique subject to talk to you about. Give us time to get ready and we really must talk about it this very day. But, before I forget, I need to pass on the fraternal greetings of the Negri Sembilan Regional Committee Political Commissar, Comrade Lau Beng. He said that he and you had not met since the 5th Plenary Session in Kulai.'

'Yes, I remember him. I'm glad he's still alive.' Chin Peng looked at his watch. 'four o'clock suit you? I'll order a special something to eat in your honour, "seven stars accompany moon".' Ah Fat was delighted, it was a long time since he'd had a meal of roast duck and dumplings.

After bathing, a change of clothes and a meal, the three senior men sat closeted together, exchanging views on how this new development would affect central planning. By 1952 Communist losses were causing considerable concern. Would this unprecedented development mark a change for the better?

They turned in at 10 o'clock, Comrades Yong Kwoh and Ah Fat almost asleep on their feet by then, the latter inwardly worried and the former happy that the Secretary General had not summarily turned down their tentative acceptance of the Lustful Wolf's potential aid to the Party. He might have done had not Comrade Lau Beng's testimony swung the balance of thought in favour of such a project.

Sunday, 15 June 1952

An emergency meeting of the full plenum gathered at 10 o'clock when Yong Kwoh was asked to give all details of his 'discovery'. It caused a great stir, as he expected it would, and he asked if the

Comrade Secretary General would call a vote to act on this *gwai lo*'s unique potential as a contribution to the Cause.

'Before we go any further,' said Chin Peng, 'I feel I must correct you, Comrade, on the use of the word unique.'

Yong Kwoh did as near a 'double take' as Communist discipline allowed. 'Com ... Comrade, not unique?'

'No, Comrade, strangely and almost unimaginably, a British sergeant from a well-known British regiment,' and he paused as he tried to think of its name. 'It sounded like "God's Brigade" but that can't be right yet I remember hearing that the officers behaved as though they were gods so it could be right. There was this *gwai lo* club in one of the towns and the officers applied to join it. They were told to appear before the committee to see if they were good enough. This so annoyed them, thinking that the person telling them to come before the committee was socially below them, that they refused to join,' and Chin Peng laughed out loud. A fly flew into his open mouth, resulting in paroxysms of coughing. *Who can thump the Secretary General on the back to cure him?* passed through many a mind. Recovered at last, he continued, 'This sergeant was caught entering the jungle with a whole load of his battalion's intelligence files. The local Min Yuen saw him overpowered by a follow-up group at the very edge of a rubber estate and being led away as a prisoner so we never did get any benefit. That and now the *gwai lo* in Seremban both point to a most favourable development for our Cause. This time we must be much more careful in every detail of the planning so that we don't have another disappointment.

'But I'll let you into another secret. You may not know just how wide the tentacles of our Party are in Asia and I have heard, by roundabout means, from as far away as Darjeeling in India, that the man you are telling me about is safe. He even has his Party membership card which he keeps more safely than his virginity,' and the Secretary General, usually severely strict, laughed once more.

'He stopped guarding that as soon as he found out his family jewels were gift-wrapped,' quipped Ah Fat. *Tradecraft, pretend to be one of the boys!*

In the end a vote was called, asking for a 'yes' or a 'no' to letting the *gwai lo* known as the Lustful Wolf help the Cause. It was carried unanimously, especially as it would be a political embarrassment to the Running Dogs and, as the Secretary General thought privately to himself, *it won't be difficult to get rid of him if he is found unsuitable.* Details of the route to be taken after leaving the Bukit Beremban area were decided upon, at Ah Fat's insistence, as he was detailed to be the new English Comrade's mentor and minder, with local Regional Committee chairmen personally responsible for his safety between stages. Ah Fat asked if the decision could be put in writing, signed and have the 'chop' of authority affixed. He was given a copy, written in miniscule writing, the easier to hide, which he had stitched into a waterproof covering: no one knew when rain or river water might render it illegible. He hid it in the butt of an escort's rifle.

After a couple of days' rest, Ah Fat and his two bodyguards started back on their return journey. At each new stage they had a new escort and the old one returned to its base. This method meant that the escorts always knew where they were even though those being escorted did not. It was a well-tried method and the safest: the policy for senior guerillas being for them never to go unescorted. Apart from being a sensible precaution in its own right, it was thought necessary to prevent any of them from trying to make an escape to surrender as had happened once or twice. In any case, those leaders whose task it was to organise and control guerilla movement, operational policy, propaganda and finance had no need to go on jungle operations themselves. The MRLA had excellent foot soldiers whose senior men had learnt their trade against the Japanese during the recent war, not that the Japanese troops in Malaya were the best the Imperial Army had. They seldom went into deep jungle and they were noisy, so easy to keep away from when contact was not wanted. In early 1948 there had been only three British battalions in the country and, while brave even to recklessness, their jungle work was not of as high a standard as that of the guerillas. Like the Japanese, they too were noisy so easy to evade and easy to ambush. The arrival of Gurkha battalions later that year was not a source of anxiety to high-ranking guerillas: the initial appearance of Gurkha troops in Malaya in 1942 had not shown them to be any better than the run-of-the-mill British or Indian troops that fought the Japanese. This was because the three battalions had been milked, bled some said, of most of their good commissioned and NCOs in order to raise and train new battalions while recruit training had been truncated. In fact the three battalions had initially trained for desert warfare and only at the last moment were they sent to the Malayan jungle – the exact opposite. They were also short of much equipment even to start with, let alone the many losses sustained during the retreat down the peninsula. In 1948 six Gurkha battalions had been sent from India to Malaya, the two sent to Hong Kong joining them a year or so later. To start with many were ridiculously under strength, with only fifty all-Gurkha ranks. Training the many new recruits to make up numbers was a hard and slow job. However, by 1952, standards had risen considerably and the guerillas were taking heavier casualties than hitherto.

The guerilla foot soldiers were mostly a plucky and hard-living lot of men whose continuous life in the jungle had given them an almost animal sixth sense of danger and a seemingly telepathic ability to communicate between themselves which allowed them to stay alive where softer European-bred soldiers would have wilted harmlessly.

I am in good hands, Ah Fat said to himself as they started out.

3

Thursday, 17 July 1952

The CO of 1/12 GR, Lieutenant Colonel Robert Williams, looked the very image of a pre-war regular, which he was. Precise, economical movements revealed both his soldierly bearing and those of a skilled sportsman, probably a polo player. Six feet tall, ramrod straight, square-shouldered and flat-stomached, he carried no spare flesh. He had an austere face with compelling eyes, thick dark eyebrows, black curly hair, a high forehead, a straight Roman nose and a clipped, trim moustache. He used half-moon specs for reading. A pleasant voice and a way with Gurkhas that the younger officers envied belied his outwardly severe looks. When, just before Independence Day, 15 August 1947, four regiments of Gurkhas were chosen for the British Army, he had been saddened by his not being one of them. Yet, as others like him, he had worried if 'the Brit Mil Machine' as he thought of the British Army, could handle Gurkhas properly. He himself, and others of his seniority, had had to wait in a British unit until promotion in a British Army Gurkha battalion became available – much slower in a contracting peacetime army than during the war – and, when it did come, it was four years into the Malayan Emergency. He hoped his personal credo, 'stand up and be counted', 'we are our own shop window' and 'react to the unexpected', would still be viable in the 'subalterns' war' being fought in the jungle.

He had read how Communist Revolutionary Warfare had three phases: passive, active and counter-offensive, this last giving the Communists liberated zones that were to be used as bases to take over control of the country. In Malaya the struggle was still active. He had read about how the French in Indo-China were fighting a losing battle although only a miniscule number of Frenchmen realised that – wasn't *la gloire* worth more than just pints of blood? He could see that British Army methods were paying dividends, but oh, how slowly. 'I certainly have a worthwhile task to tackle,' he told his wife when she joined him.

On his arrival, the battalion was deployed on operations. One rifle company was based in Seremban and the other three in separate locations, up to thirty miles distant. He had visited these 'out' companies but had been unable to meet all the soldiers as there were always at least two platoons out in the jungle on what were known as framework operations, that is to say, the company commander, in conjunction with his local police opposite number, knew where boots on the ground could exert the most pressure and keep the guerillas moving. He had been heartened to see the high standards the men had achieved. Once every eighteen months all rifle companies closed on Seremban and underwent six weeks' re-training. This included classification on the range, as many aspects of non-jungle warfare as possible and, of course, 'champion company' events, which included ferocious football matches. Re-training had just started.

He looked at his list of British officers, wondering who he could spare for an extra job that the Brigadier had suggested to him that morning. There was a buzz that the guerillas were planning something out of the ordinary but quite what was unclear. Police Special Branch, composed almost completely of Chinese plain-clothes operators – Malays were not normally suited for such work – had had word from an agent who had contact with the Regional Committee, believed to be based not far from Seremban. He got up and looked at a map on the wall. *I wonder whereabouts. Somewhere in the high hills, I expect. Probably too close for comfort.*

Relations between the Army and the Police were 'good to patchy': both were overworked and under-manned. The Police were still suffering from the effects of the Japanese war: those of their senior officers who had been interned were in poor shape. Many needed a few more years for their pension but were now 'rice-minded' so couldn't stand the tempo of work under the new ruthless High Commissioner-cum-Director of Operations, General Sir Gerald Templer, a ball of fire, who seemingly never took 'no' or slowness as an adequate answer – or for any answer at all, come to that. He was trying his best to clear out the dead wood and was on his way to being successful. 'Jointery', police, army and civil, at all levels from the lowest to the highest, was seen as the best way forward for success.

'Scrutiny of the Form ZZ General Templer instituted analysing all enemy contacts, those that result in a kill or capture and those that fail, shows a gap between what Special Branch can tell our company commanders about guerilla personalities and what the company commanders need to know about them to get a better contact-to-kill ratio. I'm worried about what details Special Branch has about the enemy, Robert,' the Brigadier had said. 'I feel that either their records may not be as up-to-date as they should be or that our liaison should be closer – or indeed both. What are your views?'

Williams tentatively agreed. 'One trouble is, sir, we army people are not in any position to know if the details they do have are, in fact, the best available. It may be that Special Branch does have all the available material but merely that the filing system is inadequate.'

'Could be, could be,' cooed the Brigadier. 'What I'm going to suggest is that you talk to the Officer Commanding the Police District, OCPD, at your next 'joint' meeting – he's a new chap, Ian Clark, ex-Indian Army but not Gurkhas, jumped in with Force 136 and is mustard keen – and I'll talk to my police opposite number, the Officer Supervising the Police Circle, OSPC, when I next meet him.' He spoke of the police in a half respectful, half pitying way, much as one speaks of Parliament. 'Speak to Clark and ask him if he'd like one of your officers on loan for, say, a week to ten days, to help him put his records into "military focus" according to Staff Duties. That, of course, includes the Wanted List but not, presumably, police "sleepers" with the opposition. The OCPD, being a wartime officer, should understand that. Put it to him kindly and don't be pompous about it. Say something to the effect that when our troops are out in the jungle they may well have a contact, a capture with whom they can talk, and names of dead or escaped guerillas could add to the immediate intelligence input before the captured man has recovered his balance. After all, our Gurkhas are much more likely to get results than any Police Jungle Squad is.' The CO was wise enough not to mention to the Brigadier, a Sapper with only European experience, that he had yet to realise how different Gurkhali, Malay and Chinese were.

Williams arranged a meeting with the OCPD and put the idea forward. After a bit of initial reluctance Ian Clark had come round to the idea. 'My Head of Special Branch is one Ismail Mubarak, known to us all as Moby, an exceptional man, actually a Pakistani – but only in his spare time, as it were – and a Chinese speaker to boot. I'll send for him.' A little later in came Moby and after introducing him to the CO, Clark said 'Moby, the Brigadier believes that your Special Branch files need, how shall I put it, "tightening up" and the CO has come to offer the assistance of a British officer to help you.'

'I suppose every little helps,' Moby said, 'and I can't see him doing much harm. Even so, I'll monitor him.'

The CO liked the cut of Moby's jib. Light brown features with a pleasant smile, his thirty years sat lightly on him. *Looks a tough character.*

'Moby, that's perfectly understood. Let me know the moment anything jars.' Before the CO left, the OCPD told him that he had come to know that there was a Captain Jason Rance in his battalion and could the CO ask him to pop round. 'Purely socially. We may have been together during the war,' he dissembled.

Back in his office, he hummed a tune as his fingers worked

down the list ... no ... possible ... no ... The choice came down to two officers. One he thought of as an excellent Company Commander, good with the men, a brilliant linguist, dedicated and hard-working who, if he could get his administrative and staff training as good as his tactics, could go far, Captain Jason Percival Vere Rance – ouch, quite a mouthful – and, from what he remembered from his record of service, had an unusual background. Spoke fluent Chinese apparently. Kept quiet about it, almost as though he was, well, not exactly ashamed of it – why should he be? – but more likely to keep it as a 'secret weapon'. He made company and battalion parties a roaring success by being a ventriloquist: he had a dummy which he sat on his knee and the absurd conversations in Gurkhali and English brought the house down every time he did it. One of his acts involved a highly coloured model krait which produced some side-splittingly funny situations.

Rance had been asked to give the Gunner officers a talk on the jungle as soon as jungle operations started in 1948. They had been absorbed and, to an extent, comforted, by it and the CO had read the notes he had used. *From the air the jungle looks like a sea of cabbages and a novice might be forgiven for thinking that underneath it is impenetrable. It is not. Under the tree-top canopy nature jostles itself to find a space to catch the sun's rays, producing a litany of sounds and a library of sights. Myriads of insects help to propagate new growth as well as slowly, slowly helping to eradicate the old. Damp soil and a mulch of fallen leaves cushion noise but retain tracks for those who know how to read them. Birds and animals are heard rather than seen. Navigation is a skill that anyone can learn: map, compass and a retentive memory along with a cool head are the main requisites. The direction of stream flow, a rise or fall in contours are normally the only aids in featureless terrain to work out one's position when lost: 'If I can't be in those two, or three, places then, however improbable it seems, I must be here,' with a dubious prod of a finger on the map. But the depth of a stream, the thickness of undergrowth, the flight of the birds, the age of a track and many other signs are always there to be read like a book by the initiated and turned to his advantage when, to most others with senses deadened and mind dulled by a depressing and endless similarity, the jungle takes over as a master who cannot be bettered. The jungle is said to be neutral: indeed so, but it is an armed neutrality which can never be taken for granted.*

Tactical movement is normally restricted to about a thousand yards an hour, while in swamp it can be as slow as a hundred. Under the canopy of tall trees visibility is also heavily restricted, often being no more than a few yards in any one direction, so the ears take over from the eyes. Jungle fighting has the characteristics of night work.

The CO had liked what he'd read.

The other choice was at the opposite end of the scale, Captain Alan Hinlea, an ex-Gunner, a remnant from when the battalion had been made into a Gunner regiment in 1948 and officers of the Royal Artillery posted in. After reverting to infantry, all but he had returned to their original units. Hinlea had stayed on to finish a 3-year short-service commission tour. The CO still didn't know what to make of him. An atheist of such virulence, so he'd heard from one of the senior majors, that not only did he not believe in any God but hated the very idea of any belief at all. Chip on his shoulder, never could tell what he was thinking. Came from a disadvantaged background. Oddball, needed to be watched. Yet there was nothing untoward to pin on him, he just somehow didn't fit in properly. Outwardly he seemed keen enough. Only a short-service commissioned officer so comparatively easy to get rid of. He was the IO, mainly engaged with keeping the Operations Room up to date, procuring maps and aerial photographs, arranging for any aerial reconnaissances needed and, of course, liaison with the Police. Well, why not him then? If he were to make a nonsense of it, it would be a good excuse not to recommend any extension of his service.

He made up his mind and sent the Stick Orderly to go to the Intelligence Office and give the IO sahib the CO's salaams.

'Sir, you sent for me.'

'Yes, I did. How busy are you these days?'

'Not all that, sir. With retraining I'm running a short course for company Int NCOs, otherwise I'm less busy than when companies are deployed on ops.'

'Good. Then I do have another job for you. A temporary one but most important ...' and he went on to explain what was wanted.

His IO kept a straight face, his mind churning. 'I see no difficulty, sir,' he answered gravely, only his north-country accent slightly more pronounced than normal. 'I needn't stay all day with the Police and can therefore look into my office from time to time to see if my Int Sergeant needs any help.'

'Fine. So away with you and, after your week to ten days, come back and let me know what you managed to do. If you do well, it will reflect to your advantage. However, at times you do have an abrasive and recalcitrant manner so if I find you have mishandled the job, put the policemen's backs up, it won't pay you any future dividends. In fact, I'll be writing your Annual Confidential Report in a few weeks' time and I'll do you a favour by giving you a warning. I've heard that you visit some nightclub, Wam Yam or some such name. Such behaviour is not far from conduct unbecoming an officer. So cut it out. And, while I'm on it, for goodness sake stop smoking those vile native weeds you seem to like so much. Cut it out, Mister, and learn to behave properly otherwise I won't be able to recommend your short-service commission be extended.'

Hinlea said nothing, saluted and dismissed himself, bursting both with supreme satisfaction at having his most difficult task, that of getting hold of what was in Special Branch, made legal, and a pulsating irritation at having a pistol put at his head, as he saw it. The importance at getting his own back 'on them' became even more starkly etched in his mind.

What fools, these imperial idiots are, he said to himself. *Real fools. Shit heads. I'll smoke what I like when I like and go to the Yam Yam, not the Wam Yam, thank you, as and when I like. Now I've got a real chance to find out what those slag-bags the police think about the comrades. I'll go and see Siu Tse on Saturday and tell her about it.* A daring thought struck him: *if she can get hold of some comrade who can help me in Special Branch, perhaps I'll somehow be able to rewrite, obfuscate or even destroy evidence*

against my new comrades when I take the real facts with me?
Worth trying however risky and difficult! He chuckled in his glee
and impatiently waited for his meeting. *Operation Janus, here we*
come!

Back in his office the CO rang Jason's company. 'Captain
Rance speaking,' came the answer.

'Rance, the CO here. The new OCPD, an Ian Clark, told me
this morning he's welcome a call from you, any time.'

'I have a clear conscience, sir.'

The CO laughed. 'I believe you, many might not!'

Saturday, 19 July 1952

After lunch Hinlea and Rance were sitting on the Mess verandah
each with a cup of coffee. It was a satisfying place, a pergola of
leafy flowers made a pleasant shield from the sun. Hinlea thought
it time to dissemble. *My instructor taught me to keep my powder*
dry and my enemy unsuspecting till the very end, until I know I've
got my best target. The truth is often a useful tool in the service of
lies. 'You know, Jason, I'm finding I'm liking this place more and
more. I'm getting used to this sort of life in a way I never really
thought I would. I like the men. I'd like to be in a rifle company
and earn a bravery award, an MC or even a DSO.'

'No harm in that, surely. Your life as the IO mucking about
with Intelligence can't last for ever.' *What's on his mind, I wonder.'*

'Jason,' Hinlea asked after a considerable pause, 'if you were
stranded in the jungle all by yourself and you couldn't shoot
animals or trap fishes, how would you survive?'

Something is *on his mind.* 'In the Burma war it was a question of roots, fruits and shoots, I can't see anything different here.'

Hinlea seemed not to have expected such an answer so asked: 'Burma. I hear you were recommended for a bravery award a couple of times yourself, Jason. Why didn't anything come through?'

Hinlea took out one of his *bidis* and lit it. Jason wrinkled up his nose at what was, to him, a vile smell. 'Alan, it's up to you what sort of fag you puff at but I think most of the Mess members would prefer you not to smoke them inside, as I have noticed you do from time to time. What's wrong with the normal type of weed?'

Hinlea forced a laugh. 'Nothing really but it amuses me. I learnt to like them when with the Indian Artillery and soldiers in my troop smoked them.' He snuffed it out. 'But back to yourself and getting no gong.'

'Oh, Alan, everything but everything, even loo paper, is rationed in this man's army. Bravery awards, so many of whichever sort every six months. If there're only, say, six MCs for the Division and seven people are written up as deserving cases, bad luck on the seventh! If there are only five deserving cases, the sixth is a lucky man.'

'So I might not get mine straight away,' Hinlea said with a laugh. 'I think I'm getting on with the language. The men don't have all that trouble in understanding me,' gesticulating wildly and muddy, shifty eyes a-gleam.

'Yes, Alan, I've noticed how hard you've been trying. Also I believe you're trying to learn Chinese. Which dialect would that be?' He knew that Hinlea did not know about his own Chinese ability.

'Cantonese,' came the answer as he absent mindedly picked one of the nearer leaves and started folding it in half. 'It is a tantalisingly difficult language and I keep on seeing think bubbles in Chinese characters as I try to speak it,' and both men laughed.

'Jason, something I've meant to tell you is that, unlike the other officers, you seem more at home with Asians than they do. How is that?'

No harm in telling him. 'I had my early childhood years in Kuala Lumpur, Alan, and although many Europeans did behave superciliously towards the natives, my parents would have none of it and we all treated each other in a most friendly way.'

Alan nodded. 'Another thing I've meant to ask. How do you manage to get music that is not on Radio Malaya playing so softly in your room?'

Jason laughed. 'Haven't you heard about my new toy?' Hinlea shook his head. 'Well, not all that new now, maybe six months old. It's something called a tape recorder that has recently taken the place of the older and more inefficient wire recorder. When I know that some decent music is to be broadcast and I have the time, I record it so I can listen to it whenever I want to.'

'Bloody marvellous. What will they think up next?'

'I don't think you've heard my "noises off", as I call them. Recently, on the range, I recorded the firing from the firing point, first rifle fire then Bren gun.'

'For goodness sake why?'

'More for a lark than anything else but just to see how loud the wretched thing played.'

'And is it loud?'

'Loud enough.'

Jason didn't tell him that, during the war, he had spent a short while with the only Nepalese battalion to go into Burma, The Mahindra Dal Nath, commanded by Lieutenant Colonel Ksatra Bikram Rana. His battalion was short of ammunition and, much to the CO's initial bewilderment but later almost mirth, he'd been sent fireworks to let off, hoping to scare the Japanese into thinking that rifles, machine guns and 2-inch mortars were being fired. The idea had tickled Jason who, remembering it, had recorded firing on the range and used it for 'enemy' firing on the 'jungle lane' that had been constructed not far from the camp when various sized figure targets – bodies or heads – appeared. It had added a degree of realism that even he had not envisaged. He had trained Rifleman Kulbahadur Limbu, his batman in the lines and bodyguard in the jungle, how to use it so he, Rance, could the easier monitor his men's reactions. Kulbahadur was also an expert tracker and one who used his nous: when, on one patrol he had been ambushed by the guerillas, he had outfought them, shouting orders for attack, '1 Platoon, move right and open fire, 2 Platoon move left,' when there had been no 1 or 2 platoons. He had been awarded a Mention-in-Despatches in the next Birthday Honours.

'How many people have you killed, Jason?' Alan asked after quite a long pause.

'Difficult to say, Alan, because in a firefight it might be your bullet that hits an enemy just after someone else's has, does that count as a kill or not? Can't say.'

'Do you like fighting?'

'It's not a question of liking or disliking, Alan. It's one's job. Many times it's a question of if you're not as quick as the other chap, then you'll be the one to die. As the old sweats have it, "it's better to make the other fellow die for his country than for you to die for yours".'

'Fair enough, Jason, but were the Japanese in Burma the Gurkhas' enemy and did Gurkhas die for Nepal?'

'In fact you could say they did. I learnt, when I visited Kathmandu in February, 1947, that the Maharaja initially forbade, or tried to forbid, all Gurkha units from fighting in Burma because he feared that the British would lose and that the Japanese would conquer Nepal as a punishment.'

Hinlea merely shook his head in bewilderment at that then changed the subject. 'I've seen how well you get on with Asians. How well do you really know the Gurkhas?'

'How much does one really know about oneself, especially when under great stress, come to that but, to answer your question, I've tried to learn as much as I can about their language as well as their history, politics and religion.'

That surprised Hinlea. 'History, politics and religion? Them's needed for soldiering?'

'Yes, Alan, the more background knowledge one has about one's soldiers the better one knows them.' *I'll see what he thinks of this.* 'Alan, how would you define those three words?'

Hinlea, inwardly struggling to give an educated answer

merely said, 'probably no different from how you do, Jason. So how do you define them?'

'History is dead politics, politics is belief without magic and religion is belief with magic.'

'My politics is my only religion,' Hinlea answered, eyes staring straight ahead, thinking *too clever by half, bloody man*. 'Here in Malaya so many of the guerillas seem to be the underdog. Do you like killing such people?'

Why is this joker so insistent? I wonder.

'Come off it, old boy. I'm no psychopath,' answered Jason with a chuckle.

For some unknown reason the expression 'old boy' caused a violent reaction. Almost without thinking, Hinlea spat out, 'As long as people can say "old boy" it shows that they have no respect for the underdogs in their own society.' Spittle formed at the corners of his lips. 'When I was in India I saw just what Britain hadn't done for the Indians: Calcutta was a disgrace to living humanity and up in Darjeeling, where I was on 15 August 1947, the upper-class snobs in the Planters Club wouldn't have lasted five minutes if they'd spoken to working-class men in England as they spoke to me,' he hissed in his pent-up anger, eyes glazing over. 'The quicker that country gets rid of all Britons, and this 'ere Malaya too, the better for the natural occupants of both countries.' He took a big breath, almost, it seemed to Jason, as if he'd forgotten who he was sitting talking to, and continued, 'If I'd had anything to do with it, they'd never have come here in the first place. Now I'm happy to help them go ...' and his voice trailed off. 'Janus,' said almost in a whisper, 'Janus, look my way.'

'My name's Jason, not Janus, and I am looking your way. Come off it,' said Jason with a laugh, wondering what had come over the fellow. *In a way this confirms my inner thoughts.*

Hinlea did a 'double take' and momentarily looked blank. Then shaking himself like a dog coming out of water, looked narrowly at Jason, eyes clicking back into focus. 'I got quite warm talking then. Forget it. Will you have something to drink?'

'No. I'm full.'

He shouted for a Mess Orderly. 'Bring me a lemonade.' The orderly brought it in a goblet. 'Take it away and bring it in a glass,' he snarled. Jason saw the orderly grit his teeth. He brought it back in a glass and Hinlea drank it in one.

'Alan, that's not the proper way to talk to a Mess Orderly. You should know better,' Jason icily said.

'Yes, I suppose so. Forgot myself,' Hinlea whined, then, in his usual tone of voice, 'I'm going down to the Yam Yam tonight. Coming with me? It's time for my weekly tournament.'

Jason hesitated, deliberately. 'Tournament? Don't get you, Alan.'

'Best of three pin-falls,' and he leered lasciviously.

Jason got up. 'You're cocksure in more than one way. I'd watch your step if I were you.' *Go to the Yam Yam? Never, even if you paid me!*

Toffee-nosed and righteous. For all his good points, he'll have to watch his step: all of them have to watch theirs, scoffed Hinlea to himself.

That evening the Battalion Stallion went down to the Yam Yam earlier than usual. He asked the barman for a large bottle of Tiger beer. Siu Tse came over to him, he put his arm round her shoulders and, in a low voice that only she and the barman could hear, asked if he could have an urgent meeting with the manager. 'He's out at the moment,' the barman said, 'and not due in till around 10 o'clock.'

'No problem with that,' smirked Hinlea, 'I have this lovely girl to dance with and talk to, to say nothing of anything else. But I really do want to talk to him about something serious. No,' he shook his head, 'I can't talk about it down here.'

Hinlea and Siu Tse moved over to their favourite corner and the barman reached for the phone and dialled a number only to be used in an emergency, not that this was one but the Sik Long was in such an excitable state he might start blabbing about whatever it was he wanted to tell the manager and be overheard. *That would never do.* 'Yap *sinsaang*,' he began, 'I have the Sik Long here,' *never use real names on the telephone*, he thought as he spoke. 'He is in an excited frame of mind and says that he must see you. I've told him that you won't be here till around 10 o'clock but were you to be here earlier, it will prevent him from blurting out too much in his over-excited state. It's in connection with that letter I took to the Bukit.' On his return he had reported chapter and verse of his meeting with those two senior comrades to the manager.

'Understood. Keep him happy and quiet,' and the phone went dead.

An hour later the barman's internal bell buzzed and he went over to where Hinlea and the woman were sitting. 'Come with me,' he said. 'I'll take you up to the manager's office. He's just come in.'

'Thank goodness for that,' said Hinlea, 'I was getting worried.' Clutching Siu Tse by the hand he followed the barman upstairs, composing what he was going to say as they went, sobered by the enormity of what was in his mind. A knock on the door; 'Come in.' The barman opened the door, nodded at Mr Yap and left without another word. The other two went in and were shown a chair each. 'Well, what can I do for you?' the manager asked, kindly but with a hard look in his eyes. He did not like being called away from what he was doing. However, coffee was ready and he offered a cup to each.

'Yap *sinsaang*, I need your help. My CO has given me a task that I must let you know about ...' and he went on to say that he had now been officially allowed to do what had merely been hoped for before. The manager's expression changed from one of boredom to one of great interest. 'I can collect all the classified information I need and, if possible, alter the records so as to be useless to the Police in the future.'

'That's wonderful news. We have to wait for the Central Committee's decision which shouldn't be long now.' Yap Cheng Wu saw that the Lustful Wolf really was ready to commit himself for, once having done what he said he'd do, if caught, he'd be so severely punished by the army he'd not see daylight for many, many years, if ever. 'Siu Tse,' he said to the girl who had said nothing so far but had looked at her man with doting eyes as he spoke, 'tell your brother to go and inform the Committee.' She nodded her answer and said, 'I'll leave here early. I can't take Alan with me, he'll have to do without me for tonight,' and she turned towards him coyly.

'So that's all, is it?' asked the manager. 'Keep in touch with us here as and how you progress with your task.'

'Tuan, sorry, yes there is one other most important point. I should have mentioned it before. I can only presume that the Special Branch staff are all staunchly against us and so will be unwilling for me to do what I want to do, unless I work after hours and, even then, I'm sure to have an escort.' Mr Yap nodded his agreement. 'Have you anyone for our Cause who works there and who, somehow or other, can ask to volunteer to work with me?'

'That's something only the Committee can let you know about.' He secretly knew that there was indeed someone buried deep there. He stood up, took the coffee pot off the heater and filled their cups, adding some powdered milk and sugar. As he gave Captain Hinlea his, he said: 'Now, drink this while I write a letter to the Committee. I have to get the details correct.'

They drank their coffee while Yap Cheng Wu wrote his letter, asking a couple of questions as he did, sealed it and gave it to Siu Tse. 'On your life, young lady, and your brother's also.'

She took the hint with a frightened look and the letter, which she put in her handbag. 'I'll get it to my brother just as soon as I can,' she said as she and Alan Hinlea left. Outside, after a brief kiss, they too went on their separate ways, pleasant and unpleasant thoughts chasing each other around in both heads.

4

Saturday, 19 July 1952

Ah Fat and his escort's journey south was exhausting, difficult
and dangerous. Late on their third day out from the Cameron
Highlands, in flatter country, they came across signs of an army
patrol: cigarette smell clinging to a stream and the tobacco not
the type guerillas smoked. Ah Fat's squad of eight, looked around,
sniffing. 'One hour ago, Comrade,' one said. 'It's not old.' Ah Fat
agreed with him. 'We must make a detour. The *gwai lo* will be
making camp not far away, probably near its banks.'

They moved away into a hillier area, found a reentrant and
settled down for the night. The escort commander was worried,
both about the enemy and the safety of his charge, a senior and
respected comrade. Normal guerilla practice, when Security
Forces were in the same area, was for moves in the first and last
two hours of daylight. He therefore planned following the axis
of the stream but on higher ground the better to escape contact
with their enemy. During the next day he sent out a recce patrol.
'Comrade, there are about forty of them,' the patrol leader said
on his return. 'About two platoons of British troops had indeed
camped on the bank of the stream.'

Contact with their enemy was the one thing they could not afford, nor did they want to delay their return journey any longer than necessary. However, on their sixth day, it seemed better to try and get well ahead of the troops who were the more heavily laden. They moved more quickly than the senior guerilla liked but he felt that, provided all necessary precautions were taken, his group could reach the next 'hand-over' place safely. Unfortunately Ah Fat twisted his ankle, so drastically slowed them up. To counter any possible contact a small guerilla patrol made its stealthy way ahead of the others.

'If you come across a *foh t'ung* tree, strip some of the bark off and, as you know, the soft inside makes an excellent bandage,' Ah Fat told the senior man. He managed to find a bonfire tree and, on meeting up with the rest of them later, soaked the thin inner layers and bound Ah Fat's ankle. By next morning he was better and the swelling reduced. They made haste slowly: *T'ung chau kung chi*, Ah Fat remembered a proverb, 'Together in the boat, mutually assist.'

Later on that day when they were walking along the side of a narrow river, one that had thin bamboo, *ningalo,* and rushes on both banks, their lead man who had gone ahead, came hurrying back to say that a platoon of British troops was about ten to fifteen minutes away, moving towards them. They moved as quickly and quietly as possible to a flank. Ah Fat, filling his canteen at the time, turned round suddenly and jolted his bad ankle severely. He tried to follow them but it was too painful. He called softly to one of his gunmen, 'I've messed up my ankle. Take my pack with you and my pistol ammunition. I'll have to hide here, in

the water. Come back and help me after the *gwai* lo have gone.'
Thank goodness I've my secret weapon with me.

The gunman took the pack and the ammunition and disappeared into the jungle, automatically erasing traces where he and the others had moved.

Ah Fat had a good knowledge of how to live, move and fight in the jungle. He always kept what he termed his 'secret weapon' with him, a 2-foot long tube of water vine. The texture of its bark was almost like a grenade and when cut, the watery sap ran out. One could have a drink of half a pint of water from two feet of it: the sap ran forward so it was necessary to make two cuts, quickly, and drain out the section into your mouth before it ran off. The only danger of cutting two feet from a vine was that it left an obviously cut piece hanging and another piece if not hidden. However, most British soldiers were not geared up to noticing such details. Breathing through the vine was of vital use if ever he was caught by a stream and had to hide with his head under water. He had used it once successfully during the war and it had saved his life. It was also of talismanic value to him.

Ah Fat felt for his tube from where he always carried it, on a string round his neck, but it was not there. *Where can I have dropped it?* he thought miserably. *I must have something else or I'm done for.* Looking round he spied an aloe plant at the water's edge: he limped over to it, hastily took a knife out of his pocket and cut a long thorn from the tall, fleshy, spiny-toothed leaves that stood higher than a man. Aloe leaves are tough and a person making his way through a thicket of them was slowed down and apt to be scratched by the thorns: the long leaves make a noise as they grate against each other. With this thorn he scratched out the pith in the piece of *ningalo*, making it hollow. He worked fast, with deft movements, hoping against hope that he could hide before the enemy soldiers appeared.

In front of him was an outsize spider's web, with the enormous black owner in the centre. He ducked under it so as not to break it, slowly turned round and, facing the way the enemy troops were coming towards him, stepped on a large stone and deliberately walked backwards into the water. He rubbed his footprints off the stone and splashed some water on it. Still walking backwards and making his way towards another aloe plant, he saw that there was one footprint he could not properly erase. He bent down, splayed his fingers and made a tiger's paw mark. Then, putting the piece of *ningalo* into his mouth as a breathing tube, silently lay down under the water, holding his nose.

He was only just in time.

'Sarge, look at this,' he heard faintly a few seconds later, 'a tiger's pug mark coming from the other side of the river.'

The guerillas, hiding in a glade, could see what was happening. The senior man had not realised that Comrade Ah Fat was not with them. 'Did anyone see what happened to him?' he asked with dismay. The escort quietly told him what had happened. 'Be ready to fire onto the enemy and draw them away from Comrade P'ing Yee, up the hill towards us. If we have to kill them don't do it by the river.'

The watching men saw an Asian with heavily tattooed arms pointing to the ground. The guerillas did not know that he was an Iban tracker from Sarawak in Borneo. British troops themselves, mainly 'townies', were not skilled in tracking. *The comrade has been seen,* the senior guerilla thought. They then saw the tattooed man bend down as though investigating, stand up and point to the large spider's web.

Ah Fat heard a voice not spoken with an English accent saying 'Not so safe here. Better move on.' The tracker had been so intent on looking near the water he had not noticed the faint scuff marks of the other guerillas. But something nagged at him.

'Better not 'alt here,' an authoritative voice called out loud enough for Ah Fat to hear. 'We'll 'alt a little way on.' The troops moved off.

After judging five minutes, Ah Fat slowly, slowly lifted his head out of the water, looked around and seeing nobody, stood up, taking deep breaths of air with joy. Up on the slope the other guerillas breathed a communal sigh of relief when they saw which way the British troops had gone and hurried back down. 'Comrade, why did you stay behind? What happened?' the senior man asked.

'When I turned round quickly to go with you I hurt my ankle again so I did the only thing possible and hid.' He passed his hand over his brow and said, 'I've got to sit down somewhere for a bit. I'm whacked. Let's move into the jungle where I can change out of my wet clothes.' They hid in a secluded spot while he put on dry ones. They had enough bonfire tree bark to put a new bandage on his ankle. 'On our way now,' said Ah Fat, getting up. They moved on as fast as the damaged ankle allowed.

The Iban tracker's mind nagged at him. *What* was *it I might have missed?* He thought back and played the scene over in his mind and minutely visualised the pug mark once more. *Got it! Two points: there was no tiger smell and,* he inwardly cursed, *the tiger's pug mark was as though the animal was moving backwards. Tigers don't move backwards ...* Ibans are mercurial people. He inwardly shrank at admitting his error and losing face. He decided not to say anything about it and anyway, his English was not really up to it. *Good luck to the clever man who made that mark: deserved to get away with it!*

Ah Fat's party was held up twice more: by planes bombing areas not far from them on one day and, on another, by artillery strafing the area they were walking through. By then the guerillas had learnt to distinguish between 25-pounder and 5.5 mm medium artillery. The former they did not fear – in fact, knowing that the Security Forces would not be moving into areas under fire, some guerillas had managed to walk unscathed through them to surrender – but the latter was a real danger.

'You're overdue," grumbled the Political Commissar as Ah Fat and his escort wearily stumbled into the camp late towards dusk, tense and tired. 'Why? And what have you to report?' Lau Beng, by nature a bully, was not only resentful at having a comrade as senior as Ah Fat on his patch, but a nagging something about him he just could not place irked him. It was too nebulous to be substantiated. But in any case he had taken a marked dislike to him, which was reciprocated but not shown. He had completely forgotten the time when a lad, with his friend Kwek Leng Joo, both having been kicked out of school for open anti-British behaviour, they had been on Kuala Lumpur station platform and had been near enough to hear an English boy in a departing train shout out 'Good bye, P'ing Yee' and a young Chinese boy on the platform shout out, 'Shandung P'aau, we'll meet again ... I know', as the train gave a jolt and moved away, 'but we'll be much older. You've learnt Chinese so well. It will save your life as you saved mine when you killed that krait I hadn't seen.' That incident had stuck in his mind but, of course, the idea that the Chinese lad was now with him in camp was too ludicrous and far-fetched ever to contemplate.

Ah Fat muffled his indignation. 'Comrade, we have made as much haste as security allowed,' came his cold answer. 'The Central Committee had to be fully briefed so as to make a decision about such an unusual and important development. That took time. On our way back we were slowed up by my twisting my ankle and we had to hide once when the *gwai lo* military was using artillery over a wide area so making movement more slow and hazardous than usual and again when a 4-engined aeroplane bombed an adjacent area. We're tired, dirty and hungry. Once I've bathed and changed I'll give you the Central Committee directive.'

'Good comrades don't complain about their bodily discomforts,' came the surly reply. Only a Political Commissar could 'get away with' such an uncouth remark to a senior comrade. 'Have you the go-ahead?'

'All in good time, Comrade. I'll let you have it once I've bathed and changed. We've been on the go without a proper break for a long time. The urgency is not so great it can't wait for an hour. I need to talk to Comrade Wang Ming also about military aspects.'

'Comrade, I'm the one who will decide whom you'll talk to,' came the niggling retort. 'I'm in charge here even though you've come from the Central Committee. Get settled in and come back just as soon as you can.' Black eyes flashed angrily.

Bloody man. So puffed up he thinks he's Lenin in high heels, thought Ah Fat, not liking or understanding such veiled hostility, but he gave a conciliatory and perfunctory, clenched-fist salute and went to where one of his bodyguards was beckoning him. *Whatever else, if I don't appear dedicated I'm finished.*

'We've got a brew of tea for you.' Ah Fat took it behind one of the huts and, leisurely sipping it with the greatest pleasure. *Nectar* he breathed silently, in English.

Washed, changed and carrying one of his bodyguard's rifle, he went over to Lau Beng who was sitting at the 'conference table' as he grandly called it, with Wang Ming. 'Comrade, be seated. Where are the Central Committee's orders? And why bring a rifle when I asked for a document?'

Ah Fat, inwardly chuckling at the Political Commissar's confusion, lifted up the rifle, a .303 taken from the body of a dead Malay soldier, turned it over and, after prising open the small recess in the butt where the pull-through was normally kept, pulled out a tightly rolled piece of waterproof cloth. 'Here you are, Comrade,' he said, handing it over.

The Political Commissar, shooting him a vicious glance, took his time in unwrapping the cloth and carefully unfolding the paper inside, straightening the sheets out on a flat piece of cardboard before studying them carefully. He must have read the whole report two or three times, so long did it take him. Saying nothing he passed it over to the Military Commander, who dutifully took his time to study it. Ah Fat knew the contents off by heart but, as was his wont, said nothing.

At last Wang Ming put the paper on the table, looked at Lau Beng and said, 'It will be tricky to bring off but it could work out properly if all involved are well briefed and careful,' was his neutral comment. 'Also nothing at all must leak to the British running dogs.'

'I was thinking of the implications as you were reading the orders,' was the snooty comment. 'Let me rehearse the sequence of events as laid down in this directive.' He looked at Ah Fat. 'It says that you are to stay in the camp here – too valuable to risk outside – until we move out with the new comrade.'

Ah Fat nodded his agreement. He had no option but to obey Politburo orders and keeping quiet might not antagonize Lau Beng as much as answering back would.

'Now we have Politburo approval we must first organise someone who can approach Goh Ah Hok surreptitiously who, in turn, will alert his sister Siu Tse who then will brief the Lustful Wolf. He must plan his own escape but I believe it best, after he has collected the data, for him to leave Seremban on a Saturday morning, if he can get away unseen, otherwise in the evening, being driven by Goh Ah Hok out to the point on the road nearest us, that old quarry. He'll have to tell Goh when he's ready. We must tell him not to wear army jungle boots but ordinary canvas shoes like we wear, he will have some to play games in, and will be the harder to follow should any *Goo K'a* ever stumble on our tracks. That should give us a 24-hour head start before the running dogs start yapping and looking for him. But they will never find him. He need not have any equipment except basic essentials and his weapon, pistol or rifle. Initially he will join us here for as brief a time as possible, then, once we are sure that he really is willing to go with us and has the details asked for, we go on to Titi, to be met by a party from Central Committee. If nobody is there to meet us, we go on to Durian Tipus and wait there. We'll be able to move much quicker than any follow-up party.' His face lit up as he realised his mistake. 'What have I just said? There can be no follow up because no one will know in which direction he'll have gone nor, as far as I am aware, none of the Security Forces knows that we have our camp here. We'll have to write all this out for Siu Tse to pass on to the Lustful Wolf.'

Wang Ming, not the quickest of brains, asked for most of that again. By then it was dark and the meeting broke off for their evening meal. After that they would normally go to bed but as time was against them, they reconvened.

'I will now write out what I want Siu Tse to do,' said Lau Beng. 'Comrade Wang Ming will stay here with me for any military points I have to include. Comrade Ah Fat, you can dismiss and go to bed,' in a different tone of voice, 'You must be worn out.'

'Indeed I am,' he replied and went over to his hammock. Waiting for sleep to overtake him he wondered just how this venture would work out. *I've a feeling that I'll have more than I bargained for* ... His mind went back to when the Japanese invaded Malaya in 1942 and had started killing Chinese civilians without any particular reason other than that they were Chinese. 'Son, don't stay around. It's much better try and join the Communist guerillas already in the jungle rather than stay here and be killed,' had been his Father's advice. 'I'm too old for that.'

'Yes, Father, I agree but I can never be a Communist.'

So his father had persuaded his son to wait a week before taking the plunge while he taught him what he termed 'tradecraft'. 'I learnt so much from Mr Rance, your friend Jason's father, when we worked together. Best I pass it on to you, especially in these troubled times.'

And a couple of years after being been fully accepted by the guerillas as one of them, honing up on the tradecraft his father had taught him as he went along, he and his group had established contact with some Englishmen in the jungle, lived and worked with them, watching them trying to work a wireless that had a battery only charged by some sort of treadle, not unlike a stationary bicycle. Then one day, in the Sungei Siput area, a long-range aircraft he later learnt had flown from Colombo in far-off Ceylon, had dropped some British officers, known as Force 136, along with arms and ammunition to help them fight the Japanese. One of the men to drop was a fresh-faced subaltern, Lieutenant Ian Clark. They had become friends. Qualities that had attracted the Englishman to Ah Fat were his composure, friendliness and the ease with which he spoke, as well as his excellent English. 'Where did you learn such good English?' Clark asked him one night after their evening meal, always quietly, never so obviously that other guerillas might draw any wrong conclusion. And out the story came: Ah Fat told him about his childhood friend, Jason Rance, and how they had played together for three or four years in pre-war Kuala Lumpur, each helping the other with a new language till both became almost bi-lingual. 'And where is Jason Rance now?' Ah Fat played back the conversation in his mind as though it had happened last week. 'I don't know, sir, I haven't heard of him again.' *Where are you, Shandung P'aau? And you, Mr Clark?*

Lieutenant Ian Clark had told him that after the war he hoped to come back to Malaya and join the police – 'such a beautiful country, if I stay on in the British Army I may never get the chance to come back again' – and that he could see a need for someone like Ah Fat to 'help out', as he put it. 'If ever you need me I'll respond. We need two code words that no one else will know about, just in case. If I do become a policeman I'll most carefully and secretly register them, presumably in Central HQ, but, if we decide on them now, so much the better – but only if you agree.' *And I had agreed.*

'What'll they be?' Ah Fat thought back to his first English friend and their nicknames: 'I'll say "Shandung P'aau" and you'll answer with "Flat Ears" in English or "P'ing Yee" in Chinese. If you make the first move, the names will be the other way round …' and he bound his face with a large sweat rag to stop him talking in his sleep. *Normal footwork even if it is my face* … and he was still smiling when he fell asleep.

Sunday, 20 July 1952

At around midday the sentry at the bottom of the camp entrance saw three unarmed civilians approaching and tugged on the vine to let the sentry at the top notify the two leaders. Soon two armed men came down and met the group where they had been stopped by the sentry. Once it was clear that two of them were Min Yuen, they were welcomed and asked what they wanted. The third man produced a letter from inside his shirt and said, 'Comrade, I've been tasked by the manager of the Yam Yam nightclub, Comrade Yap Cheng Wu, to give this to you. He said it was most important and if possible, be given the answer by return. I'm off now. Let it be given to these two.' He gave it to the oldest-looking man there and made off with a cheery goodbye and a Communist salute.

'You two stay here with the sentry while we take this up to the boss. I'm sorry but you're not allowed any farther than this,' said the oldest-looking man as went back up to the camp. Once there he sought out the Political Commissar and gave him the letter, explaining as he did that the men who had brought it were waiting for an answer to take back, there and then, and that Comrade Goh Ah Hok, the man who had brought it, had already returned.

Inwardly grumbling Lau Beng opened the envelope, then a rare smile curved his thin lips just a fraction as he started to read the details of the Lustful Wolf being officially allowed into the Special Branch office. *This is most exciting but can we really trust this unusual* gwai lo? *At least, let him do what the army has told him to do: we have had Lee Kheng as a sleeper there since our struggle started. Who can activate him ... and how best?* He called out for a brew of cold tea: he always thought better with that. *I'll write a letter to Comrade Lee Kheng here and now, explaining the situation and why and how I want him to help this Lustful Wolf, give it to the senior of the Min Yuen men to take to Seremban and somehow or other get it to Lee. One of the points I will stress is to try and get any names of police agents in our ranks* and he started putting pen to paper, gritting his teeth at the thought of any traitors. *This way we might find the traitor Comrade Yong Kwoh told us about.*

It did not take him long. He put it in an envelope, addressed it to Lee Kheng and put that into a second envelope, on the outside of which he wrote Goh Ah Hok's name. He gave it to the waiting sentry. 'Take that down to the Min Yuen at the bottom of the cliff and tell the senior man to get it delivered, just as soon as he can.'

The sentry took the letter, saluted and hurried away with it: a thin smile appeared on the thinner lips of the Political Commissar. *If this is a success it will redound strongly in my favour.* The alternative was too dreadful to think about. He put the letter away in the safe place he kept such documents and turned his mind to details of escaping once the Seremban mission had been completed.

5

Tuesday, 22 July 1952

For rifle companies operating away from Seremban, dry rations were supplied from the battalion, trucks being escorted by scout cars. Fresh rations were either bought locally or taken out by the civil fresh-ration contractor in his van. Even when 'out' companies closed on Seremban that same contractor, Goh Ah Hok, supplied fresh rations for the main cookhouse. A pleasant, smiling man, he had learnt Gurkhali and had been caught listening in to the out-companies' evening situation reports, sitreps, on his wireless. He was therefore presumed, if only for his own safety, to have one foot in the Communist camp. No proof positive, but ...

Captain Jason Rance's company's last lot had not been nearly as fresh as they should have been so, before the end of their final five-day operation and closing on Seremban for re-training, they had to be thrown away. He decided to go down to Go Ah Hok's place and have it out with him, as he mentally put it, rather than sort matters out through the battalion QM. He phoned the MTO who told him to go with the mail vehicle, drop off at the contractor's place and arrange for it to pick him up on its way back.

I'll give Goh a surprise. I'll sneak in from the back. He told the driver to stop a hundred yards short and he got out. 'Come back here for me,' he said and walked slowly up to the back premises and stopped out of sight behind an open window. He heard Goh's voice on the phone. 'Wai, wai. Goh speaking … Goh.'

Jason heard Goh's voice take on an alarmed tone. 'Tsun po fan tzi?' he asked twice before ringing off with a muttered 'sorry, wrong number.' Jason was puzzled. *Why ask about 'progressive elements' before ringing off? Makes no sense to me.*

Jason again heard 'Wai, wai, Goh speaking,' and, after listening to the answer, continued, with his tone more authoritative: 'Siu Tse, listen sister. I have a most important letter I have to give to you. It is about your special friend the Sik Long and Lee Kheng. I'm too busy to bring it over so you come over to my place and pick it up.'

The line must have been bad because three times the message had to be repeated to Siu Tse, whoever's sister she was. 'All right, then, in that case I'll send it round to the manager at the Yam Yam by hand of my number 2 and he'll give it to you. Understand?' A short silence. 'Yes, of course I know my way up to it, been enough times myself, haven't I? Goodbye, Comrade sister.'

'Comrade sister!' 'Know my way up to it.' That made Rance think. *Up to where? A direct line to a Siu Tse, little miss, a sister and a comrade. What's it all about? It might mean nothing but these days one can't be too careful.* He felt it better not to show his face and tell the battalion QM instead. The mail vehicle drove up and took him back. Once in his office he thought back to Goh Ah Hok's phone conversation. On the face of it, apart from

'comrade', there was nothing to be suspicious about yet ... yet ... there were two other points that pricked at his suspicious mind: Siu Tse and Sik Long, Lustful Wolf. Coded names for whom? She may, for all Rance knew, have many 'special friends'. *Is there*, he wondered, *more to it than I am starting to imagine – or less? And who is Lee Kheng? And 'up to' where? And whose sister? Goh Ah Hok's?* He shook his head in dismay at his ignorance. *Got it! I'll get hold of Ian Clark. I know he wants to have a chat* and, picking up his phone, asked the exchange to put him through to Police HQ. He got his answer in Malay and, following suit, asked for the OCPD. '*Siapa chekup, Tuan?*' He gave his name and was told to wait.

'Captain Rance? Ian Clark here. Is this because the CO's given you my message? Otherwise what do I put this call down to, may I ask, glad though I am to have the chance to speak to you.'

'Mr Clark. Pray excuse my butting in unofficially. Yes, indeed the CO did tell me you'd like to have a word with me: I told him my conscience is clear yet I do have something I'd like to talk to you about privately. May I come down and see you, either in your office or, maybe better still, in your quarter after work?'

'Delighted. The latter is better. How about this evening after work? Say 5 o'clock, either for a beer or a cup of tea. Both are on the menu.'

'Righty ho, see you then.'

He made his way to the Police Station in the duty vehicle and told the driver to dismiss. He was directed to the OCPD's residence by the duty constable, a shy young Malay, and, as he was at the front door, it opened. There stood a grinning OCPD.

'Saw you coming! Come along in.' They went into the sitting room. 'Beer or tea?' Jason opted for the latter and Ian called out, in English, 'Wang Tao, bring tea and biscuits.' After pleasantries and before Jason had started to tell Ian Clark about his worries, the OCPD told him just how he'd heard of Jason from one of the guerillas working with Force 136, Ah Fat ...'

'Oh, how wonderful if he's my Ah Fat,' Jason interrupted. 'How is he or rather how was he?' he asked eagerly.

'... and I operated with him till the surrender,' Ian finished off before answering Jason's queries. 'I was most impressed with his knowledge of English, how he had so obviously been happy to remember you, his childhood pal, and the names you had called each other. By the way, what does Shandung P'aau mean?'

'I was big for my age and big strapping people are said to come from Shandung and they are always called a "Shandung cannon, p'aau, so Shandung P'aau.'

'Makes better sense now.' He explained that those also were the code names they had decided upon when Ian had suggested to Ah Fat to be an agent for post-war police work – 'premature and presumptuous of me.' Jason grinned appreciatively, listening with pin-drop silence, more than happy to have news of his childhood friend and rehearsing much that lay at the back of his mind. 'And where is Ah Fat now?' he asked. 'Yes, we were the best of childhood pals. I'd love to meet up with him again.'

'So would I. I don't know where he is and I only wish I did. We're expecting something nasty to brew up quite soon and he would be a God-send. But, have another cup and tell me why I have the honour of your company?'

'Bring some more hot tea,' he called to his Chinese woman servant who came in surprisingly quickly, and they talked local matters until teacups were once again filled. Wang Tao unobtrusively 'inspected' Jason before she left. She was interested in a military visitor but knew better than to eavesdrop inside the room.

Jason told Ian enough of Goh Ah Hok's background to make sense about what he'd heard him say earlier on in the day. Three points worry me, Ian: one, the use of the word 'comrade'; one the reference to Siu Tse, meaning "little miss", sister, innocent in itself maybe but intriguing to say the least of it to link it to the Randy, no, Lustful Wolf and "special friend". It's the third person, a Lee Kheng. I wonder if you know a Lee Keng who might just be the patch of blue sky in the jigsaw puzzle, remembering that, to save his life, Goh Ah Hok must "run with the hare and hunt with the hounds".'

'Jason. You're sowing seeds of doubt in my mind. There is a Lee Kheng who is one of the Special Branch operatives, a long-term man with an encyclopaedic knowledge. His wife is the woman who brought the tea in. I know nothing untoward about him but, just suppose, most unlikely though it be, he's a long-term sleeper and that the letter to be delivered is to the effect that all the really secret stuff is to be given to this Lustful Wolf or a special friend for "onward transmission" to "them", the guerillas, through this Siu Tse, then we really will have red faces. However unlikely a scenario sadly, these days, it isn't an impossible one. I have no suspicions about him so can have no proof but ... .' and he left the rest of his sentence unsaid.

'No suspicions so no proof, I agree, but proof as such is often difficult if not impossible to be accepted by judge and jury. However, a gnawing thought is at the back of my evil mind that you may well be right. It is not up to me to solve this problem and it would be damned bad luck on any career prospects Lee Kheng might have were he as chaste as a new-born babe but ...'

Ian Clark sighed. 'You are right. But the last thing we want to happen is for the proverbial omelette to hit the fan, something I do not want, nor will I, prejudge anyone but ...'

'Two buts equal a what?' asked Jason.

Ian looked at him: 'A cover plan,' is my answer.

'Which is?'

'Somehow let's shake the tree but not necessarily to his detriment. I'll get him sent on an upgrading course and see if there are any unusual reactions.

Jason took a piece of paper out of his pocket and wrote 'Keep talking' on it. He leant over, showed it to Ian and got up, quietly tiptoeing towards the door which he opened abruptly – and in fell Wang Tao who had had her ear to the keyhole.

'That was quick of you,' said Ian as he went over to the woman, now getting onto her feet and looking more than embarrassed. In bazaar Malay he upbraided her and told her to get back to her quarters, 'I'll consider what to do with you later,' he told her as she shamefacedly left the room.

The two Englishmen sat down again, both worried. "I didn't think we'd get such fruit from the shaken tree so quickly,' Ian said, shaking his head in dismay. 'I can't keep her on and, presuming she listens in to what I say to guests or on the phone, I don't want her around any longer.' He looked unhappy as he thought of the security risks that had gone unattended.

'Is an upgrading course still your answer?' Jason asked.

'Well, what would you do?'

A mischievous grin appeared on Jason's face. 'Just suppose Lee Kheng is a good Buddhist and clean. Send him with his wife on a week's penance to, say, somewhere distant, Ipoh or Penang, from where he can't easily slip back and tell any superior he might have of what has happened to him or why. Tell him he is not being punished but, for his wife's soul's sake, she must pay a penance.'

Ian's eyes twinkled. 'I can see that your knowledge of matters Eastern is almost inbred,' he said, laughing as he did. 'I'll send them and their children on their way by tonight's mail train, with an escort.'

Before Jason left, Ian asked him why, so he'd heard, he did not use his Chinese. 'I keep it as a secret weapon,' was the enigmatic answer. 'My father thought that one of the best gifts a father could give his child was fluency in another language, preferably one known by only a handful of other British people. I have never forgotten when he told me why he himself had been so successful – "no, son, I'm not wanting to sound boastful" – was by never letting on that he knew Chinese when it was not necessary. "I'd never have learnt the secrets I did if the Chinese I overheard had had any idea whatsoever that I had a perfect understanding of their conversations. Had they had the slightest inkling, they'd never have opened their mouths anywhere near me. Keep your knowledge a secret, son, and, if you can manage by pretending only to know just enough to cope, you'll gain enormous dividends." That was the first bit of tradecraft my father had taught me and I've followed his advice ever since.'

'How did you learn it?' pressed Ian Clark.

'My father, a plain-clothes, Chinese-speaking intelligence operator working in Kuala Lumpur, Malaya, in the mid-1920s, used to take me to play with the son of his Chinese counterpart, a boy of his own age, each working day. You already know his name: Ah Fat. I was an only child, loved the fun of frolicking about with him and having even more fun with a language that my mother never learnt. I never lost tonal accuracy from those childhood days. As a child is when languages stick in one's mind. Much later, during the Burma war I was the Intelligence Officer of 1/1 GR and found it was the "wrong" Chinese when I had to contact Stillwell's Chinese Army. But I have never forgotten it. After leaving my battalion in India following partition in 1947 I joined 1/12 GR in Burma – again! Then, after Burmese independence on 4 January 1948, we moved to Malaya and once more I'm back in the Chinese language milieu.'

'It all makes very good sense.' After a bit more chitchat, Ian said 'I'll send you back in our duty vehicle. I'd rather this got no further at the moment, Jason, don't you agree?'

Jason did and as he left the premises, he happened to be seen by Lee Kheng who wondered why an army officer had come to tea. *I'll ask my wife about it,* he mused, not realising how, unfortunately for the pair of them, events had turned sour.

Next morning the OCPD opened his mail. In an envelope marked 'Secret' was a letter from Police HQ of particular interest. It had been appreciated, at the highest level, that once the Chinese squatters, the best sources of food the guerillas had, were re-settled, the supply of food would be cut off. After a slow, disruptive and expensive process it had paid dividends. Now more needed doing so a new phase of Food Denial Operations was being planned: to go into deep jungle and destroy the crops in the 'gardens' that the low-level guerillas had so laboriously sown once trees had been felled to make up for deficiencies. It had also been decided that hungry men will go where there is food and so a plan to get guerillas to surrender was introduced. To help spread the message voice aircraft were to be sent over areas where hard-core guerillas were suspected and leaflets dropped that offered safe passage out of the jungle and a financial reward after surrendering with extra money for any weapon brought in. That coincided with local elections, after all, weren't the British going, one day, to hand Malaya over to the Malayans? To make the start for self-government resonant and wide-spread, voice aircraft were detailed to let loyal citizens prepare themselves to vote – a novel concept.

The paperwork in Ian Clark's office said that surrender leaflets would be forwarded, through SWECs and DWECs – so much alphabet soup – and that the army was responsible for dropping them. He got on the phone to the Adjutant of 1/12 GR and asked him if he had had such a letter. Yes, he had, from HQ Malaya Command and, once the leaflets had arrived, they would be dropped. After all, what were army aircraft for? 'I'll let you know when we can arrange this,' and the Adjutant rang off, wondering what sort of war they were fighting.

Unfortunately, the wrong tapes were put into the plane's

loud speaker: the loyal citizens of Seremban were exhorted to surrender and the guerillas were similarly exhorted to cast their vote. Such can happen and happen it did! Result, fewer folk voted than might have done and no surrenders!

6

Friday, 25 July 1952

The Political Commissar's lugubrious face lit with joy when he was given a letter, delivered hot foot by special Min Yuen messenger. *At last we're taking a really big step for war against the imperialist lackeys,* he thought as he opened it. Yet, as he read it, his features became as ugly as a mummified monkey's, anger almost reaching boiling point:

> *We received your letter in good time. After business closed for the night, we had a meeting in the manager's office to decide just who would make contact with Comrade Lee Kheng. We decided that it would best be done through his wife, Comrade Wang Tao, the house servant in the OCPD's residence and one to be trusted just as much as her husband. We felt that during morning office hours would be the best time when the OCPD, Mr Ian Clark, would be in his office and, being unmarried, no one else would be in the house. We did not want to use the telephone just in case the lines were monitored.*
>
> *Comrade Yap Cheng Wu went round in person: it was felt*

that he could make an excuse about his license were he to be discovered. Imagine his consternation when he found that the only servant in the house was an elderly Indian cook. When Comrade Yap asked him where Wang Tao was, he was told that the previous evening the OCPD had sent her, her husband and their three children somewhere north for a week with no word of any return.

This development is entirely unexpected. We await further instructions.

As Lau Beng reached the end of the letter his stomach plunged. He was beside himself with rage and frustration. *Why? Why? Why? Now of all times, without any known or given reason, my one and only link for success has disappeared.* And not only that: adding to this bombshell his wireless had become unserviceable and the one man in camp who knew about such things had insisted that better a new set be bought rather than the old set repaired. *A chance so unique, this gwai lo and his wish to help and my part in it being known to the Central Committee ... and with all the effort of Comrade Ah Fat – although I don't like something, but what? about him –bringing back the go-ahead ... I'll look a complete fool if they ever hear that I've failed.* He put his head in his hands and thought, long and hard, knowing that in the end, anything he did or decided would have to be a joint decision taken with Wang Ming and Ah Fat, even though he himself had the final say.

He called over the nearest man in earshot. 'Comrade, go and tell the Min Yuen comrade that the message he brought with him needs serious thought which will take a day or so to resolve so go back now, empty-handed and come back in two days' time.' Then, to another man, 'Go and fetch me Comrades Ah Fat and Wang Ming.'

Ah Fat, bored almost to tears doing nothing and wondering just how he could get to warn Ian Clark without compromising his own position, that is if he had come back to Malaya after the war to become a policeman, had seen the Political Commissar's reaction to the letter. *What now?* 'Comrade Lau, you sent for me. Here I am,' he said, formally and stiffly. The Military Commander also announced his presence.

'Sit down, both of you,' said Lau Beng. 'We have a major problem on our hands,' he started off when they were seated, obviously seething with bile, 'and I can see no immediate answer. Listen to this. You both know I had sent a letter to our comrade in Special Branch, Comrade Lee Kheng, to help a British officer, known as the Lustful Wolf, who, in turn, is helping the OCPD, a new man, a Mr Ian Clark,' Ah Fat's start of surprise was only covered when he went through the motions of swatting a fly from his face, 'sort out his records.' Mysteriously, Comrade Lee, his wife, who also works for us in the OCPD's house, and children, have been sent away – no, I don't know where, why or for how long– and now there's no one who can take his place. Having gone to so much trouble and got so far, how can we abort now?'

A gloomy silence prevailed. Ah Fat's countenance did not in any way alter as his mind buzzed with a bold plan. *Shall I? Shan't I?* He jiggled his thoughts, weighing up the pros and cons, keeping silent and looking abstractly to his front.

'Comrade Wang Ming, what have you to say?'

The grizzled guerilla veteran stirred uneasily, nothing having come to mind. He merely shook his head in dismay and said, 'unless Comrade Ah Fat has an idea I can chew over, I just don't know what to say.'

'Comrade Ah Fat, your silence is unnerving me. You are deep in thought. Have you any bright ideas?'

Still Ah Fat said nothing, merely looking straight ahead without moving. *Play difficult to catch*, he thought, rubbing his hands slowly together as the significance of the occasion was turning in his mind like a slow key. The other two fidgeted, waiting for him to break his silence. 'I'm not a coward,' was his unexpected opening gambit. 'Great challenges must be met with equal greatness. Those who think of personal consequences cannot be brave. I do have an idea that goes to the limit of what is expected from a good comrade,' and he relapsed into silence again.

This was too much for the Political Commissar. 'Don't talk in riddles, Comrade, please. If you have an idea, out with it. This is deadly serious.'

'It was the name of the OCPD that put this idea into my head,' Ah Fat eventually resumed. 'I remembered I'd met him during the war in Force 136. He told me that he hoped to be a policeman in Malaya after the war because he liked the country. It seems as if he has got his wish. Ahem,' and he cleared his throat. His listeners looked at him, saying nothing, trying to imagine what was in his mind.

'How well Mr Clark can speak Malay is something I don't

know. However, you know that I can speak English well enough to sustain a simple conversation. Just suppose I "happen" to meet him and recall him as a wartime companion, it might just be possible I could get him to let me take Lee Kheng's place so help the Lustful Wolf.' He looked, first at the one then at the other, full in the face. 'If nothing positive happens we're no worse off than we are now, if something does, we're better. Of course it's a risk but better a chance of success, however remote, than obvious failure by doing nothing,' and he again relapsed into silence. *Shot my bolt now, I have* and, in his pockets, crossed his fingers, as he'd learnt to do as a boy with Jason.

Lau Beng was in a cleft stick. Without Politburo say-so such an escapade was out of the question yet it would completely ruin any forward momentum if he were to try and contact them for permission. He turned to his military commander, for form's sake. 'Comrade, your views?'

Wang Ming had almost dropped off during Ah Fat's silences and came to with a jolt. Not quite sure what to say, he mumbled, 'Oh, I agree with the majority.'

That makes two with mine as the casing vote, Lau Beng thought. *I don't like it and it gets up my nose but what else is there?* 'Right, let's say you're on. I'll have to report it to the Central Committee.' *That nag again: wasn't there another Englishman somewhere?* 'Is that the only Englishman ...'

Uncharacteristically Ah Fat interrupted him: 'Comrade Political Commissar. You seem to have forgotten my status. In your camp I accept your authority, elsewhere I don't need to.'

Lau Beng glared at him, swallowed and, tipping his chin, put his head on one side, eyebrows sanctimoniously raised, ready to disapprove of anything he heard, no matter what it was. About to say something he unexpectedly kept quiet and after a short delay, asked, 'so what next?'

Ah Fat's answer was firm. 'I'll go, as an ordinary civilian, wearing plain clothes and, of course, with no weapon. I'll need some money and some sort of documentation. The next lot of Min Yuen will have to bring me some clothes and you, Comrade, can tell them how to get an ID card, not made out in my own name. I'll decide how best, when and where, to make my contact. Please remember that I'm clever enough to dissemble my true colours and, once contact has been made, see if I can somehow, without letting on that Comrade Lee's disappearance is known by us, get myself asked to do what we wanted him to do. Of course, I can't guarantee anything. I'll take the wireless set with me and if I see that I can get nowhere, I'll come back as soon as the wireless set is mended, otherwise you can expect me back, say, in a fortnight's time. You must understand that in cases such as this, strict timings cannot be guaranteed.'

The Political Commissar looked at him grudgingly. 'Under the circumstances, I can't override you. Go and, on return, you'll make out your official report, one copy to the Politburo and one to me. When the Min Yuen comes back you can tell him what clothes to bring and I'll tell him about the ID card. Damned nuisance but what else can we do?' For once the grinding omnipresence of the Political Commissar was dimmed, his face resonating with the solitude of a long-term prisoner.

Friday, 8 August 1952

It took all of a week before an ID card, with the same name as the military commander, Ah Wang Ming, but with different characters, and some clothes were brought to the camp. A message was sent to the Min Yuen waiting below that an important personality was to be taken to Seremban and they were to obey his every order. Ah Fat changed into an open-necked white shirt, dark slacks and canvas shoes, gave his uniform to the senior man in the defence section and went to hand his pistol and ammunition into the cave.

Lau Beng gave him the wireless. 'Here're 500 dollars. Sign this receipt for them. I'll need to know how you spent the money. Fix the wireless set with our usual comrade in Jalan Channer who'll fix it for free, not that more modern shop in the High Street. The Min Yuen will show you where.' Although spoken in Chinese, he used the Malay word, 'jalan' for 'road'. The irony of the shop being in the road named Channer was not lost on the senior Communists: Captain Channer, of the 1st Gurkha Rifles, had won the Victoria Cross fighting against some Malays on 20 December 1876 – imperialist brutality against the natives.

'Shall I buy a new one if the comrade says that the set is too old to repair? If so, I'll need more money.'

'Yes. Get a model that is less bulky than this old one.'

'Comrade, I'm on my way. Wish me luck.' *At least sound as if I'm on the same side.*

The Political Commissar looked at Ah Fat, cold, basalt black eyes, almost alive with virulence. 'Good luck, Comrade, but be warned, I have ears and eyes you know nothing about and where you least expect them.'

Thank goodness I'm not one of you for real but thanks for the warning. Knowledge helps one stay alive; ignorance the opposite.

It was like a breath of fresh air to be at the bottom of the camp entrance, unencumbered by anything heavier than a pack but strange, almost unnatural, not to be carrying a weapon. The two Min Yuen who escorted him to the main road where a taxi awaited them were in awe of him, knowing his importance. Ah Fat, yet to think of himself by his pseudonym, kept silent and only when he was in the taxi did he appear to relax. 'First of all, I must put this wireless set in for repair. You will know, I'm sure, where Jalan Channer is,' a nod from the driver, 'and you,' turning to the older of the Min Yuen, 'where our Comrade's repair shop is.' More nods.

Ah Fat asked his escort where he recommended he stay while he did the job he'd been sent to do. 'After you've put your wireless set in for repair, we'll take you to a place we trust, Comrade.'

At the repair shop Ah Fat took the manager to one side, quietly to let him have the set's provenance. 'I'll have a good look at it,' he said, taking a cursory glance into its innards after taking the back cover off. 'Hm. At first glance it's well beyond its best but I'll see what I can do for you. Even if I do something with it, it's sure to break down again.'

'In that case I'll buy a new one from you, a smaller and more modern model.'

'Wise. It'll take me a day or two to have a really good look at this old set. Come back after the weekend and I'll let you know the outcome.'

Back in the car he was driven to a hotel where he booked in, using his false name. 'Before I do anything else,' he said to the senior Min Yuen, 'give me your contact details. I may need you during my stay and certainly will for my return.'

The phone shrilled several times before a sleepy voice answered, 'OCPD ... what do you want so early on a Sunday morning?' It was half past 6.

'Shandung P'aau calling. Remember? Shandung P'aau.'

An audible gasp. Pause. Ah Fat felt a tension, like a mild case of first-night nerves. Then 'Flat Ears.'

'Yes, Mr Clark. I am so sorry to call you at this unreasonable hour but the fewer people who might hear us the better. I'm glad you have your wish to be a policeman in Malaya but so sorry that you've had to deal with a sleeper in your midst.'

How does he know about that? 'What do you want?'

'To talk to you privately and soon.'

'Then we must meet. Let me think.' Ah Fat heard a low humming almost of meditation as Ian Clark thought out where best a meeting could take place. 'Do you know your Seremban and, if so, how well?'

'I had as detailed a recce as possible yesterday when I arrived so I know the nodal points,' – *he hasn't forgotten his English* – 'but not in detail.'

'Tell you what. There's a small lake not far from the Rest House. Be seated on the bench next to the bougainvillea at half past 11 and I'll stop my car, a black Morris Oxford, N 1549, next to it. I won't switch off. Come, if possible without being tailed …'

'I'm glad you're thinking like I am, Mr Clark. I'm only alive because of my tradecraft.'

'… and jump in. We'll go off to somewhere private.'

'Yes. Fine. I'll be there. Please bring a map of the surrounding area with you. I'll need to show you something.'

'Yes, I'll bring one along with me. Tell me, Ah Fat, would you like to meet Jason Rance?'

'Jason Rance did you say? My Jason Rance? Of course. Is he here?'

'Yes. I'll try and bring him with me. See you at 11.30 sharp. Bye now,' and the phone went dead.

Ah Fat put his hand set down. *Jason. My Shandung P'aau. After all these years. Can only be a good omen.*

Ah Fat's route to the Rest House started in a taxi. Halfway there he got out and went into a tea shop, watching the passers-by – no one interested – before walking on. One of his shoe laces mysteriously undid itself twice and, bending down to tie it up properly, he managed to look back between his legs. Nobody. Tradecraft. He found the bench and sat down, checking his watch.

Ian Clark's black Morris Oxford drew up and Ah Fat checked the number plate, N 1549, *That's the right one.* He saw that there were three people in it. *Will I recognise Jason?* Ian Clark drew up, not switching off and beckoned to Ah Fat. 'Hop in the back.' He'd already learnt that ecstatic greetings were not Chinese style and that the more sedate way of operating was so normal it would cause no undue interest. Only once in the car, as it drove away, did the other occupant turn round and, 'P'ing Yee, so it *is* you after so much time,' said in faultless Chinese. Ah Fat's answer was, 'Shandung P'aau, I knew we'd meet up again as I waved you away from Kuala Lumpur station in the train. And *was* I sorry to see you go,' and they shook hands, hard and tight.

'What's that all about?' asked Ian, delighted to see the two of them hit it off so well.

'Oh, we were just making sure our childhood code words were still relevant,' said Jason and told Ian what they were.

Ian laughed. 'Ah Fat and I used them this morning.'

'And now I must introduce you to the Head of Special Branch, Ismail Mubarak, known to all and sundry as Moby. He is our king-pin in the intelligence world and all our efforts would be lost if he were not with us. Moby, this is Ah Fat, that's all you need to know at present.'

Moby and Ah Fat shook hands.

'Where're you taking us, Ian?' asked Jason.

'A few miles out of town to somewhere quiet where there'll be no fellow travellers. Bhutan Estate, with a Gurkha workforce, not far from Sepang. The manager, a one-time prisoner-of-war of the Japanese, John Theopulos, has a guest bungalow. He owes us something so has most considerately offered it to us – plus cook and steward.'

'I didn't know there were any civil Gurkhas around here,' said Jason.

'Yes, John's uncle brought the original lot over from Darjeeling, coolies – not a dirty word then – from the tea gardens, in 1904. Two other estates have them.'

They drove on in silence. Then Jason remembered. 'Flat Ears, what is the significance of *Tsun po fan tzi*? I heard it used on the phone when I was eavesdropping: it was new to me.'

'It's code for asking a person if he is a comrade or not,' came the unexpected answer.

Jason leant back and, not seeming to open his mouth, pitched his voice right up against Ian Clark's left ear. 'We're in the deep end, pal,' and, so surprised was Ian that he nearly ran into a car coming the other way. He had not heard of Jason's 'party tricks'.

After meeting John Theopulos and having a drink with him and his wife, the four visitors were escorted to the guest bungalow for lunch. Conversation was general, swapping yarns about their war years, nothing serious and all 'above board'. The Gurkha waiter was delighted to be spoken to in Gurkhali by Jason as John Theopulos only spoke Malay to his workforce. After coffee they were on their own.

'Ah Fat, you first,' said Ian, 'chapter and verse. We've all afternoon so A to Z please.'

So Ah Fat held the floor, describing how his father had urged him to join the guerillas after necessary lessons in tradecraft, mentioning the part he'd played in slaughtering some Japanese which had earned him the role of Military Consultant and non-voting member of the Central Committee, then on to the visit to the Regional Committee's camp near the top of Bukit Beremban – an intake of breath from both Jason Rance and Ian Clark – with Yong Kwoh. Such an unusual visit was because the Central

Committee believed that there was a traitor – *and it is not only I who is to blame* – in the Seremban not the Kuala Lumpur area. So what was wanted was all details, *all*, the secret ones if possible, of those on the Special Branch Wanted List of guerillas. It was then that the Min Yuen had brought in details of a *gwai lo* officer who had been detailed by his battalion to help Special Branch with a revised documentation scheme and a Captain Hinlea's reported wish of joining the guerillas with a copy of the Wanted List …

'So that's who Goh Ah Hok was talking about that time I was eavesdropping,' Jason interrupted. 'That blighter Hinlea must have gone off his rocker or been drunk to get so involved with the enemy against us. Nothing of the sort would ever occur to any normal British officer no matter what class he comes from. He's an apple that has gone rotten before it was ripe.'

'Shandung P'aau, "rotten and ripe" –your words. You've reminded me to go into more details about what Lau Beng had told us at our initial meeting,' and Ah Fat told his listeners about the Calcutta conference and what had been learnt there about an English army officer's Communist leanings. 'That resulted in my having to go back to the Politburo with Yong Kwoh to see if planning would be allowed or not. It was only after my return that the Regional Committee learnt about Lee Kheng, with wife and children, being sent elsewhere so I volunteered to act instead of him,' and the other three listened spellbound. 'My task is now to try and take the place of your long-term sleeper …'

'So Lee Kheng really was a long-term sleeper?'

'Yes, Mr Clark …'

'Please call me Ian.'

'Yes, Ian. I have been tasked to take his place, help Hinlea copy the Wanted List to take to the Regional Committee when he defects as well as buying a new wireless set for the Regional Committee.'

'I know Alan Hinlea is not a pukka sahib,' said Jason, 'none of us really likes him and I don't think he has any real friends but I simply can't see him acting as your reports have him as wishing to. Although he does have some strange socialist and anti-colonial ideas, I hadn't considered them as him wanting to defect,' and he pursed his lips in disgust.

'How long can you be away from the camp without raising suspicions?' asked Ian.

'About two weeks.'

'What if we were to follow you and attack the camp after you've shown us where it is?'

'You would be unlikely to kill them all and my cover would be blown so I'd be dead before much longer. I'd be far more use to you getting back to the Politburo. In any case the camp is a devilishly hard place to attack,' and he described it, its approach, its defence and the number of people normally in it, their weapons and the two senior personalities. 'In it are the Political Commissar and the Military Commander. They don't get on well together but hide their differences as much as they can. The root of their disagreement, strangely, is not political: it is coloured because the former does not believe in *feng shui* and the latter does.' He made mention of their nicknames, Sai Daam Lo Ch'e Dai P'aau for the former and Hung Lo, for the latter and translated them. He also told them that the Yam Yam's staff's nickname for Hinlea was

Lustful Wolf, Sik Long, and that the nickname had been made known to the Politburo.

Heads were shaken and there was a long silence after Ah Fat had finished talking as the other three mulled over the many implications of what they had learnt. Then the OCPD spoke out: 'Well, details of attacking the camp are certainly premature. Tell you what, how about this: we'll say and do nothing that will make Hinlea feel we know about what he has said in the Yam Yam. By then I'll have had you, Ah Fat, documented as a Special Branch officer temporarily posted in from, let's say, Penang, to replace the fallen Lee, whom I won't take back under any circumstances. You'll be able to come and go into Police HQ as normal and we'll carry on by day with Captain Alan Hinlea helping out.' Ian Clark turned towards Moby. 'Moby, the last thing I want is to tread on your toes. *If* the Hinlea fellow is really to try and take documents to the guerillas, then he should be stopped and locked up. But, and here I want your reaction, what I suggest is that we let him see all the names on the Wanted List and let him try and make them more efficient, go through the motions, so to speak. We'll make a list of, say, five false names, listing them as our long-term sleepers with the guerillas. You, Ah Fat, can accidentally leave the list lying around or forget to lock the safe they're meant to be in. We'll see if they stay or disappear. Other than that, once you have got your wireless, either the old one repaired or a new one, bring it to me. I'll send it post haste to Kuala Lumpur where the boffins have a nippy little gadget to put inside it so whenever it is opened an Auster's beacon, I think it's called, can take a bearing on it. This means that any attack on the camp we may make *after* you're safely out of immediate danger, an Auster aircraft can find out where the main group is. It is highly secret and some of the Army Air Corps pilots don't yet know of its existence.'

Ah Fat grinned. 'Great idea. Should let us win hand down, I think the phrase is. Now, before we finish here we must put our heads together over the map I asked you to bring with you. I'll be able to pinpoint pretty nearly where the camp is.' He was given the map and pointed out where the camp was.

The others gathered round and gasped at its being so near.

'The Regional Committee is almost bound to move out as soon as Hinlea is brought there,' continued Ah Fat. 'Their move from then on will be along the courier route, there's no track as such except in places, towards the next Regional Committee at Titi, crossing the road somewhere between Jelebu and Kuala Klawang. If they cannot contact anyone at Titi, they'll make for the Committee at Durian Tipus. I can also make a fairly accurate stab at where the other committees are.'

'How can you be so sure?' asked Ian.

'Because I've already arranged that myself in the Central Committee,' he answered with a smile.

Moby had sat silently during Ian Clark's discourse, pondering on the problem from all angles. He looked around the table. 'My turn now, I like it and I don't like it but we do have an opportunity to see if really and truly this fellow Hinlea is as black as we think he is painted. The five names we give him for sleepers should not be false but those that'll sow dissention and mistrust so lower guerilla morale. As for knowing where the Negri Sembilan Regional Committee is, that is a wonderful bonus for us, although

I did have an idea of its general position. It will also be of great use to know the courier routes from there on up north.'

'Ian,' said Ah Fat. 'Before you have fixed with the battalion when Hinlea comes and starts work, you and I will have also started our own side of the job. As for me and Hinlea, I'll pretend that my English is not up to much. I've been given an ID card in the name of Ah Wang Ming and, while I'm with you, Ian and Moby, I'd like my name to be that.'

'Jason, have you any views on what we've been talking about?'

'Makes sense to me, Ian, fraught with imponderables though it is. However, what I'll try to do is probe Hinlea's intentions, obliquely to start with, and see what I come up with. Just suppose that the bloody man does scarper, the guerillas will evacuate their camp pretty damn quick so there'll be no point in knowing where it is because it'll be empty – unless they think of keeping a few men there to ambush any follow up; no, fool that I am. As far as the guerillas are concerned they will think that nobody will have any idea that Hinlea will be taken to the camp because they believe that nobody knows where their camp is. That doesn't mean the camp will be empty.' The others nodded their approval at that reasoning. He now had the bit between his teeth: 'Recapture of Hinlea, dead or alive, will depend on speed. The best way to get going will be to get to that camp just as fast as we can to start tracking Hinlea's group. Now that we know the couriers' route, we'll be able to move much more quickly and in the right direction. The idea I have at the back of my mind is to get that Goh Ah Hok fellow and force him to lead us – me, I hope, having put the fear of God, if he has one, into him,' and he gritted his teeth. 'One cannot prevent accidents of history but we must try and prevent an accident of geography. Sorry. I got rather carried away, didn't I?' and he grinned engagingly.

'Moby, shall I pretend to be a sleeper or shall I be clean?' asked Ah Fat, rubbing his hands together unconsciously after what Jason had said had sunk in.

'Oh clean, of course. If you were to get the chance to probe, then take it but don't show any indication of pre-knowledge.'

A knock on the door disturbed them. 'Come in,' Ian called out.

The Gurkha orderly brought in a tray with a pot of tea, four cups and some biscuits. 'Time for a break, sahib,' he said, smiling at Jason. He put the tray down on the table and, with another smile, said 'Anything else, just call me.' Jason translated.

'Good grief. We've been at it,' looking at his watch, 'for over two hours,' said Ian. 'Is there anything else left to discuss?'

'I do have another point,' answered Jason, 'but let's have our cuppa first. I'm dying for a wet.'

'Let's have it, Jason,' said Ian. 'Talk while you're sipping. You look a bit worried. I know we all are, but ...'

'Well, it's like this,' he began, sipping his tea. 'Other than the guerillas, we here in this room are the only others in the know. Who else, if anybody, do we tell, when and what? As a responsible army officer, surely it's my duty to warn my CO about Hinlea's plan, even though I, for one, find it almost impossible to believe it is really true. And once the CO knows he'll have to tell the Brigadier and up it'll go even higher. Thanks to Ah Fat we have some superb tactical knowledge and it would be great if we could use it properly. However, if word of what we've been talking about spreads abroad, and walls have ears as we learnt during the war, it'd be a tragedy if our potential military target flew the coop prematurely. I think, Ian, that on the police net that means the information doesn't yet go to the OSPC even though later he'll have to be fully briefed.'

The other three nodded in solemn agreement. Jason hadn't finished. 'And what is my own position here?' he asked, answering himself by saying, 'nothing official and higher authority could take it amiss if they think I'm rubber-necking. Also, despite being a childhood friend of Ah Fat, my being with him here under such unusual circumstances also poses its own problems,' and he relapsed into moody silence.

'Good points, all of them,' said Ian and Moby, almost in unison, while Ah Fat nodded once more, saying nothing. 'Let me think this one out,' and poured himself another cup of tea. 'Tell you what. Initially we'll say nothing until after our next Thursday's DWEC – Ah Fat, is that nonsense to you?'

Yes, it was.

'DWEC or giving it its full name,' continued Ian, 'District Warfare Executive Committee is for joint planning at District level and the one above that, for State matters, is SWEC,' lowering his voice to give the information clandestine force but grinning mischievously to relieve tension that was building up. 'I'll take the CO to one side and tell him everything, including your childhood relationship. You've nothing to hide, except, of course, everything!'

'And, Ian, as far as this Lustful Wolf is concerned, I'll play dumb,' Ah Fat again. 'I'll merely appear as a normal Special Branch bloke doing his normal job, probably anti-Communist, possibly not all that keen on the colonial government but liking it rather than having the Japs around or being ruled by the Malays.'

'That sounds about right. And were this Hinlea fellow to start talking about escaping into the jungle and becoming a commie, just shake your head as though you don't really believe it.'

'Point taken, Ian. When shall we start work?'

'We'll have tomorrow by ourselves and ask him to start with us the following day, Tuesday.'

'Any more points or queries?' asked Ian.

Moby had a question for Ah Fat. 'How good is the Political Commissar?'

Ah Fat thought for a moment then stretched out his arm and turned his hand upwards and downwards. 'Put succinctly, he can talk the talk but can't walk the walk. Also his intellectual dishonesty and communist upbringing mean that he has no imagination and, like all good Communists, truth has no relevance to reality.'

The others grinned in return and Moby nodded his understanding. 'Sounds impressive.'

Still not finished, Jason had yet another point. 'Just suppose Hinlea actually does disappear on his lunatic scheme and the Auster is used to spot where the group is by zoning in on to the doctored wireless set, how will the pilot know that the set has been opened? It'll be a frustrating waste of time and effort if whenever there's a flight the guerilla wireless is switched off.'

'I think I can help you here,' said Ah Fat. 'I noticed that

the Political Commissar listens in to the Radio Malaya Chinese broadcasts on the Red channel.' Jason knew that the Blue and Green channels were for English- and Malay-language programmes. 'I'm not sure but I think that there're three news broadcasts each day, at 0800, 1200 and 1600 hours. The midday broadcast may not be listened to as they'll probably be on the move then. Either of the other two might well do the trick.'

'Yes,' said Jason. 'It'll be simple enough to check on those timings. And please bear with me. I'm sorry I didn't mention either of these two points before. One: the Siu Tse we've heard about is Hinlea's Yam Yam tart *and* Goh Ah Hok, the ration contractor's sister. Whether that will have any tactical value is something we've yet to find out. And two: all our out-companies have come back to Seremban for six-weeks of re-training so we'll have enough men to deploy rapidly and, I hope, effectively *if* we have to.'

'An unexpected bonus,' murmured Ian Clark.

That wrapped the session up and it was time to go back. They went to thank John Theopulos and declined a sun-downer. Before they got into the car to drive back to Seremban, Ah Fat said. 'Shandung P'aau, you used to make me laugh when we were kids by the way you could crow at a cock and it would crow back. Can you still do that?'

'P'ing Yee, watch this,' and Jason moved over to where a cock and his hens were pecking away. He crowed three times. At the first crow, the bird looked up, at the second, it flapped its wings aggressively and, after the third, it crew back. Jason crowed three more times and had three more answers. 'Satisfied?' he asked but had no answer as the others were convulsed with laughter.

They drove off, all sadder but much the wiser. None of them spoke, being wrapped up in their own thoughts. Ah Fat asked to be put down where he had been picked up. 'The walk back'll do me good and may be a bit safer,' he said enigmatically.

'I'll tell the staff to expect a new Special Branch operator from Penang named Ah Wang Ming reporting in about 11 o'clock tomorrow,' said Moby as 'Ah Wang Ming' got out of the car. 'Bring your kit and I'll give you a billet in our bachelor quarters,' the OCPD called out. Ah Fat waved his arm in reply.

'Jason, I'll drop you off at your camp,' said Ian, 'save you a taxi ride.'

'Thank you, Ian. This really is a knotty one, isn't it? What do you think of my childhood friend?'

'I like what I saw. I like the cut of his jib. Courageous and dedicated.'

'And how! It'll be difficult to see him as much as I'd like. I feel, somehow, that our future lies together ... but quite how ...' and he left the sentence unfinished.

7

Monday, 11 August 1952

Be normal, Ah Fat told himself as he left his hotel after a dish of noodles, *you're only still alive because you've always seemed so normal to others that they have never noticed you.* Even so he did not go straight to the wireless shop. His tradecraft made him ensure he wasn't being followed. By then he had presumed that the Political Commissar's threat was an empty one but he never took any unnecessary risks – *Tradecraft!* At the wireless shop he waited until there were no other customers before asking the manager about his set. 'No good, Comrade, I'm afraid. Clapped out and, as I told you, even if I were to clean it up a bit, it wouldn't last for long before you'd be bringing it back again. No. You'd better buy this little job here,' and he produced a smaller, modern set from behind his work bench. 'Don't ask me where I got it from,' he said with a sideways grin. 'It's in good nick and should last you a long time. It uses the same sort of batteries as the other. Take it?'

'I don't seem to have much choice, do I?' Ah Fat laughed back at him. He paid for it and pocketed the receipt.

'Want a bag to put it in, I expect,' said the manager, rummaging around. He produced one with cut-away holes the easier to carry it. Thanking him once more Ah Fat left and, again circuitously, moved over to the Police Station where he reported in. The gate sentry asked him who he was and, on being shown his ID card, the new man was told to report to the Malay Chief Clerk 'whose office is just down the passage on the right.'

Mr Ah Wang Ming went and stood in front of the desk till the clerk looked up. 'Who are you and what do you want?' he asked curtly, no Malay ever needfully being polite to a Chinese.

'I'm the new Special Branch man and so must report in to Mr Clark, Tuan, before reporting to the Head of Special Branch,' he replied, politely over-addressing the Malay, now mollified a bit.

'Wait here. I'll go and tell him.'

Once in the OCPD's office, the relationship was formal. 'Mr Ah Wang Ming. Welcome. I'll take your details and then introduce you to the Head of Special Branch, Mr Ismail Mubarak.' Nothing in the tone of Ian Clark's voice gave any indication that Ah Fat, alias Ah Wang Ming, had already met Moby.

'Thank you, sir,' nor was there in the reply.

'What's in your bag? Not a bomb, I hope.'

'No sir, but it could be,' giving a twitch of a smile as he opened it and revealed a new wireless set. 'I'll leave it with you,' said, then more softly, 'for "treatment".'

Ian Clark took the bag and put it in a drawer. 'You've done well,' he said, with a wink. He picked up the phone. 'Exchange, get me the Gurkha CO, please.'

'Colonel Williams speaking.'

'Colonel, good morning. OCPD this end. It's about Captain

Hinlea helping us out in Special Branch documentation. Can he make a start tomorrow at, say, 1030? I'll introduce him to the staff and let them get on with it.'

'I'll make sure he's there on time. When shall we be meeting up next, any idea?'

'At Thursday's DWEC and, afterwards, I'd like a *very* private word in your ear, if you can spare the time.'

'Sounds fascinating! See you then,' and without waiting for an answer, he rang off.

That evening, after their meal, Ian Clark and Ah Fat went to count the number of Wanted List people in the card index box. They laboriously doctored new cards, working till midnight.

Ah Fat rubbed his brow in fatigue. 'Come to my bungalow for a beer before you toddle off to bed,' said Ian as they tidied up. 'Do you good.'

'Won't argue with that,' and they left the office, locking up behind them. After their beer, Ah Fat picked up his kit and the OCPD escorted the new Special Branch man out past the night sentry. 'We've been so busy I've not had time to show Mr Ah Wang Ming his room. Please take him over to it.'

Tuesday, 12 August 1952
Captain Alan Hinlea got out of the Intelligence Section Land Rover at the Police Station and told the driver, in understandable Gurkhali, to go back and he would phone him for his return. *I'm in the lion's den. I'm where I want to be. I can't be stopped*

now. On, on Operation Janus! He returned the salute of the gate sentry and went inside. He reported to the Chief Clerk, politely wishing him 'Good morning' in Malay, *'Salamat pagi, Inche,'* and politely asked if he could see the OCPD. 'I think I'm expected. My name is Captain Hinlea.' *So teddibly Bwitish* he sneeringly mimicked to himself, not consciously recalling where he'd picked up the phrase.

He's polite for a Mat Salleh thought the Chief Clerk, using the Malay slang for an Englishman to himself and answering his morning greeting. Mat Salleh was a legendary Malay who always thought he knew more than he actually did. 'Please have a seat, sir, while I find out if he's ready,' and off he went and, knocking on the OCPD's door before entering, told him about his visitor. 'Send him in, please, *Inche*.'

In he went and, rather too caustically for Hinlea, Ian Clark started telling him his duties, the need for security and common sense without even offering him a chair.

You're another one I'll be remembering. 'Thank you, Mr Clark. I fully understand what you want and what I have to do.' *Butter up the bastard.* 'All ready for me to start?'

'Yes. I'll take you to the Special Branch office. I've a new man, a Mr Ah Wang Ming, just posted in from Penang, to help you. Doesn't speak all that much English. *Hope he'll understand your accent.* Have you any Malay?'

Hardly any but he was learning Cantonese.

They went to the Special Branch office, where the OCPD introduced Mr Ah Wang Ming to the English Captain and showed him the card index. 'Can I make a copy for my Int files also, please?' he asked winsomely. 'It'll save me from coming down here too often.'

'Yes, provided you keep them as safely as your other confidential documents, although, at heart, I'm probably breaking all sorts of security rules.'

'No sweat. Okay, then, I'll start with this gentleman and if we have any problems, I'll come over to you.'

'We close at 4 p.m.'

'Oh, I'll be away before then but I'll come back tomorrow at around the same time.'

As Clark left, Hinlea did not see him wink at the new Special Branch operative.

Back in his office, the OCPD called for his wireless maintenance foreman, had a significant chat with him, swore him to secrecy and gave him the wireless set. *Something attempted, something yet to be done ...*

Hinlea, shown the Wanted List card index system, riffled through the boxes, noted that there wasn't a lot of information, or, rather surprisingly, any photographs. 'Why no photographs?' he asked and, without waiting for an answer, 'the cards don't look much used do they?'

'I don't know, sir. I am new here.'

Doesn't seem nearly as cooperative as I'd been led to believe. 'When did you come and where from?'

'I was posted down from Penang and only started work here yesterday.'

'No matter. Tell you what. Get some new forms. I'll copy

down these details for my own use in my Intelligence Office in the battalion and you see if you can design a better form for filling in. Include more background; education, family, when he joined the guerillas, physical details and put a space for a photograph. Somehow I'd expected much more than what's on these cards. Oh well, can't be helped.'

Hinlea started copying out the cards but, after half an hour, seemed to get bored. 'Mr Ah Wang Ming, d'you know if there's a canteen in this place where we can get a cup of tea?'

'I'm sure I can find something. Just for you, sir?'

'No, a cup for each of us. Here's some money,' and he gave him two dollars.

'More than enough, sir. I'll bring the change with the tea.' It took him longer than expected to find where tea could be bought but bring back two cups, and the change, he did. As they sat drinking it, Hinlea asked, 'What do you think of this Communist uprising against colonial Britain and how does it affect you?'

'Sir, we had so much of trouble with the Japanese, killing especially Chinese with so much being cruel and now here it is again. How can anyone like it?'

His English is not up to much for a Special Branch man.

'But to be under the colonial British,' he persisted. 'They are Europeans not Asians. How can they know what's best for you? Surely it's better for them to go back to Britain and leave the Malayans to look after themselves? In England I'd just hate to be ruled by a crowd of Asians.'

They'd put you in your place if that were ever to happen.' Oh, sir, one day that will happen but the Japanese were Asians and …'

'… and they beat the British, didn't they?' *Caught you there!*

'Sir, I don't know the answers to your questions but can we Chinese trust the Malay rulers to treat us properly and give us cit … let us be citizens?'

'Citizenship is the word. How much English did you study? If the Brits are rulers what have the Malays got to do with it?

'I'm sorry, sir. I can't answer that. How could we learn anything when the Japanese did not let the Chinese study? The British do let us go to school.'

It was an unsatisfactory conversation as far as Hinlea was concerned. He had expected to learn a lot but with this dolt it was almost, but not quite, a waste of time his coming here.

'I'll use your phone to order my transport. There's not all that much to do here. I'll come on Thursday, not tomorrow,' and he rang through to the battalion. On putting the phone down he had another question. 'Surely there're secret files about the guerillas? There's so much that's not on these cards they're only of limited use.'

'Sir, I'm only the same as a police constable. You're an officer. How can you ask me such questions? I'm sure the OCPD will answer you,' and he turned away to put the cards back in their boxes. Hinlea left the room without another word.

He's no good but there's no proof unless he takes the sleeper's bait. But he's the opposite of my Shandung P'aau.

That night Ah Fat and Ian planned to finish work on the other cards with one more session, mind-numbingly boring though it was. Towards the end, Ian said, 'I've a good mind to sow dissention among the ungodly.'

'And why not, the more the merrier, but how?'

'One way to keep any heat off you is to make someone else into a sleeper. We'll take the Military Commander's name off the Wanted List and hide it as far as Hinlea is concerned. We'll then write a really scurrilous report about the Political Commissar himself and put, at the bottom, the military commander's name in English and Chinese, so that, once it is read up in the committee camp, the one won't trust the other and the other won't understand the one's mistrust. How about that for evil thinking?'

Ah Fat burst out laughing. 'Go to the top of the class, Ian. Communism, thirty-four years of tradition untrammelled by progress and no sense of humour, and, for the record, nothing is more soul-destroying than fanaticism based on ignorance.'

'That must have taken a lot of thought,' said Ian Clark, in admiration.

Thursday, 14 August 1952

The High Commissioner's jointery was for the administration, police and military to work together at all levels, so the District Officer, always a Malay, chaired DWECs - as indeed they did SWECs – it being British Government policy for Malays to be District Officers to train them for their eventual self-rule. However, most of the impetus for Emergency work came from the British members with, sadly, little being offered by the Chairmen, yet colonial politeness and good manners usually left the Malay Chairmen not losing that all-important Oriental characteristic, 'face' – the display of public potency which makes for personal prestige.

After the meeting Ian Clark said to the Gurkha CO, 'Sir, now it's time for "your ears only". Would it suit you to come to the Police Station or shall I come up to the battalion?'

'You come to my place, Clark, and if it's as scary as you seem to be making it out to be there's that much more security in a Gurkha battalion than almost anywhere else – no, please don't take offence.'

'No offence taken, sir. I'll follow along behind you.'

They went into the CO's office, the CO telling the Adjutant that they were not to be disturbed and to warn the Mess for one extra for lunch. 'Right, Clark, fire away.'

The CO was a good listener. He made a few notes as Ian initially told him about Ah Fat, his background and work, his present task and his childhood relationship with Captain Rance. He went on to tell of the discovery of that long-term mole in Special Branch but it was only when he came to the part of Captain Hinlea did the CO's facial expression change from almost excited interest into one of firm disapproval, lips visibly tightening. 'One problem, sir, is who else to tell, when and how much. You are obviously number one, you must know now and know it all. However it's up to you to decide whether to keep it at your level or to go 'one up' and then the 'one up' will also go 'one up' and security could be badly jeopardised. I have not yet told my OSPC. So far, to be fair to Hinlea, Ah Fat, although while in Seremban he is using another's name and ID card, probably does not have proof that would be considered firm evidence in a court of law about what Hinlea is reputed and reported to have said he plans to do. Ah Fat has made no mention of anything like that during their conversations, except a request for more secret data which might or might not be coincidental. Hinlea has been asking questions about why and how the British are in Malaya and these Ah Fat parried without any difficulty, saying that the British were much better than the Japanese ever were and that the British also gave the Chinese more "social manoeuvrability", not in those exact words, than the Malay rulers would, so neither denied him nor encouraged him.' He let out a deep sigh. 'Oh yes. I should have mentioned it earlier but Head of Special Branch, Mr Mubarak, was with Ah Fat, Captain Rance and me.'

'Clark, I don't like this one little bit. How much is true, how much is gossip? Who's to tell? Also the position of Ah Fat is delicate. We must do nothing whatsoever to impede or imperil his standing with the other guerillas who most certainly hold him in high esteem from what you say. We have a military target that is well worth going for – but when? Before Ah Fat returns or after he has gone back, giving him enough time to get back to where he properly belongs?' Before the OCPD had time to answer, 'the latter, I suppose,' he said, answering his own question. He looked at his watch and gave out a long whistled whew. 'Let's go and have a pink gin or a beer, then lunch. Afterwards we'll come back here and have another session.'

At the end the CO thanked Ian Clark and said, 'I'll talk to Hinlea *after* he's finished with you and let you know what I discover and what I intend to do – or not do.'

'Righty ho, sir. And may I ask how Captain Rance, who is

also worried about his Chinese friend and feels that he really shouldn't be involved in any of this, will be tackled?'

'Good points. I'll have a word with him, too.'

Next afternoon the CO called Jason to his office and, seeing he looked worried, spoke to him kindly. 'Captain Rance, sit down and take your hat off. I understand you have become muddled up in a king-size problem, much against your will and find yourself torn between what is still not full proof and your own gut feelings. Correct?'

Jason paused so long before answering that the CO felt he had framed his statement wrongly. 'Sir, may I be impertinent and ask you for your source?'

The CO tried not to show any impatience at the query, only allowing his eyebrows to twitch. 'The OCPD, who else?'

'Good. That means that there's been no leak. Yes, there are two parts to this unforeseen situation and I'll dilate on the first, if I may.'

The CO nodded his approval. He sat back in his chair and laced his fingers across his stomach. 'Go ahead. I want to know as much as I can and we can be all afternoon. If you have any other appointment, use my phone to cancel it.'

Jason rang through to his company office and told his clerk that he was with the Commanding sahib. He then gave the CO a full briefing of his childhood in Kuala Lumpur when he'd learnt Chinese, his father's job, his Chinese friend and how he'd lost touch with him until, oh so unexpectedly, the previous Sunday.

'And which side is he on, childhood friendship apart?'

'Sir, it had never occurred to me, until your question, that he was not firmly on our side and acting, most bravely, as a long-term police agent. My father had the greatest respect for his father, they worked closely together, and yet I fully agree that's no reason why the son should think and act like his father. But, again, my gut feeling and my more intimate knowledge of the Chinese than many Europeans both make me feel he is clean.'

'Can't argue against that even though it wouldn't stand as evidence in a legal battle, as the OCPD has already opined,' said the CO, arranging his pen in a better position on his blotting pad. 'How good is your Chinese?'

'I was virtually bilingual in it as a young child and I've kept it up since.'

'But you rather keep it under your hat, it seems to me. I've never heard you flaunt it, as some Chinese speakers might. Why not?'

'My father was in the intelligence business and I can so well remember him telling me that I'd learn much more if I kept my knowledge secret. He said he'd never have had his successes had it not been for feigning ignorance in the language. I've kept to that rule.'

'And I must ask you another, rather difficult, question. I've never heard you but I gather you're also a talented ventriloquist. How come?'

Jason gave a grunt of a laugh. 'My mother was in an unusual "trade", if I can call it that, before she married. She was a ventriloquist who helped her father run a Punch-and-Judy show. She made sure that I could master that unusual art and make different voices. Quite why, other than party tricks, she never told me: possibly it was vanity and possibly so that her own gifts need not be lost after her death. She saw that I had a gift for mimicry and I suppose I have, as well for languages, in that I learn them quicker than most other people seem to,' he added modestly.

'Pre-war no regular officer would ever have had such a mixed background,' said the CO pompously. 'When I was a subaltern my first Commanding Officer told me to be sensible without being heavy, original without being eccentric and lively without being silly,' he pontificated. *Couldn't have put it better myself!* thought Jason, smirking inwardly. 'How about your Malay?'

'I'm told I speak it with a "Punjabi" accent, that's because it's influenced by my Gurkhali although I had no such accent when young.'

'I gather you have the men in stitches when you perform your ventriloquist act. Which is your favourite party piece?'

Jason looked abashed: 'The time I and my dummy have a set-to over a krait,' he said, with a nervous laugh. *I'll always remember P'ing Yee's parting shot as the train drew out. That's why I do it, I suppose.*

'Well, don't overdo it. I'd hate to think that one of my more promising officers was making himself cheap and too familiar with the men.'

All pre-war officers would say the same thing. 'Thank you for your warning, sir. When I try not to respond they seem so disappointed. But I've got your message.'

'So back to our main thrust, Hinlea?'

'He's a loner from a wretched background with a chip on

both shoulders. He seems to like me more than he does the others. Says I get on better with Asians than do the rest; seems hung up about the colonial Brits and downtrodden natives but that could be just trying to make me rise and have an argument. I don't respond. Or, if I do, not provocatively. In the heart of his heart he knows he's not officer class and he bitterly resents us as public-school snobs. He was badly snubbed in Darjeeling when he tried to become a temporary member of the Planters Club. That he did tell me but exactly what happened is something he clammed up on when I asked him for details. Stupid of me, I suppose, even to try but at least it diffused the head of steam that had so suddenly and unexpectedly blown up. His childhood was influenced by Communists and, to get his own back, so to speak, rash bravado rather than cool thinking has won his day. However, there is one devastating point my Chinese friend brought up,' and he went on to explain 'Calcutta'. The CO listened intently, nodding his head from time to time.

'Rash bravado or cool thinking, that goes along with what your Chinese friend reports, the Politburo being asked if he'll be accepted as a fighting Communist with them against the British and his wish to see what Special Branch has about the Communist Terrorists in its Wanted List. Pretty damning, I'd have thought, wouldn't you?'

'As we both know, sir, a lawyer for the government would make much of it but a defence lawyer would demand proof and not get it. For the love of me, I just can't see any British officer actually attempting what seems to be his aim. Is it sheer bravado, I wonder, or does he just want to make us feel jittery? In other words, is this his working-class background getting at us more fortunate people? Snobbery in reverse, so to speak, or an exercise of snobbery over reality?' pontificated Jason gnostically. 'He has also confided in me, sir, in plain view, that he wants to earn a bravery award. But surely he wouldn't go as far as he is reported to have gone just to be able to lead an attack on a guerilla camp himself, to win an MC or a DSO – or maybe he would.'

'*What* a poser! I agree with you in the main. For the life of me I cannot see a British officer behaving in the manner he seems to be planning while keeping us in the dark. In a way I'm in a more difficult position than you are. You're merely a brother officer while I'm his CO.'

The Adjutant asked to be excused as he had a couple of important letters for signature.

'Have you spoken about any of this with him?' the Colonel asked, putting his fountain pen back on the table.

'No, not as such, sir. What little he has said to me is, in fact, the opposite, how much he is enjoying himself, the battalion is his new life, the-men-are-a-treat-to-serve-with type talk.'

It is not often that an officer as senior as a lieutenant-colonel asks a captain for advice but Robert Williams did. 'So, if you were in my shoes, Rance, what would you do?'

'Sir, I'd wait until he's actually finished with Special Branch, call him in ...'

'Yes, I've already said I'd do that.'

'... and ask him point blank what it's all about. If he admits that he is a traitor, close arrest and o-u-t: if he denies it, see what he comes up with, patently wrong or just smells wrong or just a damned-fool practical joke to get us shivering in our pants.' *Nearly said 'shitting' not 'shivering'.* 'Until then, pretend that there's nothing wrong but remain more than ready for a loose ball.'

'I don't even like saying this but just suppose Hinlea did try and join the guerillas, have you any idea where he'd aim for or be taken, and why?'

'The why bit first: it's his background, as far as I can make out. The Communist left and the Nazi right are very much alike in their rigidity of thought. All radicals are. These people can't sublimate their frustrations so they externalise them. They convince themselves, usually subconsciously, that others are causing their miseries – "others" meaning anyone who's different from them. In Hitler's Germany they blamed unemployment on the Jews because Jews held a disproportionately high number of positions in banks, universities, medicine. They were visible, obviously prosperous and clearly different. They had different traditions, different Sabbaths, different holidays. They were an easy target. The same was true of Jews in Communist Russia. Instead of Jews, Hinlea's abominations are Britain's hierarchy, public-school educated sahibs and successful upper classes –all his opposites.'

'That seems a pretty deep analysis. I accept it.'

'As for the where, sir. I know it: the same camp where my Chinese friend came from. It is not far from here, high up on Bukit Beremban, that's the nearer of the two high mountains we can easily see from the camp.'

'And what sort of a place is it and who's there? Could we attack it with, say, a platoon?'

'No way, sir! Apparently it's a devilishly hard place to attack,' and he described it as Ah Fat had, its approach, its defence, the number of people normally in it, their weapons and the two senior personalities. 'It is the Regional Committee camp and in it are the Political Commissar and the Military Commander.'

'One tough nut but a more-than-worthwhile target. Hey ho, it most probably won't come to that, fingers crossed. Thank you Rance, most useful. As 'twas said in England during the war, "Mum's the word". Before you go, do you know what Mr Clark's Indian Army regiment was?'

'Yes, sir. He was a Dogra.'

'Good soldiers, the Dogras.'

'Did you hear, sir, that a British service type thought that DOGRA were initials for Duke of Gloucester's Royal Artillery?'

The CO burst out laughing. 'No, that escaped me.'

'I've one more before I go. When I walked up the platform to the head of the train I was travelling in to stretch my legs, I reached the engine and the engine driver looked at 1 GR on my shoulders and asked me if I had been commissioned into the Indian General Railways.'

Once more the CO laughed, lightening the tension that had started to oppress them.

'Thank you, Rance. I'll call you again if necessary.'

Jason got to his feet, put his hat back on, saluted and went to play basket-ball with his company. He almost sweated his worries out of his system during the game.

Saturday, 16 August 1952

As the Lustful Wolf entered the Yam Yam the barman noticed that he looked happier and more relaxed than he normally did. Waiting until Hinlea had made his way to the bar and was well into his first beer of the evening, Kwek Leng Joo put his head closer than normal for conversation and asked, 'How's it all going?'

'I'm more than halfway ready, Comrade,' he replied. 'I reckon I'll be ready by this coming weekend or the end of the week after. No messing. There's no bother with my getting the Wanted List and it should take only a little skill to get my hands on the secret list of Special Branch sleepers operating in the jungle.'

'I offer you my congratulations in the form of another bottle of beer on the house. Siu Tse is not due till eight.' He looked at his watch. 'She should be here soon. You're earlier than normal.'

'I need her badly,' and Hinlea laughed lasciviously.

Monday, 18 August 1952

'Ian, it's about time I went back. They're a suspicious bunch up there and I told them to expect me about now. We've prepared the secret list and it's still where Hinlea can find it *if* he really wants it. He's not got all that much to do in the copying line and, once you've got the wireless set ready, I'll have to disappear, sadly, as I'd have just loved to have had more time with Jason.'

'And I with you,' volunteered Ian, 'but it can't b e helped.' He opened his safe and took out the wireless. He took the back off it as carefully as possible. 'New batteries and I'll give you some spares. Look here, soldered behind this little whatsit is just a tiny,

tiny beacon,' and Ah Fat had to peer hard to see it. 'This will be activated whenever the wireless is switched on. It is compatible with what is carried in an Auster which can therefore lock on to it. Useful for bombing as well as reporting the carrier's position to any follow-up group or ambush placed in front.'

They said their farewells. 'Say mine to Jason, please will you, from Flat Ears.'

'Of course.'

Wednesday, 20 August 1952

'Comrade Ah Fat, I am glad to see you back,' said the Political Commissioner late that afternoon after the alert had been given when he and his Min Yuen escort got back to the guerilla camp high up on Bukit Beremban. 'I hope you managed to do all you had to and were able to guide the *gwai lo* properly to get the documents.'

'Yes, Comrade Lau Beng. Have no worries. But first here is the new wireless,' and he poked around in his pack. He handed it over, along with the receipt.

Lau Beng turned it on, fiddling with the various buttons. 'Certainly sounds much clearer than the old one,' he said approvingly. 'Come and sit down and tell me about the *gwai lo*. Did you go to the Yam Yam and how did you manage with the OCPD?'

'I feel I managed it well enough for there to be no suspicions at all. There were other members of Special Branch in the office coming in and going out so I had to play that carefully. I didn't go to the Yam Yam as I felt it safer not to. I gather that police agents visit the place now and then and I felt it would have been awkward to have gone there and done and said nothing lest the agents became suspicious and, were that the case, the comrades on the staff there might not have reacted properly. On balance I felt it better to talk with Comrade Goh Ah Hok.'

'And the Wanted List and that of the sleepers?'

'No worry there either,' said Ah Fat, mentally crossing his fingers that his answer was correct. 'There were only five sleepers and the *gwai lo* will bring them when he comes.

'And when do we expect the *gwai lo* Lustful Wolf?'

'Probably in not more than four or five days, Comrade.

'So that means he really will be coming?' the Political Commissar insisted.

'Comrade, correct.'

Friday, 22 August 1952

Captain Alan Hinlea reported to the Adjutant saying that he had finished his job there, had thanked the OCPD for his assistance and was now ready to put all the Wanted List details into Int files and give rifle companies a copy each. 'The CO told me he wanted to see him on completion of my task.'

'Wait one. I'll go and see if he's free,' and the Adjutant went and told the CO about Hinlea waiting to see him. 'Give me ten minutes. I want to clear this lot out of the way first,' and he pointed to the paperwork on his desk.

After ten minutes the Adjutant nodded to Hinlea who

knocked on the CO's door as protocol demanded.

'Come in.'

Hinlea went in, stood to attention in front of the CO's desk and saluted. The CO looked at him. 'You may stand at ease,' he said curtly then continued, 'Captain Hinlea, the OCPD has rung through to tell me what you have managed to do. So far, so good.' He saw the man standing opposite him suppress a smirk. 'However, nothing is without something else, is it?'

'I beg your pardon, sir,' large body unnaturally taut, shoulders stiffly square.

'Listen carefully. Most disturbing reports have reached my ears, no, I'm not telling you how I've found out, that you have been making stupid, almost traitorous remarks about wanting to join the guerillas, that the Central Committee has given its permission for that to happen and that your collection of Wanted List names, the job I gave you, was exactly what the Central Committee was wanting. True or false?'

Hinlea had steeled himself for such a moment. *Cover plan, always have a cover plan. Stick to my* maskirovka. 'On the surface, sir, I agree that I have behaved in what some people would consider a reckless manner and I feel therefore that I must offer my sincere apologies. However, if I tell you why some of what you accuse me of sounds true is because it is true. I have an almost insane longing to show the Gurkhas that I am brave, that, despite my poor upbringing, what I do for the battalion will benefit it as a fighting unit and me personally also.' *Go on, don't let up.*

'Explain yourself,' said the CO, intrigued with such an unusual show of passion. 'What exactly are you getting at?'

'Sir, ever since being commissioned, I have wanted to earn a bravery award,' and he laughed self-consciously, 'an MC or if possible a DSO.' *Remember 'Janus'! and that my* maskirovka *is still working well for me.* 'Stuck in my Int office I have brooded. Doing such work a bravery award could never come my way. So how to go about arranging a target, such as the Regional Committee with all its members present, for surrounding and killing or capturing them with me leading the battalion, company or whatever sub-unit you thought was needed for such an operation. In cold blood, I know that sounds ludicrous and you will be justified in punishing me for, as it were, not telling you about it, going behind your back. But, sir, I have been successful. We now know, don't we, that I am expected – yes, I fully believe that – so, if I am seen going in front of my men ... oh I know it sounds so fanciful when recited in cold blood ... success is much more likely than failure.'

'And you expect me to believe such a story, such poppycock?' *The vanity of monumental self-esteem of inadequate men; the self-arrogated right to play God, even if, in this case, you have no belief in Him, the conviction of the traitor – are you one yet? Will you be one if you can? – always right and all your colleagues are fools; coupled with the drug-like love of power ... But I must hear him out first.*

'Yes sir. If I were making it up you would never believe me. I have told you the truth and hidden nothing from you. Just because it has never happened before, or if it has I don't know about it, doesn't mean I'm not anything but utterly sincere – or indeed incredibly gullible.' *One more try.* 'If, after our attack we are successful, then, surely sir, you can give me full marks.'

The CO shook his head in disbelief. 'You're a crazy idiot, Hinlea,' he said smiling, 'Either you should be court-martialled here and now or sometime next week we'll plan and execute an operation. Call it ...' and he drummed his fingers on his desk as he thought of a name for the coming operation. 'Got it, let's call it "Operation Janus".' – Hinlea's heart missed a beat as he stood there, tense, tight, taut – 'but we can't wait till next January, can we?' and he gave a bleat of a laugh at his little joke. He did not see the 'double take' on Hinlea's face. Had he, matters might have turned out differently, 'you being the two-faced one, one face in the battalion and the other ... ', he left the remark unfinished. 'All right, Hinlea. Do you know where the Regional Committee camp is?' asked watching his subordinate's face for any tell-tale clue.

'No, sir. Of course not. In no way can I know it. We all know just how cautious that lot is and how their very survival depends on complete security.'

No, he's not bluffing. 'So what is your concept of developments?'

'I presume I'll be contacted and taken away to it. Or that I'll be told just before I'm expected to report in. I really don't know but, whichever way it happens, I surely, sir, can lead the battalion in any attack and follow-up.'

'As I said, Hinlea, you're a crazy idiot but this I will tell you here and now. If, and it's a big if, Operation Janus really comes about, you'll lead the battalion.'

Hinlea smiled appreciatively. *Got you, you miserable twerp. Pulled the wool over your bleeding eyes, haven't I?* 'Oh thank you, sir. I promise I won't let you or the battalion down.'

'Right, keep me informed. Dismiss,' curtly.

Biting his tongue, he saluted and left.

The CO leant back in his chair and closed his eyes, his mind churning. He rubbed his eyeballs then clasped his hands behind his head. *Is he just a bloody fool who needs his bottom kicking hard or just another grubby little traitor who could take a solemn oath to his Queen and country, and for his own beliefs betray us all? This next week will show us one way or the other.*

After dark Hinlea went to his room and put the kit he needed into his big pack, jungle greens, canvas shoes, underclothing, anti-mosquito oil that was so effective against leeches, soap, towel, shaving tackle, torch, waterproof cape and a bundle of *bidis*. Wearing plain clothes he took a taxi to the Police Station and said to the sentry on duty, 'I'm sorry to bother you but, so stupid, I've left my briefcase with my notes in the Special Branch office. I'll only take five minutes to get it. Please give me the key.'

The sentry, recognising Hinlea from his previous visits, fetched the key. 'Can you manage alone?'

'Yeah.' He took the key, opened the door and went straight to where he had seen Ah Wang Ming put some suspicious looking secret papers. *Got you, you whoring bastards, got you* and, as he put the list in his pocket, he danced a little jig of joy. Once outside he gave the key back. 'Must have left it somewhere else. It's not there,' he said as he left.

He went on to the Yam Yam and told the barman that he had to see the manager because he had just stolen some secret documents from Special Branch which would be discovered on Monday morning. 'So I have to go now. I'm ready to move.'

'The best thing to do,' said the manager when they met, 'is for Siu Tse to take you to sleep in her brother's house. I'll pick you up there before dawn tomorrow in my own car and take you as far as I can by road then walk you up to the camp. After that it won't be me looking after you.' He phoned Goh Ah Hok and told him to come to the Yam Yam, pick up the Lustful Wolf, take him home for the night and he, the manager, would come before dawn to take him away.'

Hinlea looked ecstatic. 'Wonderful,' he breathed. 'At what time shall we meet?'

'At about 5 o'clock tomorrow morning.'

'I'll be waiting for you, Comrade!' *The real Operation Janus!*

Monday, 25 August 1952

When Hinlea's batman went to take him his bed tea as usual at 0600 hours, he found the bed unslept in. He had a look in the cupboard and found normal uniform and jungle boots but no olive green jungle clothes and no big pack. He looked in the bathroom and saw no washing kit. Knowing that Rance sahib was a friend he went straight to Rance's room. 'Sahib, Hinlea sahib did not sleep in his bed on Saturday night or last night. Do you think anything is wrong?'

Rance, already up and dressed, put the cup of tea that Kulbahadur had just brought for him on a table and said, 'Kulé, don't go before I come back', and went across to the Mess telephone and rang the CO.

'Whoever that is and why so early?' came the testy answer.

'Captain Rance this end, sir. Hinlea has disappeared, bed unslept in for two nights, no jungle greens in his wardrobe and no big pack. I felt that you should know about it straightaway.'

PART TWO

8

Sunday, 24 August 1952

Well before dawn Goh Ah Hok's youngest daughter, carrying a breakfast tray of a cup of tea and a bowl of gruel, put her knee up to balance it with one hand and, with the other, knocked on Hinlea's bedroom door. No reply. She knocked again. Hearing no reply, she opened the door and turned on the light. She put the tray down on the chair by the bed and shook the sleeping man hard. He groaned, opened his eyes and sat up, looking round as though not sure where he was.

'Captain Hinlea, wake up. It's time for you to get up and get ready. Here's your breakfast. The time is half past 4 and you have to be ready by 5 o'clock, my father has told me to tell you, so hurry up,' she said insistently, realising that he hadn't woken up properly.

Hinlea, still a bit dazed, thanked the girl for waking him and bringing him something to eat. 'I'll go and wash my face first,' he said.

'And let your food go cold? It won't taste nearly as good, you know,' she replied, smiling, in excellent English. 'Father says he doesn't know when you'll see food again.'

'You speak very good English. Where do you go to school?'

'At King George V School and I'm in the senior class.'

'And may I ask you your name?'

'Ming Te which in English means Bright Virtue. And you'd better hurry up,' she said brusquely as she left.

Hinlea tried the gruel which was too hot for him. *I'll have to get used to strange meals.* He went and had a quick shave, left his razor in the wash room, came back and had his meal before dressing. He checked that his file of Wanted List names and the secret list were safely in his big pack. He hadn't read the secret list. There hadn't been time and, in any case, the names would not have meant anything to him. He also had a bag full of rice, a bottle of Ovaltine – a Chinese favourite – and tins of sardines for his new hosts. He didn't know if they liked sardines but he knew that the rice and Ovaltine would be welcome.

He slung his pack over his shoulder and, carrying the bag in one hand, went downstairs and waited eagerly. *Why so early?* After a while a car drove up. The driver switched off and Goh Ah Hok went outside to meet him. They came inside and Hinlea saw that the driver was the Yam Yam manager, Comrade Yap Cheng Wu, whose name he still didn't know. He glanced at his watch and saw it was a quarter past five.

In moderately good Cantonese he wished each man 'Early rising', the equivalent of 'Good morning', and the greeting was returned. 'Did you have a good night and also your breakfast?' Goh asked him. Yes, he had and was grateful for both. 'Makes leaving here so much easier. I can't tell you how excited I am,' he gushed in English.

Comrades Yap and Goh talked together earnestly while Hinlea sat to one side waiting. Then Goh looked at his watch. 'Mr Yap tells me that if you're ready you'd better be off while there's still about half an hour's darkness left,' he said.

'Yes,' said Mr Yap. 'Go and put your stuff in the boot and sit in the front seat. You will see two men in the back. They are Min Yuen comrades who will be responsible for our safely till we reach the main camp where I'll hand you over.'

Hinlea said farewell to Goh and did as told. They drove off. Nobody spoke.

About five miles up the Kuala Klawang road, the car veered to the right and turned into an abandoned gravel quarry. Yap drove over to a large tree and parked behind it, out of sight from the road. 'This is where we start walking. Go and get your kit.'

Mr Yap locked the car and joined the other three. He looked Hinlea up and down. 'Not armed, Comrade?'

'No, Comrade Yap,' he answered, taking his cue from his being addressed as 'Comrade'. 'I thought it might cause someone to be suspicious if I went to the armoury over the weekend without a good reason.'

'Not my problem. Now listen well. These two comrades will walk in front of us. We will follow on keeping them just in sight. Unless it is urgent you will not talk nor will you make any noise other than walking quietly.'

After about twenty minutes he heard what sounded like a stick beating on a tree, three spaced times, three strokes in quick succession followed by three more spaced strokes. *Some sort of signal, has to be.* Yap stopped in his tracks and held up his arm to tell Hinlea also to stop. 'That's the outer line of camp sentries,' he said, turning round to explain. They were followed by three lots of strokes, three spaced, three in quick succession and three more spaced. *The all-clear signal?* Yap moved forward and Hinlea followed him, looking round to see if he could locate the tree-beaters. They were too well camouflaged to be seen.

The one-time Gunner had never been so far into the jungle before. Mentally, the hapless fellow was not prepared for its close-horizoned, all-pervading, never-ending green of trees, vines, creepers and undergrowth. Not a gap in the tangle; it rose from the ground, trunk by trunk and stem by stem, each one crowding upon and striving to overtop the other, and tied and netted together with the snake arms of creepers into a closely woven web. Aerial roots and liana-nooses hung from high above. Leaves laid themselves out in vast terraces, fantastic umbels descended in cascades and creepers united in stout, tightly-wound, spiral columns. Vegetation teemed in the steamy twilight; great fronds broken under their own weight, ropes which had neither end nor beginning, plants with fat, sticky leaves or with hairy or scaly stems, and some with large, luxuriant flowers, exuding a strange and deathly scent. The boles of some of the big trees opened out like buttresses. It was also swampy in places and leeches prolific and squashy in his shoes and itchy and uncomfortable elsewhere. He felt overwhelmed even before he had really started. *I just can't imagine several weeks of this.*

Over the next ninety minutes, with the ground rising steadily and the jungle becoming thinner – *let's hope it stays this thin* – twice more a similar procedure was followed before they came to an abrupt, almost perpendicular slope, at the bottom of which were two armed and uniformed guerillas. The elder saluted Yap and said, 'Welcome Comrade. Is this the new *gwai lo* comrade come to join us?' Hinlea's Cantonese was good enough to understand that but he missed what was then quickly said between the two men.

The sentry picked up a thick plaited vine that Hinlea had not seen and gave it a pull. In answer a tug came above and, seconds later, another armed and uniformed comrade picked his way down steps cut into the slope so cunningly that Hinlea had not seen them either. 'Comrade Yap, good to see you,' he hailed him, giving him the communist salute which was correctly returned. 'And you are the new comrade?' said with a welcoming smile in slow, clearly enunciated Cantonese which Hinlea correctly answered.

'Comrade Hinlea, you and I will climb up to the camp where the Negri Sembilan Regional Committee will welcome you. I'll go in front and you tread where I do, otherwise you may slip. I'm empty-handed so give me your hand package.' Up they climbed.

At the top, in a semi-circle with three men older than the others in front, stood the Regional Committee, in welcome. Seldom had Hinlea been so thrilled. He'd tried to imagine how it would be but never believed it would be quite like this. He'd prepared, with Siu Tse's help, a few words in Chinese to express his happiness at being accepted and, as he stood facing about thirty men, out it came, right arm raised in salutation. 'Love live the Revolution and may I always be part of it. I am happy and honoured to be here. I am your new comrade,' followed by a spluttered, unrehearsed 'I have brought you some rice and some,' here he paused, changing into English, 'sardine fish.' Embarrassed at his inadequacy, he went and picked up the package that Yap had put on the ground, opened it and took out a tin. 'Sardine fish,' again in English and laughed at himself. 'Oh yes, and some Ovaltine.'

Spontaneous clapping, applause and laughter greeted that and the guerillas faded away, leaving the three older men. Comrade Yap took Hinlea up to each in turn to introduce him. First there was the Regional Commissar, Comrade Lau Beng. 'I was a school master in Seremban, Comrade, before I joined the Malayan People's Liberation Army. I speak some English but soon enough your Chinese will be better than my English,' and they shook hands.

The next man was introduced as Comrade Wang Ming, the Military Commander. They too shook hands.

The third man was introduced as Comrade Ah Fat, of the Central Committee somewhere in the north. Hinlea could not believe his eyes. Here, surely, was the very man who had been with him in the Special Branch office and he almost spluttered, 'Aren't you Comrade Ah Wang Ming who worked with me with the Wanted List?'

'Me? No, I haven't left this camp for, how long Comrade Lau Beng, a month or so, since I came here, have I?'

'No. You've been here all the time, Comrade.'

Ah Fat looked at Hinlea. 'What name did you say you thought I was? Please say it again.'

'Ah Wang Ming.'

'No, surely not. It can't be true. You must have met my twin. We haven't met for over ten years. How is he? In good health, I hope. I thought maybe he was dead but it seems as if he is working for the foreign devils.' Ah Fat lied with the plausibility of a trusted Member of Parliament, tut-tutting in disgust.

'Comrade Lau Beng,' said Mr Yap. 'Now I have delivered your new comrade, I must return. What do you want me to say to the three groups on my way back?'

'Tell them to come straight back here.'

'I'll do that.' He went over to Hinlea. 'Comrade, I leave you now in safe hands. You'll be safe from the army as no one can possibly know where you've gone. It'll be hard work at first but you've made the right decision. Good luck' and he offered his hand. They shook and then both of them made the Communist clench-fist salute.

'Come with me,' said Lau Beng and led Hinlea to their table and bench. 'We thought you'd get here about now and a meal is ready but first sit down and have a cup of tea. I'll have some Ovaltine, first time for months.'

After their drink, Hinlea said, 'Comrade Regional Commissar, here are the documents you wanted me to bring.' Out of his pack he took two unopened envelopes, the larger containing the Wanted List and the smaller the five secret names, and proffered them to Lau Beng.

The Political Commissar first ran an eye over the Wanted List. *I'll look at it in detail later.* He turned his attention to the secret list. It was written in English, which he could understand better than he could speak. Four names were of men who were either dead or now in other committees but one belonged to Comrade Wang Ming, with the characters of his Military Commander's written at the bottom of the sheet of paper – not 'that man' Ah Fat's as he somehow had expected. The Political Commissar's eyes bulged and his lips almost disappeared, he compressed them so tightly. *I can't credit it. Just can't be true. He's too stupid for one thing, or so deep I haven't seen down to the bottom. I'll watch him so closely, I'll know each time he farts. I'll wait for my opportunity, not now but later ... What does the Wanted List say about me?*

He thumbed through the names until he found his own: Lau Beng. 'A cruel and rather nasty man, unpopular with most of the movement, old before his time and really too stupid to be of much use as Political Commissar as he also has an inflated opinion of himself and his abilities. He has a brain like a pot-plant and the imagination of a retarded door handle. The only reason he remains as Political Commissar is that there is no one better than him to choose from and he only stays on on sufferance. Not brave. He thinks he is a Shantung P'aau but really he's only a Sai Daam Lo Ch'e Daai P'aau when you know him.'

As he read it, his temper, never a docile beast, broke all previous records for rancour and he nearly had apoplexy. He let out a wolf-like howl of rage and shook himself like a wet dog just as Hinlea was swallowing his tea, so startling him that he did the nose trick, coughing and spluttering in counter-harmony. Ah Fat, reminded of the noise hungry pigs make when food is ready, being privy to what Lau Beng was reading and happy to turn the knife, asked him from across the table, 'Comrade, are you in pain?'

The Political Commissar simply did not know where to look.

He gritted his teeth, hawked and spat. *Never, in all the time I've been working for the Party; never, by thought, word or deed; never have I had any suspicions that that was how I was thought of; never have I dreamed that anything like this would, could, happen – but happen it has.* Although he was not sure what 'on sufferance' meant, he judged that it was not complimentary. The only way he could possibly expunge such calumny was to make a success of taking this unexpected *gwai lo* comrade safely up to Titi. He had just had the biggest shock of his life and knew that his howl, unless carefully explained, was detrimental to his standing so to his authority. The look on his face was angrier than his Military Commander had ever seen it and the devastating glare of hatred that met his gaze made him feel that any remark he might make in sympathy or enquiry would not be welcome. Those cruel lips were so tightly squeezed together that they had disappeared. To those with him at the table, it was obvious that he did not want to talk. Those who had heard the howl knew that even glancing his way would invite retribution. He looked at the Wanted List personalities to see what was written about Wang Ming, but his Military Commander's name was not among them. *Why is my name on it and not his?* Then he had it, *because he's not wanted.*

Two proverbs passed through the one-time schoolmaster's mind: *convenient water, push boat* and there was nothing convenient in the here-and-now; *clear spear, easy rattle: dark arrow, hard beware*, which he took as the former meaning that his task of getting this unexpected comrade *gwai lo* successfully on the first leg of his long journey, although however 'clear' the spear was, the 'rattle' would not be all that easy and, as for the second bit, the threat from his Military Commander, *a police informer, can you* believe *it?* meant that the future 'beware' would undoubtedly be hard. He did not dare let his 'underling' stay in the camp where he'd be on his own, probably alert the military and cause no end of needless trouble. He came to a decision. Had he been less worked up he'd have sat down with his Ovaltine and thought out what to do without taking what he'd read at face value, but no ... *I'll get him and grill him alive over a slow fire when the time is ripe.* Lau Beng was now as insatiable as a cemetery and as blood-thirsty as a weasel.

I can't sit here all day and have people wonder what's wrong, so after our meal I'll order our move. He put the lists into his pocket, and jolted upright. 'Comrades, although no *gwai lo* can have any idea at all where our new comrade will have gone to so there can be no follow-up, it is only prudent for us to make as quick a get-away as possible.' He looked at his watch. 'Nearly noon. And the three groups have returned?' Yes, they had. 'So let's say be ready move at 2 o'clock. Comrade Wang Ming, give the necessary orders. The camp can be left as it is as no long-nosed, red-haired devil can have any knowledge whatever that our base is here. Once we have handed our new comrade over to the next lot, we'll come back to it. Take him to the stores and give him a spare uniform, putting his old clothes there. Comrade Hinlea, have you got a pistol with you?' *It was then that he had his brainwave.* He had never considered the possibility that Hung Lo, the Bear, was a sleeper. He knew that he was popular with the men and that he went out on ambush and patrols with them as often as he could. It had to be then that he liaised with the Running Dogs. There was no way he could do it from the camp … other than giving some sort of message to a similarly turned Min Yuen. But now …

'No, Comrade. I didn't think it wise to go and get it from my battalion armoury when there was no official reason to.'

'In that case, Comrade Wang, give this comrade the spare pistol and six rounds.'

The Military Commander, having told a guerilla to arm the new comrade, spoke vehemently to Lau Beng, 'Comrade, I cannot allow this camp to remain empty. It is against all military common sense. I refuse you to give such orders. If necessary I'll stay here myself with a small group while you go with the new comrade up to Titi and back.'

And send one of the guerillas, or you, masquerading as a Min Yuen, going and reporting in to the OCPD while I'm not here? I daren't. 'Comrade Wang Ming. I overrule you utterly and absolutely. In no way is that politically correct.'

'So you are content that I leave matters entirely as they are?'

'Yes, yes, how many times must I tell you,' said Lau Beng, grinding his teeth with pent-up frustration. '*I* will ensure everything is as it should be.'

Blood be on your own head.

In the cave Hinlea drew his pistol and ammunition and changed his uniform. Putting on his cap with the red star he exulted in his new status. *Operation Janus with a vengeance* he crowed to himself. 'Night time. Want?' asked the guerilla, showing Hinlea a plastic sheet. 'Yes,' spoken in Cantonese.

Fuming and feeling overwrought, Wang Ming accepted what he considered an unjust and unnecessary rebuke. He went round the camp as the others vacated it, not seeing the hidden machine gun left behind in the guerillas' hurry to get ready in time. It was not an obligated personal weapon so no one had individual responsibility for it. It was only later, on the move, that he realised it had been left behind.

The guerillas moved out of camp, down the hidden steps and assembled at the bottom. They moved off in three groups, the middle one containing the Political Commissar, the Military Commander, Ah Fat, Hinlea and a small escort.

The last man of the third group had a sprig of leaves with him and he used it to eradicate their footprints.

On the way the Political Commissar's mind was working furiously about his brainwave. *I know how to get rid of him legally without his men stopping me from doing so. But when?* Their route lay against the grain of the country. The main ridge above them to the north had many deep spurs with steep valleys so it was a tiring journey of ups and downs but only near water courses did the jungle thicken up to as much as he had first found it. After only two hours Hinlea realised that his journey north was not going to be easy. The weight of his pack did not worry him for he was a strong man but what did afflict him was the never-ending attack of leeches around his ankles as his canvas shoes gave no protection. He did not want to stop and dab the effective and misused anti-malarial oil onto the leeches clinging to his skin as he felt that it would look as though he was a softy who 'couldn't take it'. *None of my new comrades seem to worry about leeches so how can I?* He could see that Comrade Lau Beng was also finding the going hard work.

Shortly before 4 o'clock the group reached a place on the bank of a gushing hill stream that couriers used. The Military Commander gave orders for three men to patrol at a distance of some two hundred yards out to see if there were any Security Force traces. While they were doing that the Political Commissar switched on his wireless set, pleased with the clear reception although they were obscured by high ground on three sides. As he had expected, there was no news about the Lustful Wolf – *I must stop myself thinking of him by that name. I'll have to think up something else.*

Each pair of comrades in the protection group gathered firewood and cooked their own meal in small cooking pots they carried. The four senior men's escorts cooked theirs for them. Hinlea had given one of the guerillas his mess tin and was glad of his meal when it came, a simple one of rice and sardines. By the time he had washed his mess tin in the stream, wiping it clean with some leaves he'd picked, it was growing dark. He then rigged up a rude shelter, watching how the guerillas fixed their sleeping place, using the plastic sheet as a roof. He laid his own waterproof to sleep on.

The three leaders, with Lau Beng being more officious than usual, discussed the next day's move. It was decided eleven guerillas would move ahead along the courier route as fast as was expeditious to Titi and alert the Regional Committee there of its task to take the new comrade on to Durian Tipus. They would move off after their meal on the morrow. 'I'll brief them on how important their job is. It will make our task a success more quickly than otherwise and it will greatly redound on our Committee,' said Lau Beng, sounding cock-sure. *And make it easier to put into action part one of my brainwave by getting rid of the men most likely to come to the Bear's rescue.*

The Bear did not think of mentioning the forgotten machine gun. He was still sulking about the way he'd been treated. It was obvious that, with the camp being unlucky because of ill-fated *feng shui*, it was not his fault.

No sentries were put out as the chance of any human night movement was miniscule. Some dried bamboo leaves that crunched when trodden on as a warning of movement were cunningly placed about twenty yards out and they then turned in. Although Hinlea had had an unusually early rise that morning, he found it difficult to get to sleep. He replayed the day's events over and over in his mind, feeling extraordinarily proud of having successfully carried out what to others would only have appeared as an impossibly hopeless pipe-dream. *I've made it, I've made it.* His thoughts scuttled around like a mouse caught in a cage. *I've beaten the bastards at their own game, been clever enough to get the better of them,* he exulted. His last thought before eventually drifting off to sleep was about the success of Operation Janus.

9

'So the man Hinlea was serious after all,' spat the CO down the phone. Never one to use bad language, his most virulent oath was 'It's enough to make a puppy dog bite its tail', which he gave vent to now, making Jason smile. 'Tell the MTO to send my car round to my house soonest. I'll ring the 2 IC and pick him up. Meet me in my office at 0700 and tell the Adjutant I'll have an all-officers briefing at 0730s, with the "Officers at the Double" bugle call at 0725. Oh yes, you ring the OCPD and I'll ring Brigadier Honker,' and he slammed the phone down.

Jason went to the MTO's room, knocked on the door and went in, without an answer. 'Tony, listen to this. That rat Hinlea, the Battalion Stallion, has scarpered and the CO wants his car sent to his house now. He'll bring the 2 IC in with him.'

The MTO looked bewildered. 'Jason, you vexatious man, it's not April the first. Bugger off.'

'I'm deadly serious so "Operation Ginger" now and you'll get all the details at 0730 in the CO's office.' He moved over to the Adjutant's room where the reaction was just the same. 'Jason, I hope to high heaven you're not joking. Extra Orderly Officer if you are.'

'Paul, joking I'm not. I only wish I were.'

'Where's he gone to? Any idea?

'In all probability to join the guerillas. I've rung the CO and he's told me to tell you to have the "Officers at the Double" bugle call at 0725 for a briefing at 0730 in his office.'

'Incredible ... unbelievable,' muttered the Adjutant as Jason left to put a call through to Ian Clark. 'Ian, Jason here. Sorry to disturb you so early. This is to let you know that Hinlea has disappeared. Bed unslept in for two nights and jungle clothes not in his wardrobe.'

'Blast his eyes. What now?'

'The CO has called a briefing at 0730, is warning the Brigadier and you'll be kept in the picture. But before that, please, tell Moby *and* find out if those "secret reports" that were supposedly hidden by you-know-who are there or not. *If* they're not there, that'll be proof of where he's gone. Ring the CO's office between 0725 and 0730 to let him know one way or the other as that may affect future planning. And I'm sure your agents who know what's what in the Yam Yam can give us a steer on any unusual and untoward development there, who's missing et cetera.'

'Wilco out, as we one-time military buffs still have it.'

Back in his own room Kulbahadur was waiting for him. 'Before you go and have your own tea, Kulé, I want to tell you what I think will happen now. You heard what the IO's batman said, didn't you?'

'Yes sahib. His sahib has disappeared. His bed has been empty more than once on a Saturday night but never on a Sunday.'

'Do you know where he has probably gone? Or why?'

Kulbahadur, who like all Gurkhas did not want to talk about British sahibs, said he didn't.

'Then I'll tell you. To join the daku.'

Kulbahadur pursed his lips and remained silent, as Rance had expected him to. 'I know where he'll be making for. I also know which way he and his escort will go. I've recently been told by a Cheena, a friend who taught me Chinese when I was a schoolboy in Kuala Lumpur, who is working for the police by pretending to be a daku, that Hinlea *gora*,' – *I find it difficult to call a traitor such as him 'sahib'* – 'has secretly planned to desert from us with Special Branch documents and join them.'

Kulbahadur took a sharp intake of breath, his eyes widening as he stared at Rance, his normally expressionless face a picture of bewilderment. 'But sahibs don't do that,' he said, almost to himself, his mask of self-control slipping for a moment.

'No they don't but this one has. Sit down and listen,' said Jason, also sitting down. 'We have a briefing at 0730 and I'm sure that the battalion will be deployed. The Commanding sahib will have told the Brigadier sahib and it is quite possible that more than one other battalion will also be deployed. I don't know and it's not up to me. But, because I know where and how the Hinlea *gora* and his daku escort will be travelling, and the CO sahib knows that I know, I will ask him to allow me to track the group with four men: you, Kulé, a signaller and two riflemen. We will be armed with sub-machine guns and we'll carry rations for three days and make them last for five. We'll also open some tins of Compo rations and take out the biscuits and chocolate to use as hard tack if there's no time to cook. The lighter our load is the faster we'll be able to move. Understood so far?'

'Yes, sahib, understood,' and he repeated the bull points to Jacob's satisfaction.

'Right. The extra kit I want you to pack is that noise machine we use on the jungle range.'

Kulbahadur's eyes lit up. 'And make them think we're more than we are?' he asked, grinning hugely.

'Correct. You'd better carry it. If I go and recce their camp and get mixed up with them, you, "firing" from a flank and shouting orders, could be battle-winning. Get some new batteries and put them in before putting it into your pack. And buy a new one for my torch, which I'll take. Also, tell the Gurkha Captain sahib that what I have told you is a Warning Order only that I will confirm as soon as I can after the Commanding sahib's briefing. Plan for an "O" Group at 0800, to include you and the other three that the Captain sahib will detail. Don't say that the Hinlea *gora* has deserted, only that he's missing, and ask the Company cook to get five rations ready to eat by, say, half past 8.'

Kulbahadur saluted and marched off. It was only when he came back to pack his sahib's kit that he found the dummy krait used for the ventriloquism show. Oh, how he had laughed and laughed at that and, strangely, last night he'd had a dream about a snake. He made his mind up: *I'll take it with me.*

Only the CO and the 2 IC were married so lived away from the battalion lines. Officers under the age of thirty were not authorised married quarters or extra allowances and, in Gurkha battalions, most officers did not marry until they were majors.

Makes emergencies like this one much easier an...
to Jason mused as he thought out how he wou...
impending operation take shape.

He went down to the CO's office shortly befor...
the Adjutant telling the Duty Clerk to arrange cha...
circle around the CO's desk. He had already aske...
Bugler if he knew the call for 'Officers at the doubl...
bugle call was hardly ever sounded. Jason had only eve...
once before. 'Yes sahib. It is five "Gs" after the normal "...
call, followed by thirteen "dah-di-dahs".' The Adjutant...
relieved. It had never occurred to him that British officers h...
report anywhere at the double.

The CO's staff car drew up and out stepped two tight-lip...
and frowning officers, doors slamming behind them, almost befo...
it had fully stopped. The CO hurried into his office, looking a...
his watch. Jason and the Adjutant saluted him. He called out to
the Adjutant, 'Don't forget, the Officers Call, at the double, at
twenty-five past the hour.'

The CO, with the 2 IC standing by, said, 'Captain Rance,
this is an abomination of all that we, as British officers, have ever
stood for. Hinlea fooled us to the very end. I got on to the Brigadier
and he is seething. "I can't understand it," he had expostulated
violently. "Thought loyalty was ingrained in all army units."
He pompously added that Hinlea's talents for dissemination
outnumbered his peers' at discrimination. The CO paused for
breath. 'Let's leave the Brigadier's ranting and concentrate on
what we have to do. You were nearer to Hinlea than the others
were as well as knowing so much more about the background to

s happened, what we talked about in my office last Friday
. As we have no IO, I'm going to ask you to give the initial
ing.' He looked at his 2 IC: 'Fair enough, George?'

'Yes, Colonel. Makes a lot of sense.'

'Jason,' *'Jason' now! Normally surnames only for captains
d below.* 'In all your talks with your Chinese friend, did you
d out how they were going to act once they had their new
ecruit with them? If so, tell me in brief.'

'Indeed I did, sir. Hinlea will be escorted along the guerillas'
courier route to somewhere here' and he pointed to the Kuala
Klawang-Jelebu area on the map on the office wall, 'as they want
to go to the next Regional Committee camp at Titi and that's the
line along which Ah Fat has travelled at least twice. I can't see
them using any other route.'

'That's really good news. And have you thought of the best
way to exploit that info?'

'Indeed I have, sir. I believe our efforts to thwart Hinlea's
intention is for me to take a small group and track his party, catch
them up and shadow them without making any contact. If the
Auster can relay the group's progress backed up by sitreps from
me, then, sir, you will have virtually pinpointed their position by
the time they reach the main road. Were you to want to cross the
road and move southwest, then you'll have to let me know at once
and fix a boundary with me. That, sir, in a nut shell, is how I see
matters best developing.'

The CO shook his head in admiration. 'That's a sound plan,
Jason. In that case I will divide the operation, which I am dubbing
"Operation Janus" – although "Operation Judas" would be

more apt – into two parts, your group's and the battalion's main ambush. That's a large and dangerous, though vital responsibility for you. Apart from tracking and shadowing the group, your special knowledge of Hinlea and the Chinese mentality could pay great albeit as yet unknown dividends.' Outside the bugle blared its summons. 'Your party will be as big or as small as you think wise and effective. Your Gurkha Captain will command your company for the other part of the operation, which I'll come on to when we're all together. No point in going into it twice.'

'I had very much hoped that that is what you would consider the most expeditious method of keeping tabs on Hinlea. I can't see myself, with my few men, actually capturing and bringing him back when I'll be heavily outnumbered. However, in case matters do come to a head, I'll try and see that he remains alive.'

'Yes, alive if possible, but don't be squeamish if not possible.'

'Hoping that you'd see my ideas the way you have, sir, I have already taken the liberty of giving a warning order for my group.'

There was a squink of studded boots as their wearers, red-faced and breathless, came into the office. The Adjutant counted them, saluted the 2 IC and told him 'all present and correct, sir'. The 2 IC called the group to attention. 'Officers salute!' and the CO told them to be seated. 'Smoke if you wish.' *At least we won't have that revolting* bidi *smell*. A couple of officers lit up and the 2 IC took his pipe and tobacco pouch from his briefcase and, having filled and lit it, sucking contentedly.

'Gentlemen, this is a most unexpected briefing because of a most unexpected happening. Captain Hinlea has disappeared ...' The phone rang. 'CO.' Nobody could hear what the CO heard but all saw the look of disgust on his face. 'Thank you, Mr Clark. Proof indeed. And you'll let me know if there's anything else when your men have come back from the other quest.' Nodding, he replaced the receiver.

'Captain Hinlea, as I was saying, has disappeared and the OCPD has just rung to tell me that he has proof that he has run away to join the Malayan Communist Party.'

There was a collective gasp of dismay and everybody turned to look at one another as though it were all a bad dream.

'I have been talking to the Brigadier and we both agreed that nothing, but nothing, public can be said about this. Should anyone be interested enough to wonder why the battalion is being fully deployed at the beginning of retraining, it is because the Brigadier has decided to have a test exercise now and not at the end so we can practise what lessons emerge. He's a highly decorated Sapper who's never been in the Far East before and he has his own ideas. He's green to the jungle – sorry, no pun intended. Nor will you mention this in any letter you may feel inclined to write. But first, I am asking Captain Rance to give us the background.'

Jason went to stand in front of the maps, pointer in hand. 'Gentlemen. I'll try and keep this as short as possible. Briefly, Hinlea has been what is known as a "fellow traveller" since he was a schoolboy. His local name at the Yam Yam, where he fixed all this up, is Lustful Wolf.' There was a snickering and a few deprecatory noises. 'He has made contact with the guerillas at the highest level. This I know for a fact because one of the long-term Special Branch sleepers in the Central Committee is a school-boy friend of mine,' he was interrupted by more sharp intakes of breath, 'who also met up with Mr Ian Clark, the OCPD, when they were in Force 136. The CO had detailed Hinlea to help Special Branch to get their records in order and, before he finished, a trap was set to see if, in fact, suspicions of his treachery were merely his own "pie in the sky" or for real. From what the CO said just now on the blower, Hinlea did fall into the trap, has taken the so-called secret papers doctored to cause dissention among the ungodly and has, by now, almost certainly handed them over to the Political Commissar of the Regional Committee who happens to have his camp here,' and he pointed to near the top of Bukit Beremban. 'You can see it from the Mess lawn and, probably, with binoculars, people there can see us.

'The CO will take over directly I have finished but,' here he looked enquiringly at the Colonel – 'you're not a pawn but a bishop so carry on' – 'I'll go ahead with my own group tracking and shadowing, but *not* attacking, Hinlea and the Regional Committee. I estimate that Hinlea's group will be maximum thirty strong. My batman, Rifleman Kulbahadur Limbu, is probably the best tracker in the battalion. I will take a signaller and two riflemen. We'll travel light, on half rations, shadowing the guerillas until they come to the road around here,' and he pointed to the area between Kuala Klawang and Jelebu. 'Their plan is to move on to the high hills around Titi where they hope to join up with the next Regional Committee defence people and probably an escort from the Politburo.

'As you can see from the map, the main Seremban-Kuala Klawang road runs north of the main ridge of hills under which the guerillas will be moving. The country to the south of the main feature is rugged, thick jungle, a rough journey of ups and downs and bereft of villages except for a few aboriginal settlements. It will be a tiring and slow journey but that is the route the guerilla couriers take. I'll give them five days to reach the main road. If it takes them any longer they'll be hungry.'

He let that sink in before resuming, 'One point in our favour for finding their location is that their wireless has just had a new-fangled thingammy, I don't know its technical name, put into it that, when switched on, can be picked up by an Auster fitted with a beacon. I have learnt that the Regional Committee's Political Commissar, certainly when in his camp, normally listens to the Red, Chinese, network of Radio Malaya at 0800, 1200 and 1600 hours daily. On the move I can't say if or when he'll switch his wireless set on. Let's say that the Auster has a listening watch at these times if the weather allows. If the pilot can pick him up and give us a fix, the battalion rear link can tell me. And if the beacon in the set is not discovered, as well as getting map references from me, not only will the battalion be able to narrow down the area in which the group will cross the road in the Kuala Klawang-Jelebu area but also to move towards the guerillas and deal with them before they cross it.'.

He had pin-drop silence as he spoke. 'It is not up to me to say how many troops are needed for such a jungle-covered area. A cordon, Gentlemen, is an almost non-existent line with a soldier here and there, and 1/12 GR is certainly not big enough to block the whole area but planning will be made simpler if that method can be established.' He rubbed his forehead. 'But if, suddenly, say on D+3, no more contact can be made, that could mean that my group is the centre of attraction and that will be the signal for the battalion to move forwards to where I last reported my position which must be our boundary until any troops move south of the main road. If troops do come south of the road and we are still in contact, our boundaries must be known to all and sundry.' He said to the CO, 'Sir, that's all I have,' and saluted.

'Thank you,' said the CO. 'An admirable briefing, especially about boundaries, but I don't think that five men are enough. I'd like to think you'll have a few more than that. Your maximum?'

'Sir, tracking with eight following on behind the tracker is no problem but shadowing with eight is more risky than with five. I'll be better able to what is needed by sticking to five.'

'All right. I accept that. Anyone want to ask Captain Rance any questions? Before anyone does, I'd like to say that, up till now, only he and I, militarily, and the OCPD and Head of Special Branch, Mr. Mubarak, have had any knowledge about this. The fewer people who know about our disgrace the better, so keep it to yourselves, please. By the way, I'm meeting the Brigadier at midday.'

The 2 IC had a question. By then so intrigued with the situation had he become that he had let his pipe go out, its stem now sticking out from his fist. 'Let's suppose you inadvertently do have a contact, what will be your plan?'

'Sir, my aim is not to make contact. But were contact made, for whatever reason, and I'll take good care not to be seen, I'll just have to "play it by ear". I can always fade into the background and, with only five of us, it will be easier to remain undetected. I'll designate Fall Back and RV positions as we move along so even if we do have to split up we'll have a good chance of eventual recovery. I'll let the battalion know if I can't continue to shadow them. However, with the Auster's help and what info I've already been able to pass on, the CO can bring companies forward for a contact. If I were to have a contact, it will probably make the guerillas move forward even faster than otherwise. Which means, sir, if possible, Tac HQ should keep a listening watch for my reporting in whenever I have the chance to give you something to work on. I'll work on my proven military principles, a firm base, an alternative and a reserve.'

'It's the hell of a gamble but it might just pay off,' said the 2 IC and, to himself, *rather you than me.* He looked at Jason and saw he crackled with purpose.

'So you're almost ready to go, are you, Jason?' the CO asked.

'Yes, sir. I'll need a Land Rover at 0830 at my Company HQ. I'll give it an escort and it should be back in the lines in time for the driver and escort's morning meal.'

'MTO, copy that,' ordered the CO.

'May I borrow your phone, please, sir?'

'Yes.'

'One last point. I'd like the Signal Officer or the Adjutant to liaise with the Auster flight and tell them to be over this area here,' and he indicated a swathe of territory, 'either at 0800, 1200 or 1600 from tomorrow. The OCPD has the details of what has been put into the wireless set that the Regional Committee is using. The Auster, flying to a flank, can plot the map reference, send it to Tac or Main HQ, either or both of which will let me have it when I open up. I'll open up early morning and evening before the interference gets too bad and at any other time I have something I think you'll need to know straightaway. I think my call sign should be 1 Able and my 2 IC 1. I'll refer to Hinlea by his initials, Able How, much as I'd like to refer him as Judas.'

'I'm sure we all would,' someone muttered.

The Signal and the Adjutant made notes of Jason's request.

'Sir, if you've nothing more for me, please excuse me.'

'Of course. Rance, apart from planning to be in comprehensive ambush positions before D +5, I've nothing left to say except to wish you good hunting.'

Jason saluted and hurried off to his company. He did not hear the CO start by saying 'Gentlemen, the name of this operation is "Janus".'

Jason found his 'O' Group ready: the 2 IC, three Gurkha Lieutenant Platoon Commanders, Company Sergeant Major, Company Quartermaster Sergeant, Signal Corporal, clerk and Kulbahadur Limbu, the signaller Minbahadur Gurung and the two riflemen Chakrabahadur Rai and Lalman Limbu. They saw his normally happy face grimly hard-set.

'I have some bad, bad news to tell you,' he said after the Gurkha Captain had reported all present and correct, 'something the like of which I've never come across ever before and never would have expected from a British officer.' He looked at them, they looked back expectantly. 'The IO, Captain Hinlea, has deserted and joined the daku.' He knew that they had already heard the news of Hinlea's departure but not of his defection.

'Sahib, we don't like officers like that in our battalion. It has never happened before, how can it happen now?'

'Captain sahib, I know, I know. I hate it as much as you do, as we all do. The recapture operation will take place in two phases, my tracking Hinlea's daku group and a battalion ambush here,' and he got up and showed where on the map on the wall. 'Orders for that will be given later. I'll let you into a secret: the top police spy in the daku's top HQ was a big friend of mine when we were both children in Kuala Lumpur. He taught me how to speak Chinese and I helped him with his English. I met him in Seremban recently and he told me and the OCPD sahib, whom he had met during World War 2 in Malaya, about it. Apparently, the daku HQ in the Cameron Highlands has given permission for Hinlea *gora* to join them.'

His grim face was matched by twelve equally grim Gurkha faces.

'The police spy, my friend, knows where Hinlea will be making for.' He broke off. 'Look out of the window at that second highest mountain.' Necks craned to have a view. 'Near the top is the daku's base and that's where my group will start. I intend to track them, with Kulé's help, and hope that I can shadow them until they reach the battalion's ambush position, between Kuala Klawang and Jelebu. The daku's wireless set has had a secret receiver put into it and the Auster pilot can contact it without the daku's knowledge. That and my reporting back will mean that the battalion will have a good idea of where the daku group is so contacting them from in front should present no problem. Then we will be rear ambush but the daku won't know that either. If I get the chance to capture Hinlea having routed, killed or captured the daku, so much the better.'

'Sahib,' said his Gurkha Captain. 'Five early meals and four sub-machine guns for you and your escort and a pistol for the signaller are ready. I suggest that you, Sahib, and three riflemen each take a grenade. Also you are going on a difficult and dangerous journey. You will be in the minority. Just suppose the daku you are chasing back-track, for whatever reason, and see your jungle boot tracks. They will instantly know that they have been discovered and are being tracked.'

'So what do you recommend, Captain sahib?'

'Wear canvas shoes instead. Of course the leeches will have an easier target but with enough anti-malarial oil rubbed in, although a good sniffing man will smell it from nearby, you will be bitten much less.'

'Sahib. Thank you. Okay, lads, no jungle boots only canvas shoes. I'll go and change before I come back here for my meal. Oh yes, take a camouflage veil each and to remember that one of the most important features of an operation like this is "to react instantly and properly to the unexpected".'

While he was away the Gurkha Captain said to the four going with the Company Commander, 'If there's a way of not letting this *gora* come back, take it.'

Each man tilted his head sideways in acknowledgement but said nothing.

At 0900, after first asking the Medical Officer for two ampoules of morphia – which Jason signed for – needles, gauze and some bandages, they drove away not on the Seremban-Kuala Klawang road but down to the shop of Goh Ah Hok. Drawing up outside, Jason, with Kulbahadur following, went into the house, calling loudly in Cantonese for the fresh-ration contractor to come. Nobody came. *Don't tell me he's gone off too. I couldn't bear it.* But come he did, surprised to see Jason. '*Sinsaang* Goh Ah Hok, I know that you know where the main camp of Comrade Lau Beng and Comrade Wang Ming is. You will get out your van and take me to the place you get out then lead me and my men to the camp, *now*.'

Goh, almost totally overwhelmed to be addressed in fluent Cantonese, violently denied any knowledge of what Jason was talking about. Inwardly he was flabbergasted that the *gwai lo* officer could know anything about his 'other life'.

'Don't fool about and tell lies,' Jason said angrily. 'I'm in a hurry to get there with my *Goo K'a* soldiers.' A smell he didn't like assailed his nostrils. *Bidis.* 'I also accuse you of having had the man you call Sik Long here last night. True or false?'

Again Goh Ah Hok denied any knowledge of anything. *But how could he know the Lustful Wolf was here last night and,* another terrible thought, *how does he know that nickname?*

Jason leant over towards him and, coldly, distinctly and forcibly, 'You are a liar. Listen to this' and he cursed him in the oldest and most virulent curse all Chinese know:'*Ch'uan jia chan,* and I mean it.'

The curse means *May your entire clan be wiped out* and, in days gone-by in China, that was literally meant, no sibling, kith or kin remaining alive.

'And,' added Jason ruthlessly in Gurkhali, which he translated back into Chinese: 'I will curse you with a curse which, if broken, will result in leprosy in your entire family for seven generations.' *That sounded better than the other curse,* ngok yau, ngok bo, *evil has its recompense.*

Although the Gurkhali version was not a Chinese curse, it was too much for Goh Ah Hok. '*Sinsaang* Seong Wai, I'll take you, I promise, on one condition.' Jason was surprised that the contractor knew the Cantonese for 'Captain'.

'And that is?'

'You won't kill me if I do.'

'No, I won't,' *but I can't bespeak anyone else.* 'Did you drive him out?'

'No, no, no.'

'Who did?'

Shamefacedly and almost in a whisper, 'The manager of the Yam Yam did.'

'Go and get your van, *now, at once.*'

Goh Ah Hok brought his van out. Jason told Kulbahadur to sit in front with his kukri out of its sheath. 'If you do not carry out your promise, this *Goo K'a* will so mutilate your wife's wedding present, you'll be useless to her for the rest of your days ... and nights.'

Shortly after 9 o'clock the convoy of two vehicles moved off, the van in front and Jason's as near behind as was safe. They moved up the road that led to Kuala Klawang. About five miles up, the van moved into the same abandoned gravel quarry as before and the Land Rover followed.

'Debus,' cried Jason and Kulbahadur joined them. Goh Ah Hok, looking scared and penitent, came up to Jason. '*Sinsaang,* if the guerillas see me, I'm dead. As you are so tall may I walk behind you when we get near the camp?'

'*Sinsaang* Goh Ah Hok,' *be polite to him, he's shit scared and politeness costs nothing*, 'there will be no need for you to hide. I'm sure the Lustful Wolf and the Regional Committee will have moved out by the time we get there. In any case, as you are known, you will always be in front by about twenty paces and recognised if there are any ambushes.' He looked around at his men. 'We're going to follow this Cheena who not only knows the way but, if there are any ambushes in front of us, will be allowed to pass and we'll get to know of their presence soon enough to deal with them. In any case, it's more than likely that, by the time we reach the camp, if not before, Hinlea and the daku will have left. Driver, you may go back.'

Jason glanced at his watch. 0920. *Later than I'd thought we'd get here but no matter.* 'Move.'

Goh Ah Hok knew where the normal three ambush positions were, even so he thought it wise to skirt them, yet, when near the first one, he picked up a stick and beat it on a tree trunk, three spaced blows, followed by three quick ones then a further three spaced. No reply. He turned to Jason: 'There are no ambush positions. This means that the guerillas will have left their main camp.'

One must never take the jungle for granted. 'Move off, but as stealthily as before.' Climbing the higher ground at the end of their journey had made Goh Ah Hok breathless but Jason kept up the pressure and, well within the hour, they reached the bottom of a steep slope. 'Here there are always two guerilla sentries. Now there are none. That can only mean that the camp is empty. Do you want to go up into the camp?'

There might be some clue that'll help us. 'Yes.'

Goh bent down and lifted up a thick plaited vine which he pulled. 'The alarm system,' he explained. 'Just in case, let's wait.'

'But surely, if there had been anyone in the camp, we'd have been seen and probably fired on by now?'

'True. Can you excuse me from climbing up? There are some cleverly hidden footholds which I'll show you from here.'

This he did. 'Kulbahadur and the signal wala stay down here. Kulé, look around for any traces and find out when they left, today or yesterday, how many, and Minbahadur open up and try and contact Tac HQ, they should be open by now. You other two will climb up the steps with me.'

Up the three of them went, senses sand-papered to ultimate awareness, but there was no one at the top. Jason and the others peered around and took a good look at everything. 'Sahib, come here,' called Lalman, from a dip in the ground just at the mouth of the steep path into the camp. 'A Bren gun.' Jason hurried over to have a look at it. 'Well done, Lalman, for spotting it. How did you see it?'

'I nearly tripped on it, Sahib, as it was hidden under some leaves.'

Jason thought. *We can't take it with us. If the daku come back they'll want to use it.* 'Lalman, unlock the body locking pin, take out the breech block so it can't fire. Throw the breech block away in the first stream we cross.'

Lalman disabled the LMG and, just before they decided to

go back down, he saw the cave. 'Let's look in that, Sahib,' he suggested. In they went and had a good look around. They saw a sack which they opened – rice – and another – flour. To their surprise they also found six khaki shirts and six caps with a red star under some sacking in one corner.

'Let's take five of both with us,' said Jason. 'It may be that, wearing them ourselves, we'll be just that more likely to take the daku by surprise when we catch them up.'

'Look sahib, a rope.' It was the 'punishment rope' used for defaulting guerillas. 'We don't have one. Shall we take this?'

'Yes, it may come in handy.'

'Sahib, look at this,' called Lalman excitedly, pointing out an army issue set of jungle green and a jungle hat. Jason picked the hat up. Inside was the name 'Hinlea'. *More proof that the traitor has flown but finding his kit here means he's now dressed like a guerilla.*

Just as they were about to leave, Lalman said, 'Sahib, it's not likely that we'll use all our grenades is it?'

'Why?'

'There's quite a lot of valuable stuff in the cave, even a sort of armourer's repair place and some kerosene oil. Why don't we gather it together and make it unserviceable by exploding a grenade in the middle of it?'

'Pick out five sets of guerilla kit first, put the rest into a pile, sprinkle all the kerosene oil over it to get it alight then let's explode a grenade into it.'

Chakré took the guerilla kit out of the cave and Lalman, having sprinkled the kerosene oil over the pile, primed and placed the grenade on its inner side. By the time it exploded the three men had started their descent to join the two at the bottom. They didn't notice a package of Ovaltine lying on its side on the ground by the table. 'Sahib, was that a grenade we heard? Any trouble?'

Jason told them what had happened, then, 'Any luck with your tracking, Kulé?'

'Yes, Sahib. About thirty to thirty-five men have moved northeast. Their tracks are a day old.'

That's more than I bargained for. We'll have to be more than very careful.

'Where's the Cheena?'

'Gone.'

'Good riddance. Here, take a shirt and cap each. We may need them. Put the cap in your right-hand pouch so it is instantly ready.'

The wireless operator had made contact. 'Sunray 1 Able on set. Fetch Sunray.'

'Wilco, wait out.'

'Sunray minor on set,' came the reply a few minutes later, 'Sunray is with big Sunray.' *Yes, of course, he said he'd be with the Brigadier about now.*

'The daku camp is empty.' He looked at his map and gave the 6-figure map reference. 'In it I found Able How's jungle kit which means he is now dressed as a daku. We have found tracks for about thirty to thirty-five men, a day old, moving northeast. Roger so far, over.'

'Roger, over.'

'The person who drove Able How out and took him to the

guerilla camp was the manager of the Yam Yam and the man who drove us out in his van is the fresh-ration contractor. Over.'

'Roger, over.'

'Anything for me? Over.'

'Take care and good hunting. Out.'

'Miné, get packed.' Three minutes later, 'Ready? Good. On our way with Kulé in front.'

The 2 IC acted quickly. He phoned the OCPD with the details of the manager of the Yam Yam and the fresh-ration contractor. By the time Ian Clark went to the Yam Yam to arrest the manager he was no longer there, nor, at opening time that evening, was the cabaret girl who called herself Siu Tse. However, the OCPD did have more luck with Goh Ah Hok when he went to his shop. There he found him looking miserable. He took him in for questioning by Head of Special Branch.

Jason once more felt the wartime ganglion of tension dormant since Burma days. His thoughts became two-dimensional: his task was in the forefront of his mind while, at the back, one aspect of what he'd noticed about Hinlea's behaviour was gnawing at him like a hungry dog at a bone. *Something. What was it now?* Some twenty minutes later he bent down to tighten his laces and, as he straightened up, the sun burst through the clouds and cast a shadow on a leaf. Intrigued, he picked it up. It was folded in half. Nature does not like straight lines so only a man could have folded it. His mind raced back to when he and Hinlea were sitting on the Mess verandah and Hinlea picked a leaf off a plant and folding it in two, to say nothing of his folding bits of paper. He picked it up and sniffed it. *Bidi*! A compulsive habit but one that the perpetrator didn't realise he had was now playing into their hands. He called a halt and showed the leaf to his men, explaining its significance. 'Even if the rain does make the tracks look older than they really are, any more leaves we find that are folded and smell like this one will tell us that we are on the correct path.'

At the next deep stream Lalman ceremoniously dropped the breech block into it. *Your new permanent home*, he said to himself with a grin.

Tracking so many was easy. With the guerillas' day's start on them and their being on the move, there was not much danger in their own progress being quicker than normal, provided it was quiet. With only five of them and therefore not much human smell – tobacco, sweat – they came across more animals than they had ever seen before: several porcupines, a boar, three deer, monkeys galore and something which made them stop and stare, a python swallowing a mouse deer. 'Ten minutes halt and light up if you want to. The daku are too far away to smell issue cigarettes.'

'On,' Jason said quietly, ten minutes later, after they had watched the ill-fated deer's back legs disappear. 'On.'

After the eleven men bound for Titi had set off, the Political Commissar was not to be best pleased when the Military Commander, *and my junior*, scowling ferociously, came over to him and said, 'Comrade Lau Beng, you wrongly overstepped your authority yesterday to our base camp's security, your personal detriment and probable defamation.'

'Comrade Wang Ming, you are forgetting yourself. What do you mean by insulting me and offending correct protocol?' was the pompous reply. 'Explain yourself.'

'If you look around at our comrades and their weapons, what do you notice?'

'Weapons are not my responsibility. Why should I notice anything?'

'Think back to yesterday. You ordered us out of the camp without checking with our junior comrades that every weapon was accounted for. I was about to and you told me to move out there and then.'

Lau Beng nodded nonchalantly. *What is this dreary turn-coat getting at?*

'Comrade, where is our machine gun? Did the men going to Titi take it?'

'Now you come to mention it, no. I didn't see them with it. It is much better for us to have it.'

'I agree, so please go around and check what weapons our men are carrying.'

And, of course, there was no machine gun. Lau Beng came back to where Wang Ming was sitting. 'So where is it?'

'Still back in the camp with the bad *feng shui*. Where else? Just suppose a courier, sent from the Politburo, happens to go to the camp, happens to find it empty and happens to find an unguarded machine gun there, I fear that, however successful our undertaking, your name will not be enhanced. Losing a machine gun is an extremely serious offence but, when one is lost through arrant carelessness, no amount of excuses can avoid retribution.'

I've got you. Put the second part of my brainwave into action. 'You and your stupid beliefs. Grow up. We will have to send back most of our defence squad, Comrade,' he said, swallowing a lump of angry phlegm that had somehow risen into his mouth, in as pleasant a voice as he could master. 'We will keep our bodyguards. There should be no danger at all because, just suppose there were any *Goo K'a* soldiers ahead of us, they will be seen off by those who have gone on to Titi.'

'How many will that leave us with?'

'Nine? Us three, the new comrade and five?'

'Hm. Less of a risk than not going back at all. It will be, oh, another week to Titi and up to ten days back. Yes, send the others off now and they will, if they move really fast, be back in the camp by earliest last light today.'

'I'll just open the wireless to see if there is any news,' said an inwardly gloating Political Commissar, 'it's 8 o'clock.'

Hinlea had been surprised at the group leaving to the northeast earlier on and mystified at ten more men going back the way they'd come. He tried to find out why but the answer he got, while valid, did not please him: 'For your safety'.

There was nothing about Hinlea's disappearance on the news and at half past 8 the second, 10-man group moved off.

It was lucky that Jason and his men stopped at the edge of one clearing to allow their sight to adjust to the brighter light. They saw a lemur launch itself off the top of a tree on one side and glide all of a hundred yards to the other side, a first for them all. Lucky because, at the same time, they saw a flock of birds rise up off the trees on the far side and heard monkeys chattering. 'Someone's coming,' hissed Jason. 'Move back slowly, don't bend or crush the foliage and sink to the ground behind that undergrowth,' pointing it out. 'Watch your front and be ready to fire but *only on my orders*.' Kulbahadur stayed next to Jason.

A couple of minutes later a group of ten armed guerillas came into view. They crossed the open ground without taking any but normal precautions making for where Jason's group was hiding, looking neither right nor left as if sensing no danger. One of them called out, 'Comrade, there's a breeze here. Let's sit down for a break.' They were a few yards from their trackers.

'Good idea,' said the senior man among them. 'Packs off and light up. Not the weed that foreign *gwai lo* comrade smokes,' and Jason heard the noise of cigarettes being brought out of pockets, matches being struck and the smell of a local tobacco prisoners-of-war of the Japanese had described as 'hag's bush'.

Part of Hinlea's group? If so, why are they coming this way? Jason asked himself.

'Comrade, it seems so strange that we are on our way back after going all that way yesterday, doesn't it?' asked another.

'Not nearly as strange as that dreadful noise the Comrade Political Commissar made when the new comrade gave him those papers. I do wonder what was in them to make him howl like that. Whatever it was, the way he looked at Comrade Wang Ming afterwards made me quite scared. What's it all about, do you think, Comrade?' asked a third.

The senior comrade, a balding, slack-jawed man with a weasel face, shook his head. 'Can't tell with that lot but Sai Daam

Lo and Hung Lo don't seem to like each other one little bit, do they? I think it could be about their disagreement over *feng shui*. I think it's important. P'ing Yee keeps to himself – a nice man – but Sai Daam Lo seems suspicious of him. I wonder why?'

So he's still with the group. Useful to know.

'Comrade, comrades shouldn't really talk like that but we're on our own so there's no harm. Fancy forgetting the machine gun! Each blames the other, *feng shui* or not. And here we are to go back and occupy the camp because, were any courier to go there and find it empty *and* find the gun, someone would be in big, big trouble.'

'I agree. But why send eleven men forward to Titi before we were sent back? What's the urgency, I wonder.'

'Oh, they never tell us anything, do they? But I expect that the Regional Committee in Titi is being alerted so that they can take the new comrade on to ... where are they planning? Durian Tipus, they said.'

'So there'll only be nine people left in the group. Three senior comrades, the new *gwai lo* comrade – he's a strange one, isn't he? – and five escort. Glad we're out of it. That Sai Daam Lo is not fit and is finding walking in the jungle no fun,' and he laughed derisively. 'Cigarettes finished?' Jason, hardly daring to breath, felt that the senior comrade was looking around at his men. 'On your feet and on our way.'

'Comrade,' one man said, 'I must have a shit. I won't be long.' He moved over to the edge of the undergrowth just short of Jason's group, undid his trousers, squatted down facing his group and relieved himself noisily with a great sigh of relief. Kulbahadur had an idea – *react to the unexpected* – and slipping his hand into his pouch, took out the dummy krait and gave it Jason. Gently, oh so gently, Jason picked up a sharp twig, leant forward and, in the high falsetto voice he used for his ventriloquist dummy, shrilled, 'Shit all over my nest. I'll kill you for it,' and screwing the twig into the man's bare bottom, threw the dummy snake onto the ground beside him. The daku looked down and, with a startled yell, jumped up and tumbled forward onto his face, forgetting that his trousers were still around his legs, so splitting the seams. The others immediately made as though to see what the matter was. 'Go away! Krait! Deadly dangerous,' the scared man yelled, getting to his feet as best he could in his haste, forgetting to keep his voice down. The others edged back. Not even able to wipe himself, the terrified man pulled his trousers up and ran back to the others. The senior man said, 'Clean yourself at the next stream. Move. Quickly,' and the group moved off.

Jason waited five minutes before softly saying 'stand up'. Almost as one man, they covered their faces to suppress their laughter. Kulbahadur said, 'Sahib, your secret weapon was a sure winner. How clever of you to think of it.'

'Yes and no, Kulé,' Jason said, 'that was *your* quick thinking *and* you did react to the unexpected. Well done indeed. We had a lucky escape. If any of us had made any noise at all, we'd have had a fire-fight.' Kulbahadur went to pick up the krait and put it back in his pouch. 'Hey, you others, how long before the daku realise that snakes don't talk?' and bent double giggling.

'What did the daku say, Sahib?' Chakré asked.

Jason told them and added, 'I wonder what they'll do when

the find that their LMG is u.s. and that their store in the cave is wrecked. I pity someone somewhere sometime but it's not our problem. I don't expect that lot to come back looking for us because we're wearing canvas shoes not jungle boots.' *Whew!* 'With only nine men to track our job will be harder and even more dangerous.'

It took half an hour for the guerillas to reach the next stream where the soiled daku washed himself. He had the limpid gaze of an entirely stupid man and was normally unexcitable. The senior man said, 'Comrade, you are probably the first person ever not to die from a krait's poison.' He looked at the man's split trousers. 'You'll have to get a new pair from the stores in the cave.'

The 'bitten' man didn't seem to hear what was said. He shook his head in disbelief and, sheepishly, asked the others, 'Did I imagine that the krait spoke? Did you hear it?'

'How could a snake speak? We thought we heard you,' one of the others said.

'No. It wasn't me talking to start with.'

'Show me your buttock,' said the leader, 'and point out where you were bitten.'

With huge embarrassment the man uncovered himself. There were no marks. It then dawned on them that some dreadful and inexplicable trick had been played. What sort of jungle devil was that? The mystery made them feel uneasy. *Would worse happen?*

'Wash the shit out of your underpants and hang them out to dry. We'll stay here for the night. There's no real hurry to get back to the camp.'

The sun had gone in behind heavy clouds and it was almost too dark for tracking. Jason heard an Auster circling quite high up. He looked at his watch. 1600 hours. 'We'll stop at the next stream,' he said. They reached one within twenty minutes. 'We'll make camp up there' and he pointed the place out, Gurkha style, with his chin. 'Kulé and you, Chakré, make a short circuit of the area. Minbahadur open your wireless and try and contact HQ. I'll give you our position. Get your bashas fixed, move down to the stream for water and start cooking when the perimeter check has been made. It'll probably be too late for any more daku movement but keep as quiet as you possibly can.'

Five minutes later the two scouts found the guerillas' overnight camp. Kulbahadur looked at the ground, bent down and picked up another folded leaf and smelt it. *More proof: it smells of* bidi *and it's been folded in half. That habit makes my job just that bit easier.* He kept it in his hand. He also noticed a used piece of toilet paper –more proof were any needed as Cheena daku didn't use it.

They returned to where the others had made three bashas, two men would sleep together under one and the Captain sahib would have his own. Kulbahadur told Jason what he had found, 'Last night's daku overnight camp is near and there are no fresh tracks.' He showed him the leaf. 'Smell it Sahib.' Jason smelt it: 'yes, it certainly does make our job easier. Start cooking.' By then Minbahadur had strung the aerial between two branches and had netted the set. 'Sahib, you're wanted.'

It was Sunray himself, asking for details. Jason gave him their six-figure map reference, told him that they had proof positive that Able How was ahead of them. 'We'll get nearer them tomorrow.'

Ten guerillas moving southeast to southwest rested near us. I overheard they were being sent back to the main camp because it was unoccupied and because their one Love Mike George had been left behind. They were not at all suspicious and did not see us. I also heard that a group of eleven had been sent forward to contact other guerillas at Tare Item Tare Item. They will be moving along the axis I showed you. We are now tracking nine men.'

'Roger,' said Sunray. 'Did you find the Lima Mike George?'

'Yes and we made it Uncle Sugar. We also found their store, in a cave, quite well stocked considering and destroyed it, including Able How's hat and issue clothes.'

'Well done. You've now got fewer men to follow. Take extra care. Out.'

After their meal they lit a fire to keep wild animals and mosquitoes away. 'No guerilla would ever think Security Forces would do that. Were there any daku to see the fire they'd put it down to an aborigine hunting party. No sentries are needed.'

They discussed the day's events and the possibility of catching up with the daku on the morrow. 'Before we go to sleep, I'd like to mention a couple of points to help us track better because there are fewer daku to follow so it won't be as easy as it has been so far. There are ground signs and top signs.' The men looked at him steadfastly. 'Ground signs are foot and boot marks, broken twigs or Hinlea's bent leaves, bruised or "bleeding" roots, disturbances of insect life, grass or ground vegetation, mud left from footwear, debris dropped beside a track and disturbed water. Quite a list!' and he grinned at his men. 'Examples of top signs are broken twigs or leaves, scratches on trees, bruised moss on trees, hand holds on trees, broken spiders' webs, changes in colour and natural position of vegetation and cutting. Birds and animals moving our way also means movement is coming towards us.

'What a really good tracker like Kulé can also discern is direction of movement, number of persons - man, woman or child – making the track, time when made, loads carried or not, speed, type of food eaten and whether the people are walking backwards or forwards. I'm right, aren't I, Kulé?'

'Yes, Sahib, you are. How did you learn all that? We didn't know that you knew so much about tracking.'

Jason lifted his eyebrows and smiled. 'If I hadn't learnt it in the Burma war I'd not have been with you lot now,' and the others chuckled softly.

One of them yawned. 'Right, lads, time to sleep. One of you stoke the fire.' And, after a hectic day they turned in and were quickly asleep.

10

At dawn the guerillas 'stood to', not that any Security Force activity was remotely expected but routine was routine. After 'stand down' it was decided to have an early meal. The Political Commissar, unused to so much physical exertion, was feeling sorry for himself, legs stiff and shoulders sore. The previous day's march had taxed him considerably. He was also still beside himself with fury at the slur on his character. Nor was his temper improved when, wanting a drink of Ovaltine, he found, in his haste to move, he had left the package behind.

As for Comrade Hinlea, he too was not as fresh as he presumed he'd be: he had sweated a lot and he felt uncomfortable in his dirty clothes, his leech bites were itchy almost beyond belief and he was kicking himself at having forgotten to pack his razor.

Jason and his men also woke at dawn and not only brewed up a mess-tin cover of tea but also cooked up half the normal amount of rice for later on. 'If we do that now, heating up a tin of meat or fish will only take a short time and, being nearer the guerillas by then, also safer.'

At 8 o'clock Minbahadur opened his set and sent 'Nan Tare Roger', 'Nothing to Report'. Control passed a message saying that the battalion was to move northeast later on in the day.

They put the by-then cooked rice into their mess tins, packed up and carefully moved off, having erased as many traces of their overnight stay as they could. 'Kulé, with only nine men to track it'll be harder, won't it?'

'Sahib, only after we've passed their last night's camp.'

On they went, each man's eyes ever vigilant. Kulbahadur sighted one bent leaf, picked it up and smelt it. Bidi *and the fold fresh. Can't be more than four hours ahead of us.* At 10 o'clock, at a small stream, Jason ordered a halt for their meal. *Yes. The tracks are fresher than yesterday afternoon's.* 'Sahib, we're much nearer the daku than I thought we would be. Once we've reached their overnight camp, I'll have a detailed search.'

'Sure we've not gone beyond it?'

'Can't have. Look, the foot prints of yesterday's group that we met at the clearing are still visible.'

What wonderful eyesight.

After their meal they moved steadily northeast and, in the early afternoon, found the guerillas' overnight camp. They briefly inspected it. Kulbahadur carefully examined the tracks they were following and, after crossing the first stream they came to, turned round and spoke to Jason. 'Sahib. There's something unusual about these tracks. Some of the prints are normal but others are more pronounced. I don't know what to make of them. What do you think?'

What was it? A nag assailed him ... Got it! 'Kulé, that's what we heard the daku saying yesterday. One group of eleven men had to move forward quickly to Titi. Those tracks will be theirs.'

They moved off in a heavy storm that made going slower and which either obliterated tracks or make them look much older than they actually were. But another bent leaf, smelling of *bidi*, confirmed they were still on track. *What atrocious jungle discipline!*

At midday the main guerilla group was sitting resting. Now that he had ordered some of his men to go forward and others back to the camp, the Political Commissar felt happier. *I'll make the traitor feel safe.* He leant over to the Military Commander and said, 'Yes, that was a wise move to make. I feel happier now. We've seen that no one has been this way and, if there was the remotest chance of *Goo K'a* soldiers coming the other way, those who've gone ahead can deal with them. And if there was a battle, I'm sure that a couple of men would come back and warn us. No, I feel that everything is going well though I do have to admit that so much sitting in our camp up in Bukit Beremban doesn't make so much walking all that easy. What about you, Comrade?'

Wang Ming felt that by so unbending, the usually taciturn and caustic Lau Beng was getting as near an apology for his hasty behaviour as he was ever likely to make. 'I agree with you, Comrade. None of us is getting any younger. And I'm sure you're correct in thinking that we're perfectly safe.'

Hinlea – *Operation Janus can only be a success, however strangely it is working out* – was having a chat with Ah Fat, asking him about reduced numbers and commenting on meeting his identical twin. It amused the Chinese, who felt a marked aversion to the Englishman – but, of course, he didn't show it – and how he had been hoodwinked. 'I'm finding walking pleasant exercise,' he said, expansively, 'because I don't get out all that often. But I'm glad I've brought some stuff to keep these leeches away. I hope it'll last.'

Ah Fat understood him perfectly but had to keep his excellent knowledge of English hidden both from the new comrade but also, more especially, from Lau Beng and Wang Ming. There was no valid tactical reason to reduce the number of men; was it a devious scheme of the Political Commissar's because of 'that' secret report? Risible if so.

They heard an Auster not all that far off flying slowly in a wide circle. The others took no notice of it. Only Ah Fat knew that it was there on purpose but, as the Political Commissar had not switched his wireless on, the pilot would hear nothing. *At least the system is in place but how can I tell if it actually works?*

'Time's up. On our way, Comrade,' said Lau Beng to Hinlea.

Back in Seremban the Auster pilot rang through to the battalion to say that he had not heard anything on his beacon. 'I'll try again at 1600 hours.'

'Roger that,' said the acting Acorn. 'The battalion is just about to move off. I'll let the CO know as soon as Tac HQ has been established.'

The rain cleared and at noon Jason's group heard the Auster. At 4 o'clock they heard it again, circling only a short distance in front of them. They stopped. 'It's circling the daku's position. We'll make camp at the next water, open the set and give our sitrep.'

The nearest stream was not far off. 'Before you start cooking Chakré and I will make a short recce. Lilé, put up your aerial but be prepared to send your message by key not voice.'

Jason and Chakré moved a couple of hundred yards down the faint track the guerillas had made but saw nothing else suspicious. 'Sahib, that tree there,' said Chakré pointing with his chin. 'I'll climb it and have a look.'

He was not up it for long. Once back on the ground he excitedly said, 'I saw smoke from their cooking rising up above the trees about a half a map square ahead. Give me your compass and I'll take a bearing.' Up he went again and found the smoke was on a bearing of 37 degrees.

Back in camp Jason said 'Start cooking and we can use voice not key. Chakré has seen the daku's smoke about five hundred yards away.'

At about the same time the guerillas who had been sent back reached their old camp. 'The first thing to do is to check the machine gun. After that we'll have a good wash in the stream then go to the cave store and draw some clean clothes. Then we'll relax and cook a decent meal. With no one to bother us, it'll be more like a holiday.'

Up they went and the leader went over to where the machine gun was hidden. He made a strangled squawk to see it was not in its correct place. *Could an animal have moved it?* he wondered as he picked it up. He saw that it had been tampered with and that there was no breech block. Sweat broke out on his brow. *They'll blame us. They'll never let on it was their fault.* There was a loud shout of dismay from the direction of the cave, 'Come here quickly.' The senior man ran over and the guerilla who had shouted said, his voice hardly his own, 'Look inside. Ruined. What could have happened?'

Inside, the senior man looked around, hardly believing his eyes. He sniffed. 'Must have been a grenade and kerosene oil. Smells like it. Nothing else could have made this mess. But whose grenade? There weren't any here. This and the damaged machine gun will cause so much trouble and could be the end of us.' He sighed heavily, mind full of foreboding and the quiet thud of fear in his heart, his soul writhing like an eel on a hot plate.

'How come?' demanded another man.

'Sabotaged, how else? Nothing we can do about it.'

'I agree. Nothing at all but when the Political Commissar and the Military Commander return, we can at least say we thought of something ... but what?' asked the man who had first entered the cave. 'I have an idea. Whoever did this cannot have come the way we've come back. We'd have seen them, they make more noise than we do and there were no jungle boot tracks. Once we've had a wash let's go back down and see if we can find any footprints in *Goo K'a* jungle boots coming from the Seremban road.'

If someone else could be blamed, how much easier life would be!

Before take-off, a parcel of surrender leaflets had been delivered to 1911 Flight HQ, with a covering note saying that areas for dropping would be detailed when the battalion returned from its current operation but, if the pilot did know of anywhere a drop might be effective, he could use his initiative and drop them. The pilot for the evening search, the same man who did the midday run, took a bundle, undid it and set it on the seat beside him before taking off. He flew east-northeast with his beacon on and at 4 o'clock made a circuit in the area under suspicion. This time the guerilla wireless was switched on. The pilot was gratified to hear a ping on his headset. *Got you,* he said to himself, with a smile, looking at his map. He flew lower to try and get a more accurate fix than he had been able to at the height he had been flying before. As he finished his circuit the noise faded. He now had a good idea where the group was. He also saw some white near the top of some trees. It had been raining so was it smoke or mist? He wasn't sure if it was policy to drop any leaflets over that part of the jungle but he knew where he could. He had been briefed on the main camp below Bukit Beremban so why not there? It was not an easy place to fly near, steep country with sudden down draughts and the day was cloudy but he'd have a shot at it. He had marked it on his map and flew as near as he dared and dropped half the bundle. The leaflets fluttered out of the cockpit before being taken by the wind. Back in base the pilot phoned the battalion with the news. 'I've marked where you think the guerillas are on my map. I saw either smoke or mist. Have you got Jason Rance's position?'

Acorn gave it. 'He's not far off now. His latest sitrep said he reckoned he was half a map square away from them.'

'Thanks. I now have a much better idea of how accurate I

was. I dropped some surrender leaflets as near the Regional Committee's camp as I could safely get.'

The patrol from the main camp had only come across faint footprints of men wearing canvas shoes and, wrongly, presumed that the prints had been made by the outlying ambushes that had been recalled before setting off with the rest of them the day before, blurred by rain. On their way back they saw a one-engined plane flying low and leaflets being scattered. They had been warned never to pick up *gwai lo* propaganda but, being on their own, they decided to. Each man picked one up, had a quick read and felt, really, really inside and *not* for public discussion, that such might be an answer to their problem. 'Shall we look for more for the others?' asked one, not committing himself either way.

'If we don't they'll only ask why we didn't bring any in.'

They gathered enough for one each and went back to camp. Everyone read what was written but only their eyes spoke. In each mind was 'singly or together?'

This time both the Political Commissar and the Military Commander commented on the Auster but as they had not heard the earlier one, neither was worried. Ah Fat saw that the wireless was switched on and the plane had made a circuit. *Clever but not clever to try and cook with wet wood that causes smoke.*

That same evening the guerillas sent forward to Titi were well over half way to crossing the main road. After making simple shelters and cooking their meal, they sat around gossiping. 'What seems so strange to me,' said one, 'is our having to go forward so soon. The Comrade Military Commander was obviously unhappy about it. By my thinking they're not "comrades" to each other. I don't really understand the system although I suppose I ought to.'

'Not nearly as strange as that dreadful noise Sai Daam Lo made when the new comrade gave him those papers. I do wonder what was in them to make him howl like that. Whatever it was, the way he looked at Hung Lo afterwards made me quite scared. What's it all about, do you think, Comrade?' asked another.

The senior comrade shook his head. 'Can't tell with that lot but the Sai Daam Lo and Hung Lo don't seem to like each other at all, do they? Comrade P'ing Yee keeps to himself – a nice man – but Sai Daam Lo seems suspicious of him, looking at him with evil eyes, lips silently muttering. I wonder why?'

'Comrade, comrades shouldn't really talk like that but we're on our own so there's no harm. Fancy forgetting the machine gun! They're sure to blame each other.'

'Comrade. Something perturbs me,' said the first speaker. 'What do you think that aeroplane has been doing flying over us but circling behind as though it knows where the bosses are? Is it dangerous?'

'I don't see how it can be,' replied the senior comrade. 'No one can know about us. Probably the *gwai lo* pilot practising.'

They fell silent for a while then the senior man said, 'We don't have much food with us. Once we've crossed the Kuala Klawang-Jelebu road, let's make for that Chinese-owned rubber estate and get a decent meal and some dry rations. I know this route well.

We'll reach just south of the road by dusk tomorrow then, in the small hours, make our crossing.'

The others agreed with him and they went to sleep.

Bloody Hell! I would do a whole lot of damage to an ice-cold bottle of beer right now, Hinlea thought as his group made their bivouac for the night, cold stream water having to do instead. His day had found him more wrapped up in himself as he had plodded silently along behind the Political Commissar. Getting himself moving through the jungle without getting entangled in thorny creepers or slipping over fallen logs and not minding when getting his feet wet walking across strong currents of streams had kept his mind off any deep thoughts but now it was evening, his strangeness caught up with him. Although he had often, if only for short spells, been the only English person when on detachment with his Indian gunners, now was really the first time he was the only European in a group of Asians. The other novel experience was that, unlike such people as shopkeepers and taxi-girls who were out for his money so knew when to smile and flatter, the people he was now with were completely different in their orientation and so in their regard towards him. It was turning out stranger than he had previously imagined. His personal pride in his achievement to date would have to be his bulwark against any diminution of endeavour. *Yet*, he mused just before he fell asleep, *Janus in the abstract is my mental compass, almost my lifeblood but a protracted Janus without beer or woman will take a lot of getting used to …*

Tuesday, 26 August 1952

It had been a most uncomfortable night for the guerillas, heavy rain and thunder had interrupted their sleep early on and the cascading water had flooded their bashas. In an unusual lapse of jungle lore, they had not taken notice of the trees nearby. The heavy rain over the previous weeks had made some of them so waterlogged that the extra weight of that night's rain made them too heavy to stand alone. Around midnight they were woken by heavy creaking that heralded a fall. Everyone listened to it, every nerve tingling, knowing that a large tree was about to crash down, each man knowing that there was no chance of running away to safety. Monkeys started screaming and fall it did with a rending, tearing sound, followed by a sickening thud as it hit the ground and then stunned silence only broken by some of the smaller branches whipping down on their shelters. 'Comrades, are you all right? Is anyone hurt?' called the Military Commander. Great relief was felt when he found out that no one had been hit. It was an even worse night for Hinlea. Apart from nearly soiling himself with fear at the fallen tree, he had kept one tin of sardines in case he was still hungry after his inadequate evening meal. He had gone to sleep with one arm flung out and the empty tin hard by his hand. By midnight conditions had eased off but clothes were sodden. He woke up and one arm seemed numb. He rubbed it with his other hand and only felt rough skin. Not his own, which was itching. He was at a loss to know what to make of it and put it down to having slept on it. He tried to turn over but found he couldn't. His torch was out of reach. He lay there till it was light enough to look and see what the trouble was. To his stupefying horror, the unblinking eyes of a large python glared at him from just below his shoulder. He screamed harshly: 'Come and save me. A big snake.' Drops of sweat formed on his hairline.

A couple of guerillas came to see what the trouble was and shrank back at what they saw. For one moment they thought that the *gwai lo* comrade would be totally swallowed but then realised that no, the snake was stuck. It could not go back nor could it move forward. 'Kill it, kill it,' moaned Hinlea, by now, almost in a faint. The three senior men came to see what the trouble was: they too recoiled. The man with the sharpest chopper was ordered to cut the snake in two – 'but below the arm' – so he measured Hinlea's other arm, added a couple or so inches, and struck hard. The python squirmed with all its might and lashed its tail, but in vain. By the third stroke the body was severed. The next job was to slit the piece that was still round the arm. Hinlea looked away while it was done. He got up and staggered to the stream by which they had camped and washed his upper body. The guerillas sliced up the python to cook it for their morning meal. When Hinlea was offered a piece, he turned to one side and spewed.

The kindling they had gathered the evening before had become wet. 'No early start,' said the Political Commissar, who had found the going so hard he now wished he'd never set out. 'I think we must have something inside us before we move. Nothing will dry with this heavy mist so wet clothes are the order of the day.'

One of the guerillas said, 'Comrade Political Commissar, I heard a deer calling its mate earlier on. I'm a good hunter. As there's no hurry, may I go and try and shoot one, or both of them? Although we'll have a good meat meal of python, we can dry the deer meat to add to our rations tonight and tomorrow. Now is a good chance for something different and tasty.'

'Don't see why not. Yes, go along but try not to be more than an hour.'

The guerilla, a country boy who had lived in a squatters' area in scrubby country, could make the noise of a deer so like the real animal that the deer would more often than not come up to him. 'I'll try my best, Comrade,' he said as he set off.

Comrade Hinlea had already delved into his pack and put on dry clothes. There was a brown mark on his right arm which, although it did not hurt, offended him when he rolled up his sleeves so he rolled them down. He was not happy either, the diet was not as filling or as tasty as he was used to, his wet pack straps had rubbed his shoulders and his wet trousers had chafed his crotch. He had to walk with his legs apart, which slowed him up. In fact, having been brought up as a gunner – he hadn't taken kindly to the jibes of his fellow officers when he joined the battalion as being a 'nine-mile sniper' – he was not as used to walking longish distances as were his peers, infantrymen from the start. His incipient beard was itchy. He was almost out of his *bidis* but, even so, he tried to appear as cheerful as he could. He sounded almost jovial when told of the hunting expedition. 'Oh, I do hope he's successful,' he said, trying to regain some of the 'face' he felt he had lost by screaming so loudly at the discovery of the python.

Ah Fat was concerned that there were only being nine of them, with the Political Commissar not much use as a fighter although he was armed and Hinlea an unknown with his weapon, how would he react if anything untoward happened? *If or when?* He knew that all he had told Jason had certainly got back to the CO. Once the news of Hinlea's defection broke, immense and immediate efforts would be made to recapture him. He thought it most probable that the battalion would move out to the area where he'd told Jason the guerillas would cross the main road and so was worried about their moving into an ambush: *Will I be clobbered before I can identify myself? Would Jason be in the forefront of any battle to try and recognise me or would he have thought that I'd have already left? Imponderables.* The Auster would report back their position but how accurately? Certainly accurately enough to confirm their line of advance.

As for the Military Commander, in the heart of his heart, he was glad that his skills would not be called upon. *The Security Forces cannot know which way our new comrade has gone so won't know where to start looking for him. But only nine of us ...*

While they were waiting for their meal, Lau Beng beckoned to Comrades Wang Ming and Ah Fat. 'All in all I think we're doing well. I now feel happy that our main camp is once more properly guarded and that our comrades who have gone off towards Titi will deal with any *Goo K'a* they might meet. One thing heavily in our favour is that only we know where we're going. No one else does or can know. That makes us safe as well as being a small group making us safer still.'

The noise of an Auster was heard in the distance. 'That damned aeroplane has come back again today. We heard it twice yesterday, the second time it circled quite near us. And now there it is again. What do you make of it?' and he looked at Ah Fat for an answer.

'I don't think we need worry about that in any way, Comrade. When I was in Seremban that time I picked up a certain amount of gossip, some of which was so tenuous it wasn't worth passing on. Now it does come back to me. The British have a new batch of pilots to train and have increased their aircraft by,' and he pretended to think back, 'one or two, was the rumour? As it didn't affect me I really took no notice of it. It can be nothing more than those new pilots training.'

'Now I come to think of it,' said the Political Commissar looking wise, 'That's the only logical reason, don't you think so, Comrade Hinlea?' and put Ah Fat's answer into English.

'Probably, yes,' was his tentative reply, feeling a worm of worry in his gut. He knew that 1914 Flight had handed over to 1911 flight the previous March, so a new batch of pilots was most unlikely nor would there have been any increase in aircraft.

Back in the battalion, an 'O' Group had been called for 1000 hours. The CO had decided that only elements of HQ Company should remain back and the Adjutant to be Rear Party commander and temporary Intelligence Officer, 'Acorn' in signal speak, and revert to 'Seagull' for normal business. OC Support Company was detailed as Tac Adjutant to be the CO's staff officer on the spot.

'Gentlemen, yesterday the Brigadier and I had a long and fruitful meeting,' he began, 'although he was not at all happy at the idea of Rance and his shadowing party. However, I calmed him down. He has decided 1/12 GR's task is to ambush on the north side of the main Seremban-Jelebu road concentrating on the area between KK, that's Kuala Klawang, and Jelebu. He has ordered a company of 2/6 GR from Kluang to ambush east of KK and a company of 2/7GR from their camp near Kuala Lumpur to ambush west of KK. All four rifle companies and Support Company, with support weapons less Anti-Tank guns, will load up with five days rations and be ready to move by 1230 hours today as ever is. MTO, if you think that extra transport is needed, get onto Brigade for more. I'll detail the order of march later.

'You will be interested to hear what Captain Rance has achieved,' and he gave the gist of the last two sitreps. 'He overheard why a group of guerillas had been sent back to their original base,' and he gave the details to the intense interest of everybody. 'I hope that none of them saw our men's tracks. Yes Captain sahib?' he asked as Rance's Company 2 IC put his hand up. 'Have you a point?'

The Gurkha Captain understood English better than he spoke it so he gave his answer in Gurkhali. 'Sahib, I don't know if you have been told that Captain Rance sahib's group decided not to wear jungle books but to move out in canvas shoes. It was considered that, although the leeches might be worse, with so few numbers it would be much safer that way.'

'Good thinking, indeed, Sahib. I guess that was your idea.' He looked hard at the Gurkha Captain, who smiled and said it was. 'Well done. It could well save some lives.'

There were no questions. All trooped away to give out orders to their subunits.

The guerillas back in the main camp were hungry. The spare rice and flour in the cave was mostly inedible and the main group had taken the remaining tins of sardines. 'Comrades, gather round,' said the eldest. 'What shall we do? Go foraging in the nearest villages and risk running into the *gwai lo* looking for their missing man, go fishing or go hunting? Comrade Goh Ah Hok won't bring us anything because he thinks the camp is empty. Let's put our heads together and find a solution to this knotty problem.'

The youngest man asked permission to speak. He was given it. 'Comrades, I have a feeling that something is badly wrong with our organisation. Our two senior leaders just don't get on together, only calling each other "comrade" because they have to, not because it is a word of friendship. I ask myself why I'm here. My parents work in a small shop that sells food, fish hooks, needles, oh you know the type of place I'm talking about. I didn't know anything about Communism or any politics before a man came to the shop one night and told my father that if I didn't go back with him to the jungle, he'd find his daughter raped. So father had to send me. I don't feel anything like a comrade or a guerilla,' and his voice tailed off, tears pricking his eyes.

The others looked embarrassed. Then another man said, 'the only reason I joined was that I was hungry and stole some food. I was so scared that I felt the only place I could hide from the police was in the jungle with the comrades. Politics and Marx and that lot still bore me stiff.'

And one by one, each told his own story. Only one man was a dedicated Communist. 'So what's your answer?' he asked with all the enforced dignity of someone who finds himself the only odd man out, his tone of voice alive with malice.

As if pulled by the same string, each other produced a surrender leaflet. 'I'll get back to my shop and my sister will be safe.' 'The police won't nab me for being a thief.' And the others gave similar answers.

'When will we go?'

'Now. What else is there to do?'

'How'll we find where to go?'

'Read the leaflet. With it in your hand, the nearest police station. Let's go.'

As they left the youngest guerilla turned to the one man who said he was a Communist. 'Goodbye Comrade. Have a nice time by yourself.'

Drawing his lips together like a turkey's bottom, 'Damn you all. I'm coming with you,' he spluttered.

Jason and his men had been on the move for less than an hour when they were startled to hear a shot from somewhere to a flank, away from their line of movement. They froze and sank to the ground, taking up all-round firing positions. No more shots were heard and, five minutes later, they stood up. They looked enquiringly at each other. 'What do you think it was, Sahib?' Lalman asked Jason.

'Either an accidental discharge from a patrol making sure the area is clear or, possibly, a hunting party looking for deer or pig.'

'Deer probably,' said Chakré. 'I heard one calling earlier on.'

'Yes,' added Kulbahadur, 'I've seen tiger tracks. No wonder

the deer was frightened enough to make a noise.'

'Then that's probably why. If they've shot an animal, they'll spend quite a time gutting it and cooking it,' said Jason. 'In that case, Kulbahadur and Lalman will go ahead to see if that is what did happen. If they are cooking meat, you'll smell it before you actually reach them. Before you go, change your jungle shirt and hat for daku ones. Leave your big pack and equipment here. Don't hurry as that will make too much noise and leave traces of movement. Try not to stay out longer than you need to.'

The two Gurkhas took their equipment off, changed and moved away. The others had seen some bamboo shoots and fern tops which they picked to add to their next meal. Some ninety minutes later the two men came back, smiling. Jason had had some water heated and, on seeing them, told Chakré to make a brew. Over their sipping, Kulbahadur told them what they had come across. 'We moved most quietly for only twenty minutes and heard the daku before we saw them. We also smelt their cooking. It was a deer that had been shot, not an accidental discharge. We crawled up a short ridge that we reckoned overlooked them and, there they were, gathered around the cooking, talking and no sentries. The captain man was sitting on one side by himself. Two elder Cheena were sitting apart, not looking at each other nor talking. Another elder Cheena was sitting alone. If we made an attack now I'm sure we'd kill all nine of them with no difficulty.'

'Probably could but that's not our task. Anyway, you did well,' congratulated Jason. 'How many others are there and did they have any idea you were there?'

'No, Sahib. We counted a total of nine men in all, five

bodyguards for the four others. They didn't see or hear us.'

Jason looked at his watch. 'We'll cook our meal here and open up, letting HQ know what we've found out. One man stay up there,' he indicated a small rise in the ground to their front, 'just in case someone comes along.'

At 11 o'clock they opened up their set and gave Tac HQ their latest sitrep.

Lieutenant Colonel Robert Williams was busy with commanders of the 2/6 GR and 2/7 GR companies that had reported to him and were in the middle of getting their orders when Jason's sitrep was given him. He read it straightaway. 'This is exciting news,' and he gave them the message to read. 'How best to make those guerillas less complacent? Um ti um,' drumming his fingers on his chair arms. 'Got it.' He called in the Tac Adjutant. 'Put a call through to Seremban and tell the Auster flight OC to get some surrender leaflets and drop them …' and he gave a six-figure map reference, 'as near noon as possible.'

'Right away, sir.'

At midday, as the guerillas were happily chewing some deer flesh, with the Political Commissar listening to his wireless, an Auster suddenly circled overhead, terrifyingly low above where they were sitting. Through a gap in the tree tops they saw the pilot. It came over again and they saw him release a bundle of papers. With the shattering noise still reverberating in their eardrums, away the plane flew as bits of paper floated down. Men rushed to pick them up before the Political Commissar could tell them not to.

'Show me,' he ordered a man who had brought a few back with him and was utterly appalled to see what they were. The first thought that came into his mind was *that traitor Wang Ming.* Then cold reality hit him. *How could he have? But someone had.* He did not see his Military Commander pick up a leaflet and put it in his pocket.

'Finish your meal, Comrades, then gather around. We'll go no farther today, it's still safe here. This afternoon we'll have a self-criticism session to determine exactly how the *gwai lo* could have sent an aeroplane *here* to drop *these,*' and, nearly choking with frustration, the bile of hatred and enmity rose in his throat. *Not long now. What is necessity but a man convinced of the need? If only I had some cold tea to clear my mind properly.*

As the Auster made its two tight circuits, Jason's men looked up and saw leaflets being dropped a little way over to their east. 'Sahib, what do you think the daku's reaction will be? asked Kulbahadur.

'Can't tell till we've been and had a look. Come on, Kulé, stay dressed as you are. I'll put my daku shirt on and off we'll go. If we see some arum leaves we'll cut a couple off at the base of the stem. If there's no cover at our hiding place, we'll put one each over our head instead.'

They found some at the first stream they crossed. They each cut one and, carrying it carefully they walked with extreme caution to almost in sight of where the daku were, Kulbahadur in front. They wormed their way up the same short rise that the two men had used earlier, arum leaf in front and lay hidden from view, peering through a small hole torn in each leaf. The guerillas were about thirty yards in front of them. An obviously senior man was standing up and his men were sitting in a half circle in front of him. Jason saw Ah Fat and Hinlea sitting at one end and another man, older than the remaining guerillas, at the other. The man standing up started talking and Jason strained hard to hear what he was saying. 'Until now we have been unheard and unseen by the Running Dogs. No one other than we ourselves and our comrades has any idea of where our camp was, has any idea of where our new comrade would find us, nor has any idea of where we are going or our route. Yet a *gwai lo* flying machine has been circling round the area more than once. Of course we thought it was the *gwai lo* pilots training ...' He paused, almost theatrically. '... until today. It came twice round us, dropping this vile propaganda, full of lies. We all know how harshly the puppet police treat any of our comrades they capture and here they are talking about "safe conduct" to traitors and "payment for arms delivered" and other nonsense. But that is not the main point: that is *how did they find out where we are?'* His voice reached a scream-like crescendo and Jason saw Hinlea's bewildered expression.

So did the man talking. By now Jason, remembering what Ah Fat had told him about personalities, guessed it was the Political Commissar, Lau Beng. He had also presumed that the other older man to a flank was the Military Commander, whose name he'd remembered as Wang Ming. In his not-often-used and stilted English he looked across at Hinlea and asked him, 'How do you think the aeroplane knows we are here, Comrade?'

'Comrade Lau Beng, I have no idea. It gave me a great shock.'

'It means that someone has told the Running Dogs which way you have escaped. It is not you sent to trick us, is it?'

Hinlea's face became a mask of horror. He violently shook his head. 'Comrade, no, no, no. How can you think that when I myself did not know where your base was or by which route you would be taking me?' *My Operation Janus is sacrosanct.*

After a moment's thought, the speaker said, 'I agree with you so it must be someone else. Who?' and he resumed talking in Chinese. 'There are only two people I can suspect but only one I actually do. Shall I point him out or will you sitting in front of me point him out?'

Ah Fat's heart thumped. He had no idea of Jason's follow-up, shadowing group. *If I'm accused I'll deny everything.*

The Political Commissar asked each of the five guerillas whom they thought responsible for the aeroplane finding them. Each of them said they did not know, how could they? and what had been said previously had to be the explanation. One of the more thoughtful of them said that maybe the pilot's task was to drop such leaflets wherever he saw smoke in the jungle and, because of their cooking the deer there was rather a lot of smoke, wasn't there, it just happened that the pilot was suspicious so dropped them. Surely there was no case for 'pointing out' anyone.

'And you, Comrade Ah Fat, what is your view?'

'Comrade, I think that what the comrade said was entirely sensible. Of course the pilot could in no way know who we are or where we are. How could he? Any of our comrades opposing the *gwai lo* whose smoke had been seen would have had them dropped on them. There's nothing to worry about in my view.'

'And you, Comrade Military Commander?' said with an implied sneer that was not lost on any of his listeners. *See if you can wriggle out of this. You're the chief suspect in my mind.*

'Eh? How many times have I had hostile planes over me which have had no proof of who was under them in the jungle. I fully agree with Comrade Ah Fat. All we need to do is to keep our smoke hidden as best we can and carry on with our task as ordered.'

And the Political Commissar decided not to take any further action. *Not yet proof positive but if any more planes come over …*

The group stood up, stretched their legs and Ah Fat said he had to have a pee. 'So must I,' said the Bear and both men wandered off to just short of where Jason and Kulbahadur were hiding, neither daring to move an inch and both thankful for their arum leaf cover. Both Chinese must have seen the arum leaves but neither seemed to realise that, on a small rise, they were unnaturally out of place – no water.

As he was pissing, the Bear turned to Ah Fat and said, almost in a whisper, 'Our so-called leader, that Sai Daam Lo, is so unpredictable I've lost faith in him. What think you?'

Ah Fat, feeling that he could get the Bear thinking about 'joining' him, acquiesced in a neutral but positive manner.

'I daren't say anything otherwise I'm a dead man,' said the Bear, buttoning up his flies, 'but frankly, I'm disillusioned. We've never seen eye to eye: he can't believe in *feng shui*.'

'Keep it to yourself, Hung Lo, certainly for the present. Let's get back before Sai Daam Lo starts getting ideas he shouldn't,' and, with that, both men moved back.

Before Jason and Kulbahadur oozed back down into the re-entrant that hid them from the guerillas, Jason whispered 'Kulé, is that mess,' and he pointed with his chin, 'python skin?' The Gurkha strained his eyes. 'Yes, Sahib, I think it must be.'

Back with the others Lilbahadur was told to open the set on the next hour. 'I'll have to report what I've just heard,' and he told the others what that was. He did not need to explain *feng shui* as all Gurkha villagers had the same theory.

'Hello 1 Able. Fetch Sunray.'

'Wilco. Wait out.'

'Sunray on set. Send, over.'

Jason told the CO what the guerillas' reaction to the drop of the surrender leaflets was: obviously worried but put down to too much smoke made while cooking. 'They're short of rations and the Military Commander is disillusioned. Their morale has been shaken. Let's shake it a bit further. By 1600 hours tomorrow can you get a Voice Aircraft overhead? Talking in Chinese, telling them that their LMG had been found broken, their stores in the cave destroyed and, in English, some message to Hinlea, telling him that he had no hope of escape and that, on capture, he can expect the ultimate. You might like to make use of the fact that his private icon is Janus, I spell Jig, Able, Nan, Uncle, Sugar. Over.

'Sunray, that last is a great idea. You seem to have worked the oracle. Well done. Leave it to me. Take care. Out.'

11

No sooner had the CO taken off his head set did the Tac Adjutant, who had heard the exchange between him and Jason, excitedly call him, 'Sir, before you do anything else you are wanted urgently on the phone. The OCPD has some red hot news.'

The Colonel moved over to the phone and took it. 'Colonel Williams here Mr Clark. What have you for me that's so important? – that is before I tell you something of importance from my end.'

'Sir, in the past few minutes a group of guerillas from the Regional Committee camp we thought Hinlea would go to have surrendered. They had leaflets dropped on them yesterday and have decided they've had enough. What made them decide to surrender is that the camp was left empty with their one machine gun hidden. The Political Commissar ordered them back to look after the camp. They found the gun disabled by someone unknown and this someone had found their store in a cave where they kept dry rations and clothes. It was wrecked. They are hungry and most dispirited, and one of them has so split the seams of his trousers he looks like a scarecrow. Great, isn't it? It really shows that these leaflets can work wonders,' and he gave a throaty chuckle. 'Moby will start fully debriefing them directly.'

The CO's eyes had opened wide and his face had lit up, leaning forward in his chair as he listened to what the OCPD had to say. 'Clark, this is truly wonderful news but we must, at all costs, keep it from the press and Radio Malaya, certainly for the time being. From my end Rance has eavesdropped on a meeting held by the guerillas after the Auster dropped leaflets on them. Each guerilla was asked how it was that their position was discovered. Although they were frightened and suspicious from having heard the Auster fly over and around them, the agreed answer is that they were showing too much smoke when cooking a deer they'd shot and the pilot had merely chanced on them and dropped his leaflets, not knowing who they were so there was no need to worry. They were to press on as planned and try not to show so much smoke when cooking in future.'

'How can we pressure them even more, sir?'

'That's what Rance has also asked me. I'm about to ring Brigade to try and get a Voice Aircraft for between noon and 1600 hours tomorrow. I'll tell them to include those details you've given me as well as a warning to Hinlea that we know where he is and that traitors get short shrift when caught.'

The CO then got onto Brigade HQ and asked for the Commander. 'Brigadier, this is an open line so I'll have to be careful in what I say,' and he went into as little detail as necessary for Brigadier Honker to understand the situation. The Brigadier was hesitant and it was only the CO's most urgent pleading that now was the time to take advantage of such a golden opportunity that he gave way. 'William, as you know the details, get onto HQ Malaya Command yourself and tell them I've given you the green light to do so.'

'Thank you, Brigadier,' and the CO rang off. 'Get the GSO 1 at HQ Malaya Command for me as soon as you can,' he told his Tac Adjutant.

The call came through quickly. 'It's CO 1/12 GR here, calling from my Tac HQ. I know you're busy but I must take up some of your time with an important request,' he said almost brusquely.

'Go ahead, Robert. We've read your sitreps and understand the background perfectly. We've also had news of the surrender of some of the group you're tracking.'

'Yes, before my news, please ensure that nothing is given to the press or Radio Malaya. We must keep it to ourselves until it's all over bar the shouting. Now my news is about the dropping of the surrender leaflets earlier on today. Captain Rance managed to overhear how the guerillas have reacted to them. He has told me that they are definitely "windy". They are only guessing at how they were found as they'd presumed they were undetected. They had a self-criticism session and came to the conclusion that their cooking a deer they had shot on damp wood had caused too much smoke which the pilot had seen as he happened to be passing overhead, rather than having any pre-knowledge of their position. Rance saw the look on the face of the commander and said that, although he appeared to agree with that conclusion, he is most uneasy.'

'Extremely interesting but how incredible. Don't tell me the guerillas were speaking in English.'

'No, in Chinese. Rance is bilingual.'

'How extraordinarily fortunate. So what are you leading to?'

'Rance wants a Voice Aircraft over the area, telling the guerillas about the surrenders, their plans are known about, they are virtually surrounded, their LMG is useless and the stores in the cave store destroyed. He says their morale has been shaken but it needs to be broken. Also, Rance tells me that Hinlea has "Janus" as a personal icon which happens to be the name I have given to the operation. Hinlea won't know that so, if possible, he needs to be told something to the effect 'Icon Janus broken".'

'I like your idea and that tidbit about Janus, but my boss may have reservations,' Colonel Kenny said. 'Your operation has been put out as a training exercise for damage limitation purposes. I don't think that the Crabs' – he was referring to the RAF whose nickname came from the colour of their uniform, crab-fat grey – 'are too keen on helping an exercise. Also, a tape has to be made and that ensures publicity and it takes time. Inter-service bumbledom, I'm afraid, old chap.'

'Richard. Great shame if the opportunity is allowed to slip. I've heard that there's a brilliant Chinese propagandist in Special Branch HQ, I don't know his name but you'll know who I mean. Couldn't he hold the microphone and talk out of the aeroplane as it makes a circuit without the tape business – and you then, in English, tell turncoat Hinlea that his time's up?'

'Of course I'll try but I can't promise. It'll be up to the GOC.'

'He was my instructor at the Quetta Staff College in '44 ...' but the line was dead.

The guerillas bound for Titi reached the jungle edge below the Seremban-Kuala Klawang road an hour before dusk. Although tired and hungry, they were pleased with their progress. The leader said, 'You two, go out to the rubber estate between us and the main road, just in case there are any indications of *gwai lo* or *Goo K'a* troops. We won't prepare for the night until you return.'

Off they went and half an hour later came back. 'Anything of interest?' asked the senior man.

'Not really, Comrade. The only tracks we found were for a couple of grown-up elephants and a baby one. We went forward and found them grazing. In case they smelt our cooking or we bumped into them later on we shooed them across the road. By the time we get near the coolie lines, they'll be a long way ahead of us.'

'Well done. Now, listen. We'll move off at midnight.' Boastfully he looked at his watch with the luminous hands – he was one of the few 'rank and file' men to own one and he was inordinately proud of it. 'That'll give us good time for a rest and to get food from that estate we always try to stop at. There's not much else between there and Titi.'

On the north of the main road 1/12 GR, plus the other two companies, were in ambush positions, mostly facing south. It was a moonlit night without many clouds. The three platoons of Jason's company were stretched along a laterite road that led to the coolie lines where, it was rumoured, guerillas got rations.

They had taken up their positions at dusk and, shortly after 10 o'clock, one of the riflemen, Ganeshbahadur Rai, felt breathing in his ear. He thought maybe it was his Section Commander come to see if he was asleep. Another breath. He moved his hand up and, instead of feeling a face, he felt the end of an elephant's trunk. He looked up and there an elephant loomed over him, behind him his mate and behind her a calf. *Brahma, Shiva, Vishnu, come to my aid*, he breathed silently. '*Ustad, Ustad*,' he whispered hoarsely to the Corporal a few yards to his flank, 'Help me, help me.'

The NCO was as much at a loss of how to help the man at the elephant's feet as was the man himself. He saw the elephant wave his trunk then gently and quietly step over the prostrate rifleman, one leg at a time, his mate and his calf moving round, not over, his body. After they had gone some way towards the jungle, the NCO went over to the rifleman, by now emulating *rigor mortis* in his fright, and tried to cheer him up. 'I don't know if elephants normally move by night,' he said, 'but I do know that they hate treading on anything like a body. In fact,' appearing to be wise after the event, 'you were in no danger.'

The rifleman didn't, couldn't, reply.

The Corporal continued, 'I expect they'd come from the thick jungle to the south of the road because of man-made movement there. It could be the daku, the ones that the Commanding sahib said that Rance sahib had earlier on sent a message about. Some of them crossing the road here and moving north to Titi.' Still no reaction. 'Oh wake up. The elephants have gone. Ganesh is the elephant god; you are Ganeshbahadur. You could never be hurt by another Ganesh,' he extemporised. 'That is a good omen. Now, before very long, I expect the daku will come. Be ready,' and with that encouragement, he crawled back to his position and waited expectantly.

Wednesday, 27 August 1952

And, at 1 o'clock in the morning, some eleven armed and uniformed men were seen moving along the road, towards the coolie lines. The Gurkha Captain, with the middle platoon, had given strict orders not to open fire until either he gave a fire order or opened fire himself. As the eleven men drew along side, he shouted, 'Fire.' LMGs and rifles immediately blazed.

The gun group got four of them, three more were killed by rifle fire and four managed to escape.

'Cease fire!' shouted the Gurkha Captain. 'Close on me.'

As they gathered round the NCO who had watched the elephant step over Rifleman Ganeshbahadur Rai called him over. 'Told you so, didn't I?'

Rather shamefacedly the soldier nodded but didn't reply. The Gurkha Captain ordered the corpses to be gathered and laid together by the side of the road.

Battalion HQ had heard the firing and ten minutes later headlights were seen approaching. The Gurkha Captain stepped into the middle of the road and waved the vehicle down. Out got the CO and saw seven corpses lit up by the headlights.

'Well done, Sahib,' he said as he got out. 'How many came?'

'Sahib, we only counted eleven. There may have been more behind but we killed seven of them. The other four ran away. I'm sorry we didn't kill them all.'

'No worry, Sahib, no worry at all. The other four ran into our next lot of men in ambush and were caught. I've got the Cheena Police Inspector from Kuala Klawang police station debriefing them now. They are the group that left the party that is with Captain Hinlea on their way to Titi to prepare for the next part of his journey.'

'Sahib. What wonderful news. And is our Rance sahib safe?'

'Oh, I hope so. We all hope so. Stay here till the police come for the corpses then go back to your bivouacs and have a brew up.'

The CO went back to Battalion HQ. Police vehicles came to take the corpses away and the company moved back, rejoicing greatly.

As soon as the CO knew that the GSO 1 would be in his office, he spoke to him about the night's success. 'We must include that in the Voice Aircraft's broadcast, Richard. We can't let such a golden opportunity pass.'

'No, we simply cannot allow that. This and the surrender are Aces on Kings. I'll fix it. G'bye.'

'Mr Too. Good morning. Thank you for coming to see me so quickly and at such short notice. I hope it's not too much of an inconvenience to you.' Colonel Kenny got up from his desk and went to shake hands with a man for whom he had the greatest respect.

'Not at all, Colonel. It is a pleasure to be of use now and again,' said with a huge grin.

'Sit you down. We have a most unusual, intriguing and sensitive problem to deal with and, quite frankly, we'll be lost 'without your advice.'

'Sounds interesting,' replied Mr Too, sitting down with a chuckle. He was a short, balding, bespectacled Malayan Chinese of thirty, with quick, decisive gestures, a perfect command of English and a round face perpetually creased in smiles. His flair for understanding Communist words and activities was of the greatest use in battling the guerillas. He knew that some of them were genuine, others were in the movement to hide from the civil authority and others forced into it by threats and which ones needed which approach for success.

'Interesting to a degree not normally come across in our work. I'll brief you,' and Colonel Kenny, as succinctly as possible, told him everything to do with 'Operation Janus'.

'So to recapitulate: a largish party set out from Bukit Beremban to take this strange British officer on the first stage of his journey to the Central Committee, it is being shadowed by a Chinese-speaking British officer who has reported that the group has split into three with only nine men left in the Command group. There seems to be bad blood between the two senior men. Morale is uncertain. Ah Fat's position is, or could be, on a knife edge, especially if that beacon is discovered. And you want me to tell how best to put the wind up them so that they'll surrender. Is that it? And to think up what is the best message to give them for that from a Voice Aircraft.'

'Yes, Mr Too. That's about the sum of it.'

'I suppose it's best that they be urged to go forward towards the Kuala Klawang-Jelebu road with their leaflets otherwise they'll be dead men. And, in case the Political Commissar has made them destroy the leaflets, another drop is required.'

'Yes. I hadn't thought that far ahead.'

'What will Hinleas's penalty be if and when caught?"

'The answer to that is way above my pay scale, Mr Too. At my level the last thing we want is to get the press involved. It *has* to be hushed up it's such a sensitive issue. I expect that, if captured alive, he will be held *incommunicado* under the tightest supervision, flown to Britain where the authorities in the War Office will have to decide.'

'So back to the present. It's not for me to decide what to say to the renegade Hinlea but I'm more than happy to make up something to broadcast to the guerillas.'

'And I hope you won't mind; I'd like you to go up in the Voice Aircraft and, when the pilot signals you're over the area, talk into the loud speaker. I plan to be with you and talk to Hinlea myself. I'll ask the RAF to go round thrice so you can have your spiel at least twice.'

'Now, that's something I've always wanted to do, go up in one those planes. Can you give me official transport to get to the airfield?'

'Sure. I'll fix it. I've asked the RAF to be over the target at 1400 hours so take off will be shortly after 1330. Have an early lunch and come back here by 1230, please but first ring Mr Mubarak in Seremban for names. I gather the Regional Committee Political Commissar and the Military Commander are there.'

'No problem for the time or for the names which I know already.'

After he had returned to his office an idea struck him. He

reached for his telephone directory and found the number he was looking for. He dialed. 'Ismail Mubarak speaking.'

'Moby. It's Too Chee Chew calling. A quicky. Can you give me the nicknames of your nearest Regional Commissar and Military Commander?

'Of course,' and knowing them off by heart, he gave them. 'You know that they disagree on *feng shui*? The Regional Commander thinks it's nonsense and the other believes in it. I hope your question in a good cause, Too Chee Chew.'

'Couldn't be better. Thanks a lot,' and he rang off. *Now, what's that all about?* Moby wondered.

Earlier that same morning the Political Commissar felt he had to encourage his small group so, after they had packed up and were ready to go, he said, 'We came a good long way yesterday and I reckon we'll be able to cross the main road sometime late tomorrow. By now our forward group will have made contact with the Min Yuen comrades in the coolie lines so we'll be able to have a good meal and put some dry rations in our packs.'

'Yes, Comrade Lau Beng,' said the Military Commander. 'I've come to that conclusion also.'

'And you, Comrade Ah Fat, what ideas have you?'

None that I can tell you. 'I agree with you,' he said, lamely, rubbing his hands together as he spoke.

That put the Political Commissar in a good mood. 'I'll check the news before we set off,' he said, looking at his watch, 'in five minutes' time.'

He opened his set on the correct wave band for the Chinese

news. The 8 o'clock time signal chimed and the broadcast started. 'This is Radio Malaya. Here are the headlines ...' There was nothing of local interest so Lau Beng closed the set and had just stared to give the order to move when words were obliterated by the arrival of another Auster dropping more leaflets on their position before zooming off. 'Leave that muck where it is,' Lau Beng screamed, 'or you'll be severely punished.'

Only Ah Fat seemed to realise that there had been no smoke to guide it in.

'Let's move off now,' said the Political Commissar, deeply worried but keeping it to himself. 'The quicker we start the better.'

Hinlea's mind was in a whirl. Another worm, this time of fear, turned in his gut.

The Wing Commander answered the phone. 'Staff Officer to the Air Officer Commanding speaking.'

'I'm the GSO 1, Lieutenant Colonel Kenny, calling from HQ Malay Command. We spoke yesterday about a possible sortie with a Voice Aircraft. I think it was you I spoke to.'

'Yes, it was,' said scowling at the mouthpiece. 'The Air Vice Marshal needs a bit more convincing as to the need to have people in the plane, rather than a tape.'

'Yes, I suppose it is unusual. If it weren't so vitally important, from our point of view, we'd never have broached the subject.'

'No, I suppose not.' The Wing Commander was not a brown-job fan.

'My GOC has asked if I can have a word with the AVM. We don't have much time to waste. May I come over now, please?'

'I can't stop you, can I?' said in an ungracious tone of voice.

'I hope you can't. If it's not me, I'll have to ask the General to go himself.'

'No, come round yourself. I'll warn my Lord and Master.'

The RAF was under a great strain to meet every army requirement and it was galling to the airmen that most of their tasks were in support of what was an infantryman's war with no dashing piloting needed. The GSO 1 was ushered into the AVM's opulent office and saluted. 'Good morning, sir. I'm sorry to be such a nuisance but needs be and all that.'

The AVM didn't get up but indicated a chair, frowning. 'Have a seat and tell me exactly why a normal mission is needed at such short notice and without the customary tape. If you can convince me, I'll authorise it.'

'The situation is one that has never happened before, sir. A British officer has joined the guerillas and is being escorted up north to join the Politburo,' he saw the AVM's eyes narrow to mere slits and heard his intake of unbelieving breath, 'and we desperately need to enforce a surrender before bloodshed: this is not, in fact, an exercise but for real. We have a Chinese-speaking British officer shadowing the group and he has overheard what the guerillas have said about the dropping of leaflets. He raided their main base, which they'd left temporarily unoccupied, and wrecked enough havoc there that when part of the main group went back they were so dismayed that, with the aid of surrender leaflets, they surrendered yesterday.' The AVM was, by now, intensely interested. 'Part of the group that was sent forward to arrange onward transmission and rations was obliterated in the early hours of this morning. With a Voice Aircraft overhead, we can try and persuade the remainder to surrender, with the Regional Committee Political Commissar, Military Commander and the renegade British officer. I'm sure they won't know of the fate of their other two groups as we have not released any details to Radio Malaya or the press. Once they've been apprised of the real situation by the only quick and sure way possible, a Voice Aircraft, our hope is that they will surrender. And the target in the jungle is so remote no one else will hear it.'

'My dear Colonel, what an extraordinary story. Why was this not spelled out yesterday?'

'The killings and captures had not taken place so the urgency was not quite as pressing but, in particular, the fewer people, especially the local press, who know that a British officer is trying to become a guerilla, the better. It would be a massive victory for Communist propaganda were this to be made public.'

'Point taken. I'll certainly authorise it. When and where do you see it actually taking place?

'This afternoon, around here,' and he stood up and showed the AVM on the map on the wall, 'I hope the aircraft will circle overhead three times. Mr C C Too, the man behind all our positive thinking towards how to combat Communist propaganda, will talk to the guerillas and I, personally, will have a message for the traitorous officer.'

The AVM called in his Wing Commander and told him that authorisation was given for a civilian – 'yes, he'll sign the blood chit' – and the GSO 1 to go up in a Dakota Voice Aircraft and each make a personal broadcast at 1400 hours. 'Got it?'

Yes, the Wing Commander got it. 'Last minute addition to normal crew briefing will be at 1315 hours and take off at 1345.'

The GSO 1 thanked the AVM most sincerely. 'That this should ever have happened is unbelievable. But happen it has and now we'll be able to put an end to it before anything worse can eventuate.'

The nine men were totally overwhelmed when a Dakota aircraft suddenly started circling round them and their hopes irreversibly shattered when a voice started talking: 'Comrade Lau Beng, Comrade Wang Ming, Comrade Ah Fat and other comrades, listen well. All those of your men who returned to your camp on Bukit Beremban have surrendered. They found the machine gun made useless and all the kit and the rations in the cave store destroyed. Bad *feng shui*. The guerillas you sent forward to Titi have all been killed or captured. You are surrounded. You have been followed all the way and strong ambushes are in position to eliminate you once you reach the main road in front. Listen well. We'll send you more surrender leaflets in case you ordered the others to be torn up. Surrender and live. Ignore this warning and die ... like dogs.'

The listeners were dizzy with red-hazed rage. Only Hinlea, not understanding the words, was unsure of the actual message although he felt that now nothing made sense. He was soon put out of his ignorance when the Dakota came round again. An English voice this time: 'Captain Hinlea, your plans were fully known about before you turned traitor. You have been followed ever since you left Seremban. Those sent back by your new leader have all surrendered and those sent forward have either been killed or captured. Come out and surrender. Don't pretend that you can do otherwise. Listen well. Otherwise you'll die ... but what a way to go! Farewell Icon Judas.' Hinlea explosively fulminated against his unseen tormentor then, head madly in a whirl, sat down in a near catatonic state, mind buzzing like a fretsaw.

Jason also heard it: *Icon Judas, almost good as dead.*

The message in Chinese was said twice and Hinlea's once before the Dakota flew off leaving behind a frightened and bewildered group of tired and hungry men. The guerilla soldiers had sat down, looking dismally at Comrade Lau Beng who was now emotionally drained. That last bit so infuriated Hinlea that he started shrieking obscenities in stomach-churning rage. The others looked at him and he realised he'd made a fool of himself. When finally he had calmed down, 'What do we do now?' he asked Ah Fat who merely shrugged his shoulders and said, 'Surrender or die.'

The senior guerilla soldier, a squat affable man, saw how utterly lacking the Political Commissar looked and plucked up enough courage to say, 'Comrade, you got us into the situation, you now get us out of it. You told us nobody else knew about our task but you were wrong. How did others know? Please tell us?'

Something is so wrong. Something does not add up. Not even that traitorous Hung Lo could have arranged all that, could he? I can't put my finger on it. What or who is it? the Political Commissar cursed to himself. 'Comrades, I can't tell you. For once I'm in the dark. We'll continue until this evening by when I hope to have an answer. Move,' he snarled.

With heads bowed and with no spark, the group ambled off, all of them gut-churningly worried, Hinlea especially so. He felt lonelier than he had for ages, a superb example of someone who had the impossible combination of incurable stupidity harnessed to unattainable visions, with too wide a cultural fault line.

All that time Jason and his team were never more than two hundred yards behind. When they heard the Dakota Voice Aircraft they did not stop but continued forward. Jason reckoned correctly that the noise of the aeroplane would drown any excess noise they made. After the first Chinese message had been delivered he briefly translated it to his men and he also put the English bit aimed at Hinlea into Gurkhali for them. 'So they know about us now,' said Rifleman Chakrabahadur, solemnly. 'We'll have to be even more careful.'

No one contradicted him.

They came to a small rise and there below them they saw the guerillas. *Crestfallen and crushed* went through Jason's mind. 'Listen lads. We're not quite equal in numbers but we're more than equal in spirit. Someone, either Hinlea or the daku chief may, at long last, realise that the Auster has only swooped low when the wireless set has been switched on. From the look on their faces each is wondering which of them has arranged for that to happen. It could well be that this evening someone will have the bright idea of looking into the wireless set, finding the secret, what do you call it? beacon thing, and then my friend Ah Fat will be in big trouble. Let's stay close until this evening, just in case. Too close to cook so biscuits and chocolate for our meal.'

The Voice Aircraft landed at the aerodrome and taxied to a halt. The two passengers moved up to the cockpit and thanked the pilot. 'A great job. Just what we wanted. Thank you very much,' said the GSO 1, putting his hand out to shake the pilot's.

The pilot took off his gloves and gave a lop-sided grin. 'You're welcome, sir, but please don't ask me to do it again, unless it is as important as today's seems to have been.'

'I'll try not to. I expect once is enough. Was it all that tricky?'

'Yes, the down draft from the mountain side as we were circling at near to stalling speed was a shade too hairy. At times there was nothing on the clock but the maker's name.'

'Anyway, many, many thanks,' and the two of them walked down the steps and made their way to the dispersal area where Colonel Kenny's driver was waiting for them. 'Get in Mr Too, I'll drive you home.' Once settled in the car, Kenny asked him exactly what he'd said and, on being told, nodded his head appreciatively. 'Neither of us wants a bloodbath.'

Back in his office the GSO 1 put a call through to CO 1/12 GR. 'Robert, just to let you know that, from our side at least, the mission was successful. A well thought-out message was delivered to the guerillas telling them that they were surrounded, their people either surrendered or dead or captured, and that they too had better surrender. As for Hinlea, wait, I've got a copy of it in my pocket. Ah, here it is ...' and he read it out. '... "Farewell Icon Judas." That last was a bit melodramatic but I felt it wouldn't do any harm.'

'Thank you, Richard. I think we'll soon know, one way or the other, if your efforts will have paid dividends.'

Dividends and penalties would be the order of the day – and night.

The dispirited guerillas found a place to doss down for the night. They now only had rice and a sprinkling of dried fish to eat. ''Right, gather around comrades,' ordered Lau Beng, trying to sound as if he was in charge of the situation. 'We've got to thrash this out.' He turned to Hinlea and said in his careful English, 'Comrade, first I'll talk in Chinese to my men then to you.'

'Yes, Comrade, I'm as worried as you are.'

'Right, let's start. Comrade Wang Ming, I am deeply suspicious of you. Quite how you have manipulated your influence with the police of the Running Dogs is, at the moment, beyond my comprehension,' said in a silkily threatening tone of voice.

The Bear looked at his political boss in uncomprehending astonishment. 'Comrade, are you out of your mind? Have you no notion of what nonsense you are uttering. Me a police spy? Ludicrous.'

'No, Comrade, not ludicrous. Look at this. I've been keeping it for such a moment as this,' and, so saying, he pulled the secret list out of his pocket. 'This is the list of police sleepers that our new comrade brought me from the police Special Branch secret files. It has your name on it. Look,' and he thrust the list under the Military Commander's nose.

The Bear read it, deliberately tore it up and threw the pieces on the fire that had been kept alight to keep off mosquitoes. 'That's what that nonsense deserves and that's what it's got.'

The response outraged the Political Commissar.

Hinlea, recognising the list, was appalled even though he did not know that the Military Commander's name was on it.

The Bear, looking dangerous now that he was thoroughly roused, turned to Ah Fat for support. 'Comrade Ah Fat, doesn't such an accusation strike you as absurd and obscene?'

'Why, yes, Comrade Wang Ming. It's obviously nonsense ...'

'Then who's to blame?' queried the Political Commissar, butting in.

No one spoke. The quarrel and the query were far above the heads of the guerilla soldiers.

'Comrade Hinlea, who do you think is responsible for the leaflets being dropped on us, for the Voice Aircraft telling us the dreadful news which, if true, means the death, capture and surrender of our comrades? Who *can* it be?'

And then the answer came to Hinlea. 'I think I have the answer, Comrade Lau Beng. Did you notice that the Auster only circled us when you were trying to listen to the news?'

'No, yes, oh,' muttered Lau Beng is confusion. 'Ye ... yes, now it does occur to me. But why?'

'Comrade, give me your wireless set, please.'

Uncomprehendingly he did. Hinlea took the back off and looked inside. It was still light enough for him to make out a small silver-coloured fixture hidden behind the valve. 'Comrade, look at this. This is the answer, surely.'

The Political Commissar squinted at it. 'What is it and why are you showing me?' he asked diffidently, not being technically-minded.

'Because, in the aeroplane there must be a similar device that acts when your wireless is switched on and gives it our position. There can be no other answer.'

Voices were raised loudly enough for Jason to hear and, from his hidden position, to see the two senior comrades and Hinlea turn as one man and accusingly look at Ah Fat.

In as menacing a tone of voice as he could muster, the Political Commissar hissed, 'Comrade P'ing Yee ... .' He was interrupted by Hinlea. 'Are you calling me? My name's Hinlea, not Pinlea.'

'No, P'ing Yee.'

'Pinlea or Hinlea to me. Which do you mean? Don't you know me bleeding name after all this time?' *What the devil's wrong?*

The Political Commissar took a huge breath. 'No, not you. Keep quiet.' He started again, 'Comrade P'ing Yee,' and was interrupted by a loud snort from an abrasive Hinlea. He was ignored and the Political Commissar continued, '*You* changed the wireless, *you* must be responsible for the leak of information. Explain yourself.'

Jason had to give his old friend his due. With nonchalance bordering on boredom – *tradecraft* – he said, 'I brought it back as it was sold to me. Rather than your being worried about Comrade Wang Meng being a traitor, I should start asking whether the comrade in the wireless workshop is the traitor.'

The thought obviously had not struck Lau Beng. 'So you didn't check it?' he snarled.

Ah Fat was enough of an actor to be able to laugh out loud. 'Comrade, be reasonable. Is checking the inside of a new wireless set something that a normal buyer would even think of doing?'

Stalemate. Silence. *I've won through!*

It was Hinlea who queried Ah Fat's pitch. 'I don't know why you use a name that sounds like mine but I don't believe that the man who helped me in Special Branch, an obvious friend of the OCPD, is Comrade Ah Fat's twin. No, no, no. It could've only been your bleeding self.' In his excitement his north-country accent made his English difficult to understand. 'Comrade Lau Beng, he's the bloke responsible. You must punish him, here and now. Kill him.'

As the respected military advisor of the Central Committee, it was no easy matter for the Political Commissar to give the order. Despite being told surrender was the only option for their safety, even survival, he still felt somehow he simply had to hand this *gwai lo* comrade over to the people at Titi.

'No, I can't.'

Hinlea's pent-up frustration broke under the strain. Dirty, tired, hungry and seeing his carefully nurtured high hopes and years of careful planning not just in jeopardy but totally ruined, without further thought he reverted to prototype. 'Then I'll flatten the bastard and make him talk,' he shouted, jumping at Ah Fat and giving him such a punch in the face, kick in the stomach and another kick into his testicles, that the wretched man collapsed writhing on the ground, screaming in agony. The enraged man was pulled off his presumed opponent.

Jason had one thought. *He doesn't know I'm here. I've got to let him know* and, to the surprise of his men, threw back his head and crew loudly, three times. *I hope he gets the message.* His Gurkhas lay as low as they could and Jason heard one of the guerillas say, 'Not often a jungle fowl comes as near as that.'

'Comrade Ah Fat. Were you responsible for that list? I'll get the truth from you if it's the last time you'll ever utter a word,' snarled Lau Beng, almost beside himself in primordial frenzy and pent-up frustration. 'Who's got some twine for putting a fish hook on?' He was given a long piece. 'Cut it in two and tie the traitor's hands and feet around the back of that thin tree there,' and he pointed it out. 'Let him spend the night contemplating the future after he has confessed. We can do nothing without a confession – and tomorrow morning we'll get one. He has to know what was written in that secret report.'

Comrade Lau Beng ordered his men to pick Ah Fat up. They half carried, half dragged the stricken man to the tree, stood him against it and tied his hands and feet at the back. He was only just conscious and in excruciating pain. Hinlea went up to him and knocked his head hard against the tree trunk. The battered man passed out.

'Get settled in,' the Political Commissar ordered everyone. 'We all need sleep.'

Jason pin-pointed where the Political Commissar lay down.

That night, as he turned first on one side and then on the other trying to get to sleep, Lau Beng heard Comrade Ah Fat moaning deliriously. He cocked his ears and distinctly heard *Shandung P'aau, Shandung P'aau. You speak Chinese so well. It will save your life as you saved mine when you killed that deadly poisonous krait snake I hadn't seen.* A childhood echo stirred uneasily in his mind. *That English boy at Kuala Lumpur station all those years ago with his Chinese friend seeing him off.* And the obscure, never-quite-justified nag that had irked him like a loose tooth for so long suddenly leapt clear. *Got it, at long, long last! That's why I've never trusted him. That's who the traitor is. Only he could know what was written on that thrice-cursed secret report so he'll be the one who arranged that doctored list that impugned me so vilely, without any doubt. I'll get my own back trebly tomorrow morning.* Only then did sleep come, deep and sweet.

None of Jason's men stirred for an hour then, speaking very softly, he said, 'Listen well. I've got a plan. I don't like leaving my friend like that. At midnight Kulé, Chakré and I will go and untie him. I'll talk to him and the two with me will, quietly, quietly, bring him back here. The jungle night noises will cover any sound we may make. I will then have a word with the Political Commissar before coming back here. With me so far?'

A collective whispered 'yes'.

'Tomorrow morning, at dawn, Kulé will put on my noise machine, shouting orders to 1, 2 and 3 platoons to move left or right. The other three, with me, all wearing daku kit as we've got on now but mouths covered with our camouflage veil, will run up to the camp, I shouting "beware" in Chinese, and we'll kill the guerilla soldiers. Lilé, you leave your wireless set behind a tree. I'll want you as one of my killers. By the time that's done, I'll have disarmed the other two and tried to overcome Hinlea. Only if I can't, will one of you shoot him, preferably first in the legs so he can't run away then in the arm so he can't fire. Make sure your magazines are full and carry spare ones in your pouches. Think it over and ask any questions you may have.'

There were none.

Jason picked a leaf from a vine, unscrewed the cap of his torch and put the leaf behind the glass. *Just in case.*

Thursday, 28 August 1952

At midnight Jason and his two men moved to a flank and approached Ah Fat's tree from behind, so cautiously that no one heard. There was enough residual starlight as well as the phosphorescent glow of decomposing vegetation to guide them. Ah Fat was leaning forward, hands, arms and shoulders a blaze of pain, knees buckled, feet numb but delirious no longer. 'P'ing Yee, P'ing Yee, Shandung P'aau here. Come to rescue you. Don't make a noise.'

Ah Fat gulped and looked up. *Not dreaming.* 'I knew you'd come, Shandung P'aau, I knew you would. I heard the cock crow. Thank you.'

Two Gurkhas came to hold him up, one switching on the torch which he held cupped in one hand the better for Jason to see while he carefully cut the cord holding the bound man's wrists and feet with his kukri. The Chinese lurched forward and was saved from hitting the ground. 'P'ing Yee, these two men will help you hide. I'll join you in a few minutes. I've something else to do first. Try and make as little noise as possible otherwise I can't guarantee your safety – or mine. Oh, by the way, what's the nickname of Comrade Lau Beng?'

'Sai Daam Lo Ch'e Daai P'aau. Small gall-bladder bloke, big cannon.'

'Got it,' and repeated it.

They let his circulation restore movement, Ah Fat grimacing silently at the pain, before helping him away.

Jason cut some leaves and crept away to the Political Commissar's shelter, skirting the others. Holding the leaves in front of him, he softly said, 'Sai Daam Lo Ch'e Daai P'aau. Wake up. *Ch'uan jia chan* – May your entire clan be wiped out' – making it sound as though the voice came from in front of the sleeping man, not behind him. Lau Beng groaned to semi-awareness. He saw nobody. 'Sai Daam Lo Ch'e Daai P'aau. *Ch'uan jia chan.*' It came again. He fully woke up and looked around. 'Who are you? I can't see you,' he croaked, wondering whether he was awake or suffering from a bad nightmare.

'I am the ghost of Ah Fat. He has disappeared from the tree you so wrongly tied him to. I will guide him to get his revenge in the morning. You will die with your eyes open for what you've done to me.' Jason knew that to die like that meant to carry one's regrets of doing wrong to the grave. He was also playing on the fear many Chinese have of devils and ghosts, nor was he wrong. 'Go and look for me. Ha, ha, ha. I won't be there. Ha, ha, ha. Too much bad *feng shui* in your old camp catching up with you. Ha, ha, ha.'

Thoroughly awake and in mortal dread – despite all Communists repudiating anything of the spirit, primordial beliefs and fears still lay dormant till roused – the Political Commissar got up and moved towards the tree where Ah Fat still should have been. When he was gone Jason felt for his pistol, found and, wrapping his handkerchief around it – *better not have my fingerprints on it* – unloaded it, putting the bullets into his pocket. He slipped away unseen and joined his men. Ah Fat was lying on a groundsheet and Lilbahadur was massaging his wrists with rifle oil. 'Shandung P'aau, this is the second time you've saved my life. How can I say thank you,' he said so softly it was almost inaudible.

'I know no one whose life I'd rather save than yours, P'ing Yee. Listen, don't worry about the noise in the morning. Go to sleep now.'

Back in the camp a frightened and bewildered man returned and lay down trembling. *How could a man so tightly and securely tied have disappeared?*

At a quarter to six, Jason nudged Kulbahadur. 'Kulé, get the noise machine out of your pack. Exactly at 6 o'clock start firing.'

'I'll be ready, Sahib.'

'You others, ready?' Yes. 'Move as quietly as ghosts, following me.'

On the hour heavy firing broke out, waking the sleeping men. Shouted orders for platoons to move were heard. Pandemonium! Before the guerillas knew what was what, Jason and his men charged towards the camp, running on the upper side. 'Escape or you're dead. We're being attacked. Hurry, hurry. Help, help.'

The still sleepy guerillas got up and, groping for their rifles, were shot down, all five of them, four dead, one badly wounded in the leg. The Political Commissar was completely flummoxed when his pistol did not fire. 'Drop your weapon or you're dead,' Jason shouted to the Military Commander in Chinese and in

English to Hinlea,' then, at the top of his voice in Gurkhali, 'Cease fire. Close on me.'

Wang Ming, seeing he was completely overwhelmed, dropped his weapon, took his surrender leaflet out of his pocket and, holding it in one hand with his arms above his head in surrender, stood still.

Hinlea recognised Jason's voice. 'Jason, you filthy bastard. You ... you, I'll kill you,' and, moving with the intense speed of a pouncing cat, he raised his pistol. As he was about to shoot, Jason dropped to a crouch and Chakré knocked Hinlea's arm to one side as he fired. The Political Commissar, hit in the foot, added to the noise by screaming. Jason, for once, lost control of himself. He threw his weapon on to the ground and leaped at Hinlea, eyes fixed on the barrel of his pistol. He grabbed it with his left hand, his fingers gripping the warm steel, hand and wrist twisting counter-clockwise, pulling downward to inflict the greatest pain. He threw his right hand – fingers curled and rigid – into Hinlea's stomach, tearing at the muscles, feeling the protrusion of the rib cage. He yanked up with all his strength. Hinlea screamed and fell, thrashing about in agony. Jason heard him mutter, 'Janus, Janus, you did look the wrong way.'

Jason came back to his senses and saw his men staring at him. 'Get those two Cheena still alive and see they don't run away. Lilé, go back and get the rope from my big pack, bring it back then open your set.' And to the Military Commander, 'As you have surrendered go and stand with Comrade Ah Fat.'

Hinlea recovering a little, checked his pistol, took aim and again fired at Jason who, just in time, dodged. The bullet pinged harmlessly overhead. Kulbahadur, his weapon at the ready, emerged from having had his 'battle', took aim at Hinlea and, without another thought, shot him through the head. A death spasm caused the fingers to close and, with the safety catch already off, his finger pulled the trigger hard enough to fire the weapon. The bullet somehow hit the wounded guerilla in his right eye, killing him instantly.

Lilbahadur brought back the rope and Jason ordered Chakré and Lalman to tie Lau Beng by his wrists and ankles. 'Bandage that foot as best you can, Chakré,' and, wiping the sweat off his face, he called to Ah Fat. 'P'ing Yee, if you can walk, please come over here. Take Lau Beng's pistol, using a cloth so not to touch it with your hands, note its serial number. I'll witness it. We'll need it for his prosecution.'

At Ah Fat's appearance Lau Beng was dumbstruck in amazement: *a man or a man of a ghost?* Ah Fat looked at the bound man: 'Lau Beng, comrade no more: in due course I'll have to let the Central Committee know just how badly you committed yourself. You were always too stupid for your own good.'

Lau Beng spat his disgust, almost apoplectic and hardly able to mouth anything coherently. 'I blame you, not Wang Ming, for this tragedy. If it's the last thing I'll ever do, it'll be to track you down and kill you,' voice trembling both with fury and pain in his foot. '*Ch'uan jia chan*' – May your entire clan be wiped out.

'You never really meant anything you said unless it was for your personal benefit, not the Party's. I discount your oath as I have inwardly discounted almost everything I have heard you say. Anyway, for your possible interest, I am, in fact, a Christian so your oath has no power over me. And, for the record, you were never nearly as good as you thought you were. Let's hope the *feng shui* of your prison cell is appropriate. Keep quiet.'

Ah Fat's cold reply stayed with Lau Beng until the hangman's rope was tied round his neck a few months later.

Lilbahadur called out to Jason, 'Sahib, I've netted the wireless.'

Having put the headset on, Jason said, 'Hello One Able. Fetch Sunray.'

'One Able, wilco. Wait out,' crooned the operator.

'One Able, Sunray on set.'

'Sunray 1 Able. I have had an unexpected but successful contact with the daku. My men have killed figures six, including Able How. Roger so far? Over.'

'Roger over.'

'I have captured the Regional Committee Political Commissar who was shot in the foot by Able How whose death antics shot and killed the one wounded guerilla. My childhood friend suffered some battering but is safe. We have no casualties. Over.'

'Roger. Extraordinarily well done. What next?'

Jason had by that time worked out his position and gave the map reference. 'I will stack and cover the corpses and suggest that a Sugar Baker [Special Branch] rep comes ready to photograph and finger-print them if policy is to bury and not carry out, otherwise please detail carrying party. I have rations only for today. Request a pick-up party to me Able Sugar Peter with a bottle of rum. There should be no more hostiles so movement can be fast. All details later. Over.'

'Sunray. Wilco out.'

Jason called to his men, 'Change out of daku clothing before anyone from Battalion HQ reaches us. You probably know that such a tactic is not allowed and what the eye does not see the heart does not grieve. Let's have a brew.'

What an ending! That misfit Hinlea caused more trouble to more people in a shorter time than most people can manage in a lifetime but, in the end, he was about as successful as a blank file on leave, Jason thought while the water for their tea was being boiled. They gave a mess cover half full to each prisoner – Lau Beng refused his – then sat down, drank theirs and relaxed, supremely content.

As they waited, Jason had an idea. After the Military Commander had drunk his tea, Jason beckoned to him. He cautiously moved over. 'Sit down beside me. P'ing Yee also come here.' Cautiously, so that Lau Beng could not hear, Jason said, 'Officially you have surrendered. I also heard you say that you were disillusioned ...'

Against his better judgement, the Bear interrupted, '*Sinsaang*, how could you have done? Impossible!'

'No, not at all. You had a pee near two arum lilies. I was hiding behind one of them and heard you say so.'

The Bear's startled expression should have been captured on film. *It never occurred to me that those two arum lily leaves were out of place!*

'May I suggest that, once we get to Seremban, you ask Special Branch and the OCPD if you can join the staff and work for the Government? I'll recommend you.'

After a long silence, an ungrudging 'Yes' was the answer.

Monday, 1 September 1952

Excitement in Special Branch had been intense at the arrival of Lau Beng and Wang Ming on the previous Friday, brought in by Ah Fat – whose appearance had been explained to as few people as necessary that he was in his Special Branch mode – and Ian Clark had gone into a huddle with Moby. 'Shall we let Wang Ming see those who served under him and see the reaction?' Ian had asked.

Moby thought that one over. 'I have an idea, Ian, that might work better if we let him kick his heels for a couple of days.'

'What's that, Moby?'

'I'd like to get him into a frame of mind forming a 'Q' Group composed of the men who surrendered with Jason Rance as his leader.' He paused, looked at Ian and said, 'If you think there's any mileage in it I'll give C C Too a bell and ask him to come down here on Monday and talk to them about it.'

'Moby, I've been so busy what with one thing and another and you have with debriefing the people who recently surrendered that I forgot to mention that Jason Rance phoned me after he came back and told me that he had already spoken to Wang Ming, whom he also called the Bear, just on that subject and that, of his own accord, the idea has been accepted.'

'Even better but I'd still like C C Too with us. We don't have a secure phone but I'll put our point to him in such a way that he'll be more than intrigued to come down.'

'Yes, and I'll get Jason in as well. He'll have some good ideas, I expect, being such a shrewd operator.'

And so it was, that Monday, most secretly, under C C Too's

supervision, that the Bear and the surrendered guerillas entered into a pact, having sworn the most solemn oath a Chinese can swear, that the group would be forgiven any previous bad behaviour, promised pay on a regular basis at the rate of a Special Constable with new names and supporting documentation at the end of their 'service'.

The final outcome was that Ah Fat was to be the 'political commander', using the 'Q' Group where it was thought best while the Bear would be the tactical commander. The Bear had one request: if ever the Shandung P'aau had any special operation to consider, he, the Bear, would be only too pleased to be under his or P'ing Yee's command.

Jason had two points: one that he could not guarantee being allowed to or even be available to undertake any such operation; his other was that if such were allowed, it should have its own code name. After much thought, he suggested Operation 'Blind Spot'. Ah Fat suggested that it were better to use the physical *Maan Tim* rather than 'blind in the mind', *Sam Lei Maan Tim*, which was too cumbersome. C C Too fully agreed with this. Eventually approval was given but only as a 'last resort' if all other methods were seen as either useless or unacceptable. But first of all, it was decided that Ah Fat would go back to Central Committee, give a doctored report of what had happened and volunteer to go back and re-establish the Negri Sembilan Regional Committee. All military operations in the Kuala Klawang-Titi area were discreetly suspended while Ah Fat and three of his 'Q' Team made contact with the Regional Committee there. That done, the 'Q' Team men were to return and Ah Fat go on up to the Central Committee as it was normal for such people.

The sentries around the camp of the Central Committee were surprised to see five figures coming up the hill towards their camp. They recognised only one of them, Comrade Ah Fat, not the others with him. They let them pass into the camp. Ah Fat reported to the General Secretary, Chin Peng, who expressed surprise at not seeing the expected *gwai lo*.

'Where's the new comrade, the Lustful Wolf as we've been calling him? We were all expecting him around now? Why is he not with you?' he asked, almost churlishly.

Ah Fat looked straight at his questioner, feigning sadness and dismay – *tradecraft: Operation Blind Spot!* – and shook his head. 'Oh Comrade, let me give you the bad news, the bad, bad news straightaway: something went so very wrong. All our group, except me, were ambushed and killed. The *gwai lo* comrade was killed as were many other comrades, less Comrade Lau Beng who was wounded and captured. It was only by the grace of Lenin that I was saved by having surprisingly contacted another comradely group when I went to shoot deer with a comrade. I took them to one side so that the group with the Lustful Wolf could continue without their knowledge. It was then that the disaster occurred. I stayed back only long enough to find out details of any casualties then moved on to Titi with my own escort. So thankful to be alive and back with you, can hardly be said forcibly enough. When I've changed and had a rest I'll go into details of what happened.'

'Well, that is indeed a grave disappointment and completely unexpected. I hope the Running Dogs have been acutely embarrassed even without their captain not joining us. There has been nothing on the wireless about a British officer being killed or any other casualties. If there was anyone to blame, tell me now who he was.'

Remembering the golden rule of all Communists: blame the absent or, better still, the dead, Ah Fat said, 'It was Lau Beng – hard to believe, isn't it?'

'We'll have a plenum tomorrow when you can explain it all. I'm only so pleased about one aspect,' and Chin Peng looked at Ah Fat straight between the eyes, 'At least you weren't involved in any way.'

My tradecraft has let me win through.

Saturday, 13 September 1952

Re-training was over and on the Monday rifle companies would once more be deployed away from Battalion HQ. Lieutenant Colonel Robert Williams had asked Captain Rance and his four men round to his house for a drink and to say a private and personal thank you for their outstanding military prowess. No one mentioned that Hinlea's death had, in fact, solved a lot of unpleasant problems. 'A much misguided man, Jason,' the CO said. 'I had never thought he'd get killed. He never should have been commissioned. Your final summing up of him?'

Jason had a flash of inspiration. 'I remember my first head master when I went to England telling me that it takes three generations to make a gentleman and the hapless Hinlea wasn't really even the first generation.' He paused and had another flash: knowing how the CO's mind worked, he felt a biblical quotation would satisfy him. 'Sir, I forget the exact words I read in St. Matthew's gospel but I'll paraphrase them: "One cannot expect grapes from thorns and figs from thistles".'

The CO bowed his head slightly in reverence to a gospel being mentioned. Before they left, he led Jason out onto the verandah. 'Listen, Jason. You have saved the army and the regiment from a great and soul-searing disgrace. You have incurred danger beyond the dictates of duty but under no circumstances can this become public knowledge. No bravery awards can be made. A thick, dark, heavy curtain has to be drawn over these recent events, never to be pulled back. I hope you understand.' He paused, as though making up his mind. 'I shouldn't really tell you what my senior officer told me but I will: I asked the Brigadier if he'd support bravery awards for all five of you but,' and here he faltered slightly, 'he refused, point blank. Rather pompously, I thought, he said "The Army, like the Royal Academy, desires docility in her children and even originality has to be stereotyped".' Jason thought the CO looked rather forlorn as he said that.

The Colonel cleared his throat and continued, 'Your empathy with the men is as irrefutable as the shorthand of the Recording Angel. You have the indispensable virtues of humour, humility and honesty but sadly, in this instance, the only record will be on your confidential Record of Service. Apart from wearing enemy uniform which is strictly forbidden under one of the Geneva Conventions, the only law you have broken is the Law of Averages.'

It was Jason's turn to bow his head, if only to hide his facial expression. 'Thank you, sir, for those kind words. I share your feelings. I could never have done what was done without my Gurkhas. I merely guided them. They have already come to terms with what is good for the regiment. Their proverb says it all.'

'Which proverb? I can't call one to mind.'

'Pure gold needs no touchstone, nor a good man any adornment.'